HOW A LOSER LIKE ME
SURVIVED
THE ZOMBIE APOCALYPSE

STEVEN BEREZNAI

Jambor

First Printing: 2017

ISBN (print) 978-0-9958690-0-4

ISBN (ebook) 978-0-9958690-1-1

Jambor Publishing

Cover design by Joey Wargachuk

For Craig Dale. Thanks for being a bro, m'kay?

Special thanks to Joey Wargachuk, for all the magic that he weaves, and my mom, for her always keen editorial insights.

The battlefield is a scene of constant chaos. The winner will be the one who controls that chaos, both his own and the enemy's.
—*Napoleon Bonaparte*

PART 1

CHAPTER 1

"It is not the strongest of the species that survives, nor the most intelligent, but the ones most responsive to change."

Steph looks at me after I finish reading the quote off my laptop. She leans against the chipped kitchen counter, waiting patiently for the kettle to boil—and for me to make my point. It's unclear which will come first. Steam starts to rise from the nozzle, and a low whistle fills the room.

"That's how I want to start my blog post," I explain.

She's wearing pink scrubs. They're a loose fit, but they can't hide the shapely curves of her hips and the firmness of her breasts. Her sleeve tattoos poke out, bright swathes of golden yellow, emerald green, and brazen blue; it's a kaleidoscope of intertwining flowers, vines, dragonflies, and bees. Girl loves her pollinators, buzzing from flower to flower. Nature's man sluts I once called them, to which she shrugged, "Disposable drones, ruled by their queen."

It was that convo that inspired my current blog post. Steph is my muse, in all sorts of ways. Fools might describe her as pretty, but, having memorized the pattern of freckles across her cheeks and woken up to that slightly too large nose on countless mornings, holding her in the crook of my arm while she informed me of the alkalizing benefits of vegetable juice, I know the truth. The woman is gorgeous.

I realize I'm staring.

"Take a picture," she teases.

"You're deformed," I say, resuming my work.

"Marry me," she says, setting the kettle aside and twisting the mismatched knob on the stove to turn off the element.

"I'll think about it," I reply. I glance at the ring on her wedding finger. The rock is modest, like our home, like our car, like our jobs, but when I proposed, she said yes.

"So, since you asked," (she didn't, but she smirks indulgently as she pours the water into a mug, filling the room with the smell of hibiscus) "the reason I can't start with that quote about the strongest of the species is I thought Charles Darwin said it, but he didn't. I mean it *sounds* like something he would have said, and it sounds like something he *should* have said, but, according to Quoteinvestigator.com, it was some Louisiana State University business professor who said it, at a social science convention of all places, and it's been misattributed to Darwin ever since."

I turn the laptop around so Steph can see the damning evidence on the website devoted to savvy things that luminaries like Oscar Wilde and Genghis Khan have (or have not) said, which I recycle, peppering them into my blog posts so as to look smarter than I am. She nods "uh huh" as she dips the bag of herbal tea in and out of the mug of steaming water.

"Slow day at the office?" she asks, lifting the tea bag by the string and dropping it into the sink with a splat.

She knows me well. I've got an acute case of Wikipedia blabber mouth. That means I worked out, stretched, and ran through some mixed martial arts exercises (I've recently gotten into weapons fighting, 'cause yeah, I'm bad ass like that), and I still had time to surf for conversation starters. It's an old habit.

"Three cancellations," I admit. "Weird week for that. Everyone's sick. Or their kid. Or their maid."

"Hospital's been cray cray too," she says. "That weird thing that's been going around. Everyone's super edgy." She tunes out for a second. "You still get paid?" she asks, returning the convo to my day. Unlike some people, she's democratic that way.

"Yes, ma'am."

She sighs. "I should become a personal trainer. No catheters and your work clothes are sweatpants."

"This from the woman whose power suit is a pair of pajamas?"

"Jealous?" she asks.

"Kinda," I confess.

This is one of the games that we play end-of-work-day: who has the better job. Today, it centers on comfort clothes. Yesterday, we focused on perks. She won for her access to prescription medication samples, narrowly beating my Lulu Lemon discount. I assured her I wasn't just dating her for the anti-inflammatories. She said "thanks," then put in an order for a new Yoga mat.

These are the good days. On others, her eyes will be puffy, and I'll know that some kid lost her battle to leukemia; or a five-year-old's been brought in high on meth; or some parents flipped out because they needed to blame someone for the caprices of life and death as a disease slowly eats away at their child right before their eyes.

On those days, I hold her close, and I tell her about the menopausal women in my Pilates class complaining to me about hot flashes and collapsed pelvic floors. On these days, I win for worst job ever, because she suddenly can't imagine doing anything other than working with sick kids.

"So, what's the blog post about?" she asks, taking out a jar of raw almonds from the cupboard. The lid makes a grinding sound as she forces it open. "Survival of the fittest?"

"Kinda," I say. "I was going to write about how Teddy saved my life when I was going through a hard time as a kid."

We both look over at Teddy, who occupies a place of honor on our new Ikea couch. The couch has modern lines and a neutral charcoal palette. It's so crisp, we're almost afraid to eat on it—almost. Teddy is a stark contrast. He looks like he's fought a war. If being the Keanu to my inner demons counts, then he has. Teddy is my childhood Teddy bear. His fur is yellow, rubbed raw on his belly, and patchy and matted in places; around the face, it hangs and protrudes at whimsical angles over his jet black button eyes, which have been sewn back on more than once.

"Interesting," she says. "So, the blog post is about the importance of mental and emotional resilience."

"And turning points."

"It's definitely revealing," she says.

"Bad idea?" I ask. "I could go with Confessions of a Binge Eater."

She thinks about it, munching on almonds. "No. I like Teddy. And sometimes you need to face your past to leave it behind."

She holds an almond and aims it at me, tossing it high in an arc. I move my head right and catch it between my teeth. I hold it there, sticking out from my incisors. I point at the seed (it's technically not a nut) with both hands, arms spread wide, my grin speaking for itself.

"You're not as awesome as you think," she smirks.

"Yeah, I am," I snort, crunching down on the almond.

She takes a handful of almonds and fires. They smack me gently, skittering as they hit the peeling linoleum floor.

"Abuse! Abuse!" I shout, holding my arm up as a shield. As I do, I marvel at three things.

One: that I'm cocky enough to tell the most beautiful woman in the world that I am awesome.

Two: for at least three seconds, I believe it.

Three: when that caught in the moment attitude fades, only half of me feels like a fraud.

I'm making progress.

CHAPTER 2

A few hours later, I'm shirtless in bed, finishing up the blog post. I'm wearing an arrowhead necklace that Steph gave me after we went to an exhibit about Native Americans. The chord is leather, which I've had to replace twice because of overwear. I even shower with it. I suck on the arrowhead like a soother and scratch at the butterfly tattoo on my shoulder.

The tat is a simple design, especially compared to Steph's mass of ink, just an outline that looks like a single Japanese brush stroke. My hand is hovering over the POST TO BLOG button. Soon, the world will know about the weirdo acne-prone kid (me) with the scrawny arms and saggy belly, who stared at his feet so much, he had a slouch by grade eight. He wanted to be Han Solo (or at least R2D2). At best, he was a bumbling C3PO, constantly bleating "Master Luke, Master Luke" in his sissy, synthetic voice.

I reread it one more time.

If I'd been born in the era of the cave man, and it was left up to natural selection, I never would've made it to adulthood. As it was, I barely survived the tribal world of grade school, my legs so inwardly rotated that gym class and recess were a nightmare. When it came to dividing into teams even the so-called weird kid with braces got picked before me. When it was my turn to stand on the mound, or take to the court, or grapple on the wrestling mat, I invariably threw up a little in my mouth. It's not the most obvious beginning for a personal trainer.

But what I lacked in athletic ability and social acumen, I made up for with gumption. I knew how to dream, and the girl who first sparked the kindling of my imagination was one Jenny Fitzgerald.

Picture it: grade eight. Afternoon recess. The air is crisp with an early winter bite and a young boy's hope. She stands before me in all her 12-year-

old glory. She has a dancer's poise, winter jacket to her knees, puffy pink mittens warming her hands. Bedazzled earmuffs clip her blond bob like a tiara. I slouch, oily skin blistered with whiteheads, palms sweaty despite the chill, croaking to this playground princess, "Will you go out with me?"

Around us, children scream and run about the school yard. "I was thinking we could go see a movie this weekend," I add. The end of recess bell hammers the air, an extended interlude to draw out her silence, followed by that moment of partial deafness as the ringing stops. Kids sprint to line up for class, and she says to me, "But I thought you were gay."

So much for my strategy of the past two weeks, asking her every day how her ballet lessons were going and complementing her on her choice of outfits, all the while building up the nerve to ask her out.

I explain to her that I am not *into boys. She looks unconvinced. I emphatically assure her that I am* into *girls. One in particular. She looks at me like a vegetarian forced to eat veal tartar. Finally, she responds, "Can't. Busy."*

"What about next weekend?" I ask.

"Can't, busy," she repeats.

"How about..."

She holds up her hand to stop me from finishing my sentence. "Can't," she emphasizes, "busy."

There are no words to capture the fog horn whomp, whomp devastation that I feel. I'm in a haze for the rest of the day. On the bus, I hear my name, and Jenny's, and kids laughing. Someone passes me a note. On it is a stick figure of me getting ass-fucked so hard by another stick figure that my stick self is splitting in half. My name and the word FAGGOT are in bold capital letters. I crumple it in my hand, staring out the window. I think to myself, I know *when I'm not wanted.*

That night, lying in bed, the stars shining through the skylight in my attic bedroom, I decide to kill myself.

That will show her. That will show them all.

An image comes to mind, of me hanging from a rope about my neck from the fire escape outside my room. Jenny Fitzgerald will be at my funeral. She'll cry for me, clasping my headstone with her puffy pink mitts. She'll lay her bedazzled earmuffs on my coffin. Most importantly, she'll wish she'd gone out with me when she had the chance.

I get out of bed and find a suitable length of rope in the basement. My dad uses it to tie things to the roof of the car. I take it upstairs and open the door to the chill early winter air.

I loop one end of the rope around the fire escape, using the knots I learned in sailing camp (I was just as useless on a boat as on dry land, but knots I could practice on my own, without the pressure or criticism of kids who absorbed these physical skills like a sponge. In sailing I got a C-, out of pity, I think. In knots, I earned my A+.) As I yank on the rope, I already know it will hold. The other end I turn into a noose.

I stare at it, then I put it around my neck, getting a feel for its weight and rough texture. I look back through the door into my room, and I meet Teddy's button eyes. I've never been more scared.

Tomorrow, *I hear him say to me inside my mind, which is, of course, just me talking to myself.* Tomorrow will be a better day.

"You don't know that," I whisper back to him.

Of course I do, *he answers in my head.* Tomorrow's comic book Saturday.

I'm so beat up inside, I completely forgot—I made it to the weekend!

It would be stupid to kill yourself now, *Teddy reasons in that way that only Teddy can.* Wait until Sunday night.

He's right. I'm shaking as I take the noose from around my neck and hide it in a dresser drawer. That was the beginning of Teddy as my savior and alter ego.

Sunday night, *I assure myself, my hand still on the drawer's handle.* You can kill yourself Sunday.

I echo this thought the next day as I wait in line at the corner store with the latest copy of The X-Men. Sunday night. You can kill yourself Sunday night. *It's a mantra, my lifeline, helping me to hold on for just a little longer —which is long enough. As I idly scan the magazine rack, I find my miracle: a copy of* Muscle & Fitness *magazine.*

I stare at the muscled male model, with a large-breasted blond draped over him; my mind goes blank. The dude looks like a real life replica of the jacked heroes in my comic books, the kind that attracts women with big boobs in bikinis. I can't even process.

Obviously, I'd seen the pixelated "skinny guy gets sand kicked in his face" ads in the back of my Marvel comics, promising guys like me the key to building a better body. But compared to the pumped bods in this muscle mag? Fuck you, very much, Charles Atlas.

I buy this flexoholic's digest without a second thought.

My parents give each other worried looks as they see me pouring through the muscle rag on the living room floor. They sit down next to me.

"So, you know that your father and I love you very much, no matter what, right Marty?" my mom says.

I nod, fixated by what's before me: the promise that anybody (translation: even me) can look like a superhero, and in my hands, for $2.99, is the blueprint for how to achieve it! I just have to follow these steps—mind blown.

"So, is there something you want to tell us?" my dad asks, as I practically salivate over Arnold Schwarzenegger—more worried looks.

"I want to start working out," I reply, not even looking up.

From the corner of my eye, I note the parental expressions of relief. They buy me a weight set that very day.

As it turns out, there's a lot more to getting in shape than what any single magazine contains, particularly a hardcore bodybuilding one that ignores functional fitness—especially back in those days. In some ways, I did myself more harm than good, overtraining chest and biceps, which would lead me to a shoulder injury that stalled my training for too many years.

And yet, as an adult, I would go on to overcome that as well.

I'm no 'roided out bodybuilder, nor even a fitness model, but I have actual delts, biceps, and abs, along with a solid social media following (shout out!). My legs are very much a work in progress, but they're improving. When I wear a tank top, I get the occasional look—and not just from gay men in their 60s. Not the worst for a guy who barely got through phys ed and once thought to end it all.

So, what was the actual blueprint, both mental and physical, that took me from contemplating pre-teen suicide to become the man I am today, who is even engaged to the woman of his dreams? More on that in my next post, so stay tuned!

I'm about to type TO BE CONTINUED... when I hear Steph swearing like a sailor with Tourette's. The arrowhead falls from my mouth and bangs against my chest. The warm metal is wet with my saliva.

"God damn mother fucking cocksucker cum dump ass licking piece of shit!" she shouts from the bathroom, the words practically slurring one into the other. If this verbal torrent were coming from my ex, I'd tense and freeze like an abused dog; one that hopes to remain unnoticed for fear of becoming the target of her wrath. But this is Steph.

The computer is off my lap, I'm reaching under the bed and grabbing a Filipino short sword, and I'm sprinting to the bathroom door before I've even registered that I've moved. I'm expecting a raccoon that's climbed in through the shower window.

Instead, she's staring at the mirror, stripped down to her underwear and a teeny tank top that shows off the lines of her stomach. She's pointing at her reflection; it's like she's rehearsing for an upcoming community theater production of *Sybil.*

"I will not take this from you, you stupid cow," she shouts. "You're not the boss of me!"

If I didn't know better, I'd say she was arguing with her mother. I search for Steph's cell, but it's nowhere in sight. Does she have a blue tooth device stuck in her ear? Her mouth juts open in an *oh no you didn't* kind of way. She holds up a finger in warning, and says to her reflection, "You're the one who needs to shut up!"

Her other hand clenches her toothbrush tighter and tighter, turning white.

"Steph?" I say.

She turns at the sound my voice and hisses at me, the muscles in her neck and jaw yanking her visage into a demonic mask. I hold up my free palm peacefully and carefully lower the sword to the ground.

"Steph, you okay in there?" I ask.

I have to clamp down on my desire to envelop her in my arms. If she's having some sort of episode, that might freak her out more. As a sometime sleepwalker, I should know.

"It's me, Marty," I say.

I'd like to think that it's the familiarity of my voice that reaches through to her. She looks at me weird.

"What?" she asks.

"Really?" I ask back.

She blinks, confused. "Do you need to take a shit or something?" she asks. "Use the toilet downstairs, dummy."

"Uh, no," I reply. "You were shouting. At the mirror."

She takes a few moments to process this, looks ready to deny it, then as if remembering a dream, she nods.

"Oh, that," she says, laughing nervously. "I was just goofing around."

She won't look me in the eye when she says it, and her hand's shaking as she squirts toothpaste onto her brush before shoving it into her mouth. I stare at her as she slides the brush back and forth between her cheeks. She spits and then looks at me. Toothpaste is drooling down her chin. She winks playfully. "Gotchya!"

It takes me a moment to process that she was messing with me the whole time. I smile, shaking my head and power wagging my finger at her, giving her the *naughty, naughty* sign. "Okay. That was pretty good, I'll give you that."

She smiles back. It strikes me as strained, but the thought is gone the moment she gestures her lithe arm from her head down to her toes. "And, you get to spend the rest of your life with this," she winks.

"Can't wait," I say, drinking in the sight of her, which is when I notice the nasty bruise on the outside of her supple thigh.

"Honey, what's that?" I ask, pointing at the purple blot. "Are those teeth marks?"

I take a step forward to get a closer look, and she shouts at the top of her lungs, "None of your goddamn fucking business!"

Again, if this were my ex, I'd slink away like a whipped mutt, afraid to move in bed for the rest of the night for fear of accidentally touching her, or rousing her fury in some other way, but this is Steph—emotional, fierce, pigheaded—but kind, giving, and nurturing in equal measure. So what the hell is going on with her?

She claps her palm over her mouth as if that's the only way she can control it.

"Are you okay?" I ask.

She nods, slowly lowering her hand.

"I'm rattled," she admits.

"Talk to me," I say, stealing one of her favorite lines.

"Role reversal much?" she asks.

I shrug in a *look at me evolving into a better man* kind of way.

"This kid bit me today at the hospital," she says. "I swear she came from a doll factory—black hair in tight curls, freckles, super-long lashes. I'm talking capital-A adorable. But she was an animal. She was an effing honey badger."

"Honey badger don't give a shit?" I ask, referencing a hilarious YouTube nature video of the most vicious mammal in the world, narrated by what sounds like a drag queen.

"Honey badger did *not* give a shit," Steph concedes with a tilt of her head. "We had to sedate her. The parents *seemed* concerned, but I have to wonder what's going on in that home."

"I'm sorry," I say. "That sounds rough."

She shrugs. "Workplace hazard, I guess."

"Why didn't you tell me before?"

Her brow creases in confusion. "I don't know. I just…forgot. Emerg' has been that crazy. More than usual. Psyche ward is overflowing. We're running out of sedatives."

She pops the lid off of a bottle of Xanax.

"Fuck," she says. "I meant to refill that a week ago."

We have a drawer full of Saint John's wort, GABA, and other natural mood stabilizers, but sometimes a person needs the hard stuff.

I close the distance between us. My hands are huge on her tattooed arms as I grasp her and pull her closer, kissing her on the forehead. She smiles.

"I missed a spot," I say. I'm about to lick off the toothpaste that's dribbling down her chin, when I catch a whiff of rotting garbage, which must be coming in from the open window. I hesitate, and she gets the upper hand.

"Oh, gross," she says, putting her palm square on my face and shoving me out the bathroom door. She gives me a *you're a hopeless dork* look. "Go play with your swords," she says. "I'll be out soon."

I pick the blade off the floor and turn back towards the bed. I do a few moves, pretending I'm disarming someone. From the corner of my eye I see her spit in the sink. Her saliva comes out pink with blood. I shout over my shoulder, "You need to start using that Waterpik I bought you. Your gums will thank you for it."

She gives me the finger.

I return to slicing the air.

"Love you too!" I reply playfully. And, I really fucking do.

I take a few more stabs at unseen foes, then slide the blade into a sheath and put it under the bed. I crawl beneath the sheets, assuming a sexy Calvin Klein underwear model pose with which to seduce my lady. Then, like a typical guy, I promptly fall asleep.

Six hours later, I wake to the sound of running water. I need to pee like there's a fire to put out. My morning hard-on is an annoyance as I rush to the bathroom.

I notice the tap running but that's not my priority. I leave it as I sit with relief on the toilet and start counting down from ten to help topple my erection, at least enough for me to pee without turning my dick into a fountain. (I once stood in the tub and proved to Steph that a guy can piss fully hard. She was not amused. It was my first lesson that in a relationship winning is sometimes losing.)

By the count of eight, my erection has gone from 90 degrees to 80. I reach over and turn off the faucet. My dick is down to a 3/4 semi, and I notice the toothbrush on the counter. The bristles are mangled and thick with dried blood.

Someone really *needs to start using that Waterpik*, I think. I'm playing with the arrowhead necklace about my neck.

I'm only half hard now. Technically, I could push my dick down below the edge of the toilet seat and let 'er rip, but it's then that I see something on the cracked tile floor. It's a tooth. An entire molar, including the root, with bits of dried blood on it.

"Steph?" I call.

I look to the bedroom. The blanket on her half of the mattress is tucked in. Did she even make it to bed last night?

"Steph?!" I call again. Silence replies.

My hard on is completely gone now, and I start to pee with a strong, steady flow.

CHAPTER 3

I flush the toilet and stand and pull up my pajama bottoms, all in one motion, not even bothering to tap tap. I call for my fiancé, "Steph?"

No answer. Outside, the sun is poking above the horizon. I hurry to the hall. I see bloody fingerprints on the banister.

"Steph!" I yell.

My instinct is to rush down the stairs.

Take a sword, my inner voice instructs. I'm being ridiculous, but as my martial arts instructor says, *If something seems off, be ready to fight.* At which point he likes to smack the side of the head. I grab the Filipino fighting blade from under the bed.

I inch down the stairs, half naked, blade in hand, careful to step over the stair that creaks. There are more bloody prints on the wall and railing.

Downstairs, I'm greeted by the smell of brewing coffee. The normalcy of that one simple thing lets me breathe easier—until I turn the corner and see the kitchen itself.

What the...?

It looks like *this* is *Where the Wild Things Are.* The fridge and freezer doors are ajar. A puddle is forming on the floor. All over the peeling linoleum are cartons of egg whites, thawing meats, and bags of salad. Random cabinets and drawers are pulled open. Cutlery is arranged on the kitchen table in the pattern of a flower. Bloody handprints are everywhere.

How the hell did I sleep through this? I wonder. What possessed her? And where the hell is she?

I step quickly across the kitchen floor. A sputtering spray from the coffee machine hits my bare arm. It burns. Coffee grounds overfill the filter basket as it brews black sludge.

What is going on?

"Steph!" I shout.

I stop next to an umbrella container by the back door, leading from the kitchen to the yard. I ignore the umbrellas and pull out a sturdy wooden rod. It's about 3/4 of an inch thick and three-feet long. I hear Steph's voice in my mind.

More self-defense? What if our home invader finds the stick?

My reply: *That's why we keep steel in the bedroom, baby.*

I'm no longer feeling so cocky. There's a half-eaten chicken on the floor. The bones are gnawed. I see a hint of white in what's left of a thigh. It's another tooth. On the counter, I see an empty pill bottle. Did she take them?

"Steph!"

The door from the kitchen to the backyard is open by an inch. I pull it wider. In the rising sun, I finally see my fiancé. She's dressed in her slinky tank top and panties. There's an odd paleness to her skin, making her veins stick out with a sickly blue cast. Her tattoos look practically fluorescent.

"Steph?" I say. "Steph, honey, are you okay?" She doesn't seem to hear me.

She's crouching down and hunched over something. It's hard to get a good view, but the tail gives it away. It's a Golden Retriever. She loves dogs and keeps hounding me to get one. If it will get us back to our normal life, I'm happy to say "yes" because now I am truly scared.

The dog is on its back, paws up, and one would assume that she's rubbing its belly. But so many things are off. I can see bloody handprints on her thighs. The dog isn't moving. Its tail isn't wagging. Its eyes stare unseeing at the sky. There's a crunching sound and low growls, but not from the dog. They're coming from the love of my life.

"Steph, you're really freaking me out," I say.

I walk slowly, my bare feet sinking softly into the dewy grass. My grip tightens on the stick in one hand, the short sword in the other.

I gag on the smell of rot.

How can she stand it? I wonder. When my paleo protein shakes turn me flatulent, it's she who drops an A-bomb of Febreeze in my wake.

"Honey, I need you to look at me," I say.

I'm almost on top of her. Her bare feet are scraped, bloody, and covered in dirt. I set the sword and stick on the ground. *We're going to get through this*, I assure myself. I put a hand on her shoulder. "Hon…"

Her neck twists around. Something snaps, allowing her to turn her head further than it should—not quite an *Exorcist* 180 degrees, but close enough. Her eyes bulge, bloodshot like she's smoked a dozen reefers. Dripping intestines hang from her mouth. The Golden Retriever's belly is ripped open, its rib cage cracked. Blood and organs are everywhere.

"Holy shit!" I stumble back, tripping over a soccer ball (her thing, not mine—my parents had to pay me to go to soccer practice, and I still quit after one game). I land on my ass. I grab the stick and sword and quickly skitter away.

She stands, towering over me, and takes a single zombified step in my direction. That's when I finally get it, and I start to laugh. She stops. I laugh some more. I'm laughing so hard my right side starts to hurt. A corner of her mouth twitches into the semblance of a smile. *Ha!* I think. *Made you break character!*

"Okay, you got me, you twisted broad," I say. My grin is ridicu-licious —ridiculous *and* delicious. "You *will* pay for this, but shit, woman, who did your makeup? Klaus? I thought he was still in LA. And the dog. Babe, this is good."

In fact, it's too good. *How the hell am I supposed to outdo this?* All I can think is: *challenge accepted*.

For now, I just enjoy. Fake guts hang from her mouth. If we weren't already engaged, I'd ask her to marry me on the spot. When we're finally ready to combine DNA to have a kid, I can't wait to see how whack he/ she/ze turns out. Steph takes a stumbling step towards me. I egg her on, gesturing with *come and get it* fingers. She's owning the part. Even that smile, twitching at her lips, is killer-clown creepy, and it looks like she's been chewing on her own lower lip, where a chunk of flesh appears to be missing. The illusion is a definite mindfuck.

"If nursing doesn't work out, I think you've got a solid plan B here," I say. "Zombie extra, that's a thing, right?"

Another shambling step, and she closes the distance between us. Her arms reach for me. The smell of rotting detritus slaps me as she gets closer.

"Holy hell do you reek!" I say as bits of "dog guts" drop onto my leg.

I'm half tempted to let her grab me and pretend maul me, but as much as I like role play, I'm not convinced that this is the one to get me hard. Plus, I've got a client this morning, and my lady smells like a Bangkok sewer.

Still, I've got five minutes to horse around, and I want to get back at her—at least enough to show some semblance of dominance. I mean, I can appreciate a woman putting my testes on a platter as much as the next sensitive new age guy, but I would like my manhood back. I hook one foot around her ankle and then press my other foot into the knee of the same leg, and down she goes. I direct her weight off to the side of me.

We've done this move on each other many times before. Today, it goes south at warp speed. She lands on her arm, and there's a sickening crunch.

"Oh shit!" I swear.

I drop the weapons and roll her over. There are tears in my eyes.

"Baby, I'm sorry! I'm so sorry! Your arm is it..."

It's clearly broken. A bone is poking out. I'm such an asshole! The stench of rot is stronger than ever. I don't care. Her hair's in her face. She lashes out blindly with her good arm, fingers catching on the arrowhead necklace about my neck. She rips it off, looks at it in confusion through the strands of hair veiling her sight, then tosses it aside.

"Steph, we have to get you to a hospital."

The word hospital seems to resonate with her. She is a nurse, after all. She nods. I nod back, mirroring her, letting her know I'm right here with her. I leave the weapons on the grass and get my arms under her.

"You're going to be okay," I say, lifting her up, hugging her against me. I'm not sure how we're going to explain the zombie look to the emergency doctor, but whatever. From what Steph tells me, they deal with way weirder stuff than this, usually involving an object in an orifice.

She stares into my eyes.

"I'm so sorry, baby, I'm so sorry," I pant.

Her jaws open wide. If I didn't know any better, I'd say she was about to...The thought puffs into genie smoke as my foot catches on an automated sprinkler head. I trip. Steph bounces in my arms. Her jaw snaps shut on empty air. My foot hits a muddy patch. I slide. I could try to right myself, but if I fail, Steph may go flying. Better a controlled fall, like we've practiced.

My knees bend, and my hips go sideways. Instead of fighting the momentum, I ease into it. If Steph had done as I'm doing, her damn arm wouldn't be broken. I know better than to say this to her—not until the cast comes off.

My movement practice is paying off. It's about to be a textbook landing. Steph growls. Her good arm is cobra quick. Her fingers are pythons clenched about my throat. She squeezes. *What the what?* I gasp for air, land hard on my knees, and I drop her onto her butt. She doesn't let go, though. My vision's going. I panic, and autopilot takes over. My hand grasps her wrist and twists it—just enough that she can't help but release my neck—except she doesn't. It's like she doesn't even feel what I'm doing to her. I twist a bit harder, then harder still. She should be in agony, but nothing. *Her other arm's broken, fuck face*, I berate myself. *Of course, she can't feel this. You planning on breaking this arm too?*

Her teeth chatter hungrily as she starts pulling herself up towards me. I press down on her chest with my forearm, but it's like I'm trying to hold back a slowly moving freight train.

How can she be this strong?

From the corner of my eye, I see the fighting stick. I grab it, and I realize the answer to my earlier question is, yes. I'm going to break her other arm, because as much as I'd rather die than ever hurt her, I know she could never live with herself if I let her kill me while in this psychotic state. I suck in the tiniest amount of air, but it's not enough. I see stars.

I don't know if I can do this, I whine.

You have to. It's Teddy's voice. That bear has no fucking mercy.

I swing, and part of my mind notes that something's off. The stick is too heavy, the shaft too thick. I see a glint of metal in the morning sun and realize too late, I didn't grab the stick—I'm swinging the Filipino short sword. It's so sharp it slices clean through Steph's arm. I expect her to scream; she doesn't. I should also be screaming as I stumble back, but her fingers are still tight around my throat. Even cut off from her body, she's trying to strangle me.

Is this a reflex? part of me wonders. Like a chicken running around with its head cut off?

I drop the sword. Her grip on my larynx is weakening, but it still takes both my hands to yank off the one of hers. I hold her severed forearm.

Holy fuck, I cut Steph's arm off.

I stare at the engagement ring on her finger. Even detached from her body, Steph's hand is still clawing at the air.

I need to get her arm on ice, I think, praying to God it can be reattached.

She's snarls and rushes me, jaws chomping hungrily. This isn't some prank. This is more than psychosis. She's full on rabid.

Oh shit!

I dodge and shove Steph away from me—an under-appreciated tactic in the martial arts, but well understood by any kid on a playground. She smacks into the fence. I wince.

"Baby, I know you're still in there. Just hold on," I say.

I reach for my pocket to grab my phone to call 9-1-1, but I'm in my pajamas. The phone's inside, and the love of my life isn't done with me.

This isn't real. This has to be a nightmare. Why can't I wake up?

Steph takes a ragged step toward me. It looks like she's pulled something in her leg. Sirens wail. One of my neighbors must've called the police and, *please God*, an ambulance.

She growls and bites at the air. Her breath smells like she's been drinking swamp water. That crooked smile is frozen on her face. She keeps hobbling towards me.

"Steph? Honey?"

I set her arm down in a patch of dandelions. I pick up the stick and the Filipino sword. I'm ashamed the moment I do. *What do you think you're going to do with that sword? Butcher your fiancé even more?* I gently press the stick into her chest, just above her left breast. Her perky, dark nipples show through her bloody white tank top. The plan is to keep her far enough away from me that she can't hurt me, and, at the same time, avoid hurting her—anymore than I already have. *You don't even need the sword*, I tell myself. Still, I don't drop it. *Why don't I drop it?*

I hear more sirens, some drawing closer, some fading away, but none stop in front of our house.

What the fuck is taking so long?

She growls, reaching her severed arm at me. Her broken one just hangs there. Blood drips, thick and black as tar. She steps forward. I dig my heels into the lawn, promising to pull up every goddamn dandelion if I can just get us through this, get her to a hospital, counter whatever the fuck is fucking her up, and her arm...*Oh, fuck me, her arm!*

The one I cut off, it's lying there, in the grass, fingers curling in like a dying insect.

She keeps stepping forward. The stick bends a bit. I hear a squelching sound. To my horror, the stick straightens as her flesh gives and the wooden rod pushes half an inch into her body. Gooey blood oozes out, so thick with coagulant it seems impossible that it can even be circulating.

She steps closer, the stick pushing her shirt into her by another half inch, dangerously close to her heart.

"Please, baby," I say, retreating just enough to keep from killing her. "I need you to step back."

What you need to do is change your fucking tactics, I rage at myself.

"Help! Andy! Sam!" I cry, hoping my neighbors will hear me. One of them does. Someone's banging on a second-floor window one house over. It's Sam. His balding head gleams, and his belly hangs out of his open bathrobe. He presses himself against the window, smacking his palm against the glass. Half his face is chewed off.

For a moment, Steph looks up at him, and her jaws grind together. It's as if she's saying, "back off, this one's mine."

Sam's got a pathetic look on his face as if, once again, he's being left out by the "cool kids"—as he would teasingly refer to us. *They're called hipsters now, dear*, his wife would tell him. The incongruous thought flicks through my mind as the sound of a shotgun explodes the air. Sam's chest tears open, and the force blasts him through the window. He falls from the second story to the ground. Steph grows frenzied at the sound and with a surge of force jerks herself forward. Her shirt rips, and the stick stabs straight through her heart, coming out her back.

"Steph!" I shout. And then, "Steph?"

She should be dead, but she isn't. Her jaw's almost on top of me. The rational part of my brain is a frozen computer screen—unable to process. Another part takes over. I press my foot into her solar plexus and shove her away. She staggers back, off of the stick, and falls to the ground. With shaky movements, she gets back up. Her growls are now joined by Sam's. Through the chinks in the wooden fence, I see him lumbering towards our yard. A part of his upper torso is missing. His left arm dangles by ligaments and strips of muscle. His good arm tries reaching over the fence.

Steph is limping toward me.

"She's not your wife anymore," a woman says from across the yard.

I look up. It's Janine—Sam's wife of fifteen years. She's in a bathrobe, smoking shotgun in hand. She stares down from the shattered window.

She's my fiancé, I want to say, but the semantics seem pointless as Janine points the weapon at Sam and blows his head off.

"The woman you knew is gone," she repeats in a deadened voice. Her eyes glisten. "Stephanie is dead."

Janine turns from the window and walks away. It's just Steph and me. I'm panting, staring at the love of my life, my better self. From the corner of my eye, I see Sam's headless torso.

"Please," I say to her.

The tears burn my eyes. She lumbers forward.

"Come on Steph, show me that you're in there," I beg.

Her teeth chatter. I drop the stick.

"I'm begging you."

She steps inside striking distance. Still, I hold back. I place the tip of the sword under her chin.

"Don't make me do this."

She steps closer, and the blade slides into her. I'm *not* doing this. At least, that's what I tell myself. She's walking right into the sharp steel. It's angled up. Another step. The weapon goes deeper. She doesn't even flinch. Black tar oozes out of her and down the sharp edge. She takes one last step. I cringe and look away, but too slowly to block out the sight of her face, a bridge of freckles across her perfectly too large nose, impaled on my blade.

She makes a strangled sound. The thick tar that is her blood must be caught in her throat, but as the blade pierces her brain it's the change in her weight that catches me off guard. She goes heavy, all at once, yanking my arm down as her body crumples. She slides off the sword, smacks her cheek on a patio stone, and lies there.

My Steph is dead.

CHAPTER 4

I stare without seeing. The automated sprinkler system, installed by the previous owners, jerks to life. It flicks droplets of water, creating a mini rainbow over Steph's severed arm.

You need to move, my inner voice—Teddy—tells me. The weapon slips from my hand and clatters against a patio slab. She's gone. I killed her. I see something shiny against a dandelion—it's the arrowhead necklace. I pick it up. It sweats sprinkler water. My fingers shake as I tie it around my neck. It gets me moving, sluggish, but moving, and objects in motion tend to stay in motion. Physics says so.

Inside, surrounded by the kitchen mess, I try calling my parents. The call fails. I try calling my brother. The call fails. I try calling Gary, then Devon, then Chris. They all fail. Finally, I dial 9-1-1.

I get an automated message.

We are currently in a state of emergency. Take shelter indoors, in a secure location. Lock all doors and windows. STAY OFF THE STREET. More information and instructions to follow as the situation develops. This is a recording.

I think of Janine blasting a hole through her husband's chest. I think of Steph lying in the backyard. The sound of sirens still fill the air—too many sirens—some are near while others grow distant. I look out the front window. A plume of smoke rises into the air a few streets over. The neighbors, Angie and Doug, are packing up their minivan with blankets, suitcases, and coolers. They shove their three kids, aged four through eight, into the back seats. I open my front door and step out.

"No, Claire, for the last time, you cannot bring your Barbie camper," Angie says to her kid.

"But I always bring her when we go to the cottage!" the six-year-old complains.

Angie grabs her by the arms. "You need to stop arguing! Do what Mommy tells you!"

She picks the kid up and roughly straps her into a seat. The little girl starts wailing. Angie ignores her. "Doug, do you have the camping stove?"

He holds it up, piling it in the back.

"Guys," I say, "what the hell is happening?"

Doug looks up. "Marty, you gotta get out of here, man."

An idea pops into his head. "Get Steph, get your swords, come with us."

Angie stops. "Doug, what are you doing?" she asks in a stage whisper.

"The guy has swords. What do you think I'm going to do if we have to fight," Doug demands of her, "throw a keyboard at them? I'm an accountant for Christ's sake."

She looks at me, in my pajamas, shirtless, splattered with Steph's blood.

"Where's Steph?" she asks.

Doug's noticing the blood now, too.

"She's in the backyard," I say.

I feel the tears welling in me. They stream down my cheek.

"She came at me," I say defensively. "I didn't know what to do."

"Oh, man," Doug says, shaking his head, "I'm sorry, about Steph, and...look, this isn't personal, but you can't come with us. You might be infected. You understand, right?"

I do not understand. I do not understand any of this.

"I'm a father," he adds by way of explanation. "I have to look out for my kids."

Angie slides the minivan's door shut. The way she looks at me...

"Infected?" I ask. The word pierces through my grief. "What do you mean?"

"We gotta go, get up north, while we still can," Doug says, getting into the driver's seat.

Angie looks at me with pity. "I'm sorry Marty. About Steph, and...good luck."

24

They're backing out when panic sets my legs on fire. They're leaving me. Alone. I run towards them like a maniac.

"Tell me what's going on!"

I bang on the window, and Doug hits the accelerator. The tires squeal.

I run after them futilely, bits of rock biting into my bare feet. Their kids stare at me, terrified. I stop in the middle of the street, panting. They disappear down the street of small homes. All that's left of them is the smell of exhaust.

I stand there, a once dominant life form sinking in tar. *I have no fucking clue what to do.* I feel the dark place swirling around me, seducing me with the delusional notion that if I do nothing, I can do nothing wrong.

CHAPTER 5

I limp back to the house. The bottoms of my exposed feet burn as the adrenaline tapers. I approach my front door, and my neighbor Janine steps out of her house. She's got the shotgun she used to put down her husband.

What she said earlier rings in my ears. *The woman you knew is gone.* I see it all happening again, Steph coming at me, the sword sliding slowly into the underside of her jaw, Steph's cheek smacking against the ground. I make a choking sound. Tears burst from my eyes. Janine nods once in understanding and says, "Fuck this."

She puts the shotgun to her mouth—I witness it in profile—and she pulls the trigger. The boom deafens. Her brains spray through the open door behind her. She wobbles and falls.

"Fuck!" I say, sucking back my tears as I escape inside, slamming and locking the door behind me as if that can shelter me from everything that's just happened.

I pull the drapes across the windows. Teddy stares at me from the couch with his black button eyes.

I turn on the TV. A news channel shows images of tanks entering city streets, firing on a mob of what a female anchor is referring to as "the seemingly undead."

The anchor says, "...Istanbul." The images shift from the domes and turrets of a mosque to New York's Times Square, followed by the Arc de Triomphe, Rome's Coliseum, San Francisco's Golden Gate Bridge, Moscow's Red Square, then Tokyo, Sydney, Tehran, Tel Aviv, Abu Dhabi "...all have been affected, with more reports coming in from agencies around the world."

"Fuck me," I say, my leg twitching next to Teddy.

"...authorities believe that whatever it is, whether this is viral or bacterial, or some form of neurological toxin, that it's transmitted through bites," the anchor explains with practiced measure. Underneath, her voice trembles. Even her bouffant updo, glued together by hairspray, seems ready to unravel. "People are being told to stay indoors until the military and police can get the situation under control."

I look at my phone. There's a slew of missed calls that have only just come through. My parents have tried ringing three times. Nothing from Gary. My GBF. My bro. *Is he even still alive?* Yes, it's Gary. He's alive. I try calling my parents. No answer. I try Gary. No answer. I try my brother. No answer.

Fuck.

"If you've been bitten," the anchor continues, "health officials say the best thing to do is to lock yourself in a room, preferably with no windows, or perhaps your basement, if you have one. Isolate yourself. Protect your family and your community..."

I think of Steph, of the bite on her leg, of how stupidly cavalier I was last night. If I'd done something instead of being such an idiot—just dozing off—she might still be alive.

You're the one who should be dead.

The voice chills me. This isn't Teddy. Teddy's my inner cheerleader. This is that other voice. She-Who-Must-Not-Be-Named. I take a deep breath.

"That's just your self-saboteur talking," I say to myself. One of the shrinks, at the place, called it that, assuring me we all have one. Mine just happens to sound like my ex-girlfriend. She's an early warning sign that I'm slipping. The trick, the doc assured me, was to teach that part of me positive self-talk. I hear my ex's biting laugh. My throat and abdomen tighten.

"I need to check myself for bites," I say to no one.

In the bathroom, I strip off my blood spattered-pajamas and step under the steaming shower. It burns, but I don't turn it down. Will it disinfect me? No clue. The pain feels good. I grab a loofah and soap, and I start scrubbing the dirt and blood off of my arms and chest. I scrub harder than is necessary. The water runs pink and grimy around my feet. I see something in the corner of the tub. Is it a thermometer? I pick it up. It's a pregnancy tester. My heart hammers. Was Steph…Were we going to be parents? I stare at the diagram printed on it—one line means not pregnant, two lines means pregnant. There are no lines. Steph went to the trouble of buying the tester but never used it. Was her period late? Wouldn't she have told me? Or was she afraid of getting my hopes up? I'll never know.

I whip the tester against the tile wall. The plastic snaps.

I press my face into my palms; I sob uncontrollably. The sound is foreign coming from my adult lungs— an animal caught in a steel trap. I don't know how long that lasts, but, somehow, under the hot spray, I feel the release of my grief—for now. I turn off the water, yank open the shower curtain, pat myself dry, and step in front of the mirror.

Were we going to be parents? The thought is a nail in my temple.

I search my body, front and back. The loofah has left me looking like I have a full-body rash. There are scrapes, bruises, and even scratches. Nowhere do I see any teeth marks.

I should feel a sense of relief. I've been given a *Get Out of Jail Free* card. I wait for my inner saboteur to say something, to try to drag me down into the dark place, but she's gone quiet. I'm numb all over.

I go to my room and dress in clean clothes: cargo pants that Steph forbade me from wearing except for yard work, a t-shirt with the X-Men logo on it, and fresh socks that I free from a Costco pack. My phone rings as I'm pulling them on. I snap it up from my bed.

PARENTS, according to the display. I thumb ACCEPT CALL.

"Mom?" I say.

"Martin, thank God you're alive!" I hear my dad's voice on the other end. My insides turn raw, and I fight a sudden wave of tears.

My dad sounds ten years older than when we spoke just a few days ago. "Martin, you've seen what's going on out there?"

"What is it?" I ask, although why a retired engineer would have the inside scoop, I have no clue, except that this is my dad, the smartest person I know, the guy who fixes things and makes everything better.

"People are saying so many different things, I don't think anybody knows," he replies. "How's Steph?"

I cry, mangling my reply.

"It's all right son," Dad says. "It's all right."

I wipe the tears away. "Is Mom okay?"

"I..." my dad hesitates. "I had to lock her in the bathroom."

"Did...did she bite you, Dad? They say that's how it spreads."

"No, I'm fine, I'm fine, but..."

His voice trails off. "Your brother. Nancy. The kids."

I can't breathe for a moment.

"All of them?" I ask.

"Mischa was bitten by some kid in his kindergarten class. Nancy was telling your mother about it yesterday. Then he went berserk. Bit his brother and sisters. The last I heard they were all headed to the hospital. That was before we knew what this was, and before it really started to spread. I haven't been able to reach them since."

Everything throbs. I can't even...

I hear a loud banging from my dad's end of the phone. There's a crash.

"Oh, shit," my dad swears. The man *never* swears.

"Dad? What is it? Dad?"

"It's your mother. I have to go. I love you son. *We* love you."

"Dad? Dad!" I stare at the phone. CALL ENDED.

"Fuck."

I try to call him back. Three times. Each time it goes to voicemail. *The person at this number can't take your call right now. Please...*

I hear the beep.

"Dad, call me. It's Marty. Call me, Dad." I press END CALL.

He's dead, my ex's voice of doom assures me with a know-it-all's hint of satisfaction. *You're all alone.*

He's alive, I reply unconvincingly.

I should go to him. That's what a good son would do, even on the slightest chance that he's locked himself up in his room. And Mom? What's become of my mom? I don't know why, but I always thought my parents would die together in a car accident. I look out the window. Plumes of smoke rise in the distance. More sirens. Honking. Dogs barking. At least, I think they're dogs. I turn on the TV in our room— news shots of clogged highways. My dad is six hours away by car. Under the circumstances, he might as well be on the moon.

He's gone, my ex says to me with the weight of an anchor about my waist. *They're all gone.* I can feel myself sinking. My feet are heavier and heavier. Collapsing on the spot seems like a viable course of action. I feel the shadows of the dark place swirling around me.

Gary, I think. *Gary will know what to do.*

I press his number, and a pic of his poster boy face pops up on the screen of my phone. The call goes nowhere. No service.

Go to him, Teddy says.

I could, in fact. Right now, he should be at The Box with a morning class. It's protected by concrete walls and a thick gate. There are worse places to hole up.

You'll never make it, my ex says. She flashes the proof in my mind. Sure, I'm a trainer. Compared to a plump housewife, I'm the epitome of health. But, when stacked up against the other trainers at my gym, I burn out first, bench press the least, and finish last. I sometimes feel like I can barely stay a step ahead of our clients.

You're the best of the worst, she concludes. I sometimes wonder what I'll do when people figure it out.

You could just kill yourself, the Saboteur suggests.

The thought makes me freeze—because she's right.

CHAPTER 6

I consider my options. I can stay here, hiding like a kid who locks himself in a closet as a house fire closes in; I can go out there, like an amateur surfer paddling towards a tsunami; or, I can take my ex's advice, and follow Janice's lead.

Whatever I decide, I must first lay Steph to rest. I'm not leaving her body to rot on the back lawn. She can do that underground—like a civilized person. The thought makes me smile. Steph would've laughed at that. She'll never laugh again.

I go downstairs, past the mess in the kitchen, out the door, and I pick a spot in the yard where the earth is soft.

It takes a few hours to bury her. I take my time, despite the events in the outside world. I cradle her body in a sheet, lowering her down into this pit. I'm cried out by the time I place her childhood Barbie beside her. The thing has mangled punk-rock hair and permanent-marker tattoos. Next to the Barbie, I place the mystery pregnancy tester. Finally, I climb out. I shovel, and the sound of dirt landing onto her thuds in my ears. My final words to her are simple. "I love you. More than life. See you soon."

Inside the house, I place a bottle of red wine on the kitchen counter next to a bottle of Steph's sleeping pills. I normally don't touch them. They give me the sweats, crazy lucid nightmares, and have made me sleepwalk. I pour a glass of wine and lift it up to Teddy.

"I guess this is it," I say.

I shove the oval pills into my mouth when I glance at my phone. 1 MISSED CALL. FROM GARY.

I grab the phone. I try to call him back, but service is down again. CALL FAILED.

Just end it, my ex says. *You're never going to make it. You're one of the weak. Sure, you tricked me into dating you, but when I saw through you, I dumped you like the piece of garbage that you are.*

The pull of the dark place grows stronger.

I stare into Teddy's button eyes. The meds feel like marbles in my mouth.

If you kill yourself, he says, *she wins.*

Those are the magic words that break her spell.

I spit the pills into the sink. The sleep aids skitter down the drain like insects. *Jesus H,* I think—because this is going to be *really* hard.

Teddy stares at me from the couch. I shake my head at his button eyes. "You can wipe that self-satisfied smirk off your face."

I pick up my cell phone and start typing a text message to Gary.

Broseph, if you get this, if you're still alive, if you haven't left town, if you have nowhere else to go, meet me at The Box. I love you, man.

I press SEND.

A moment later a red exclamation mark shows up next to it. MESSAGE FAILED.

I think of my ex, always chipping away at me.

"Fuck you," I say to that corner of my brain where her voice lives. "I can do this."

I hope to hell I'm right.

Being deeply loved by someone gives
you strength, while loving someone
deeply gives you courage.
—Lao Tzu

PART 2

CHAPTER 7

According to TED Talks, turning a crises into a game can help a person triumph. Maybe it can even help a loser like me.

Step one: adopt an identity.

I can't let my Saboteur mindfuck me. If I'm going to get to The Box, I need to be my baddest bad-ass self. Teddy is not going to cut it.

"Let's do this, Rambo," I say, calling on the persona I've created to get through super-tough workouts. I open the closet and Vietnam vet myself by wrapping a rolled-up, red bandana around my forehead—one-man-army style.

Step two: rally allies.

I resend the message to Gary.

"Dear God, you fucker, please let him be alive."

Step three: identify the bad guys.

That feels redundant.

Step four: power-ups.

Down in the basement, my so-called man cave, I turn on a flickering light and cross the worn shag carpet that we swore we'd tear up six months ago, passing a wine rack (mine) and a beer fridge (Steph's). Next to it is a homemade wooden cabinet, sealed with a massive padlock.

I unlock the cabinet. The double doors part. My collection of knives, short swords, and throwing stars are arranged like art in a gallery.

"You are on a mission of vengeance, redemption, and to save the ones you love," I say, committing to my persona.

In a flurry, I unhook the swords and knives, attaching them all over my body in specially designed holsters. I leave the throwing stars.

You'll just hurt yourself, my ex warns. I hate to admit it, but she's right, especially if I'm under pressure.

In the garage, I load up Steph's Prius with nutrition bars, protein powder, and coconut water. A magnet clatters to the ground as I pull a picture of Steph and me from the freezer door. In the pic, I'm hugging her from behind, both of us outfitted in our autumn sweaters, big smiles on our faces. I slide the picture into my pocket.

I scoop Teddy off the couch. Teddy goes in the car's passenger seat, rolls of toilet paper at his padded feet. I throw in a first aid kit and as many non-perishables as I can find. There isn't much—some cans of chick peas and lentil soup. We believed in fresh food.

I check my phone. Nothing from Gary. MESSAGE FAILED. I resend it. I turn on the car radio. My ears burn with the zuck-shaw sound of static.

"Shit," I say, clicking it off. Maybe my ex is right. Maybe I am fucked.

I press the white button on a black remote. The garage door opens behind.

I back out, into a world that's become a horror novel. An old man, whose name I never bothered to learn, peers at me from the second floor of his house. He holds the curtain back. He's in a tuxedo, a glass of champagne in one hand. The other makes the peace sign at me. I pass another house, where a single mother is loading a car in the driveway. Her muscled teen son stands guard with a shovel, while his little brothers hand things to Mom.

"Good job, boys," she says.

Many of the houses are quiet, and I wonder, *Did they get out?* The cars out front would indicate no. *So, where are they?*

I turn the corner and speed towards a blinking traffic light. I'm almost at the intersection when I hear the wail of sirens. I hit the brakes, and my seatbelt catches me as a convoy of police cars speed by. They disappear down the highway. I look and listen, but no more are coming. I turn onto the highway, leaving the enclave of homes behind me.

The police are heading towards the beaming skyscrapers of downtown. Smoke rises in plumes from dozens of unseen fires. I go in the opposite direction. I wait to hit traffic—like I saw on the news. I join a few straggling cars, but that's it. Maybe most people fled along the freeway. Or maybe I'm among the last to make it out.

I think of those quiet homes behind me and what might be incubating within.

I pass the occasional car going the other way. I flash my lights at them in warning. What scares the shit out of me is they also flash their lights at me. I try the radio and get a signal this time. From channel to channel, I get a mashup of conflicting information: stay in your homes; go to the nearest emergency station; don't engage the infected; be prepared to fight… This is followed by a list of public buildings that have been militarized, including city hall, some schools, and recreation centers. Nothing near me. Nothing in the direction that I'm headed.

I see half-built condo towers rising in the distance. Off to my left, cranes scratch the sky like skeletal fingers. To one side of me is the lake, on the other, a sound barrier made of concrete. A graffiti artist has tagged it with a biblical verse, recent enough that the city hasn't power washed it clean.

And I will punish the World for their evil and the wicked for their iniquity, and I will cause the arrogance of the proud to cease, and will lay low the haughtiness of the Terrible. Isaiah 13: 9-13

"Well, fuck you very much, Isaiah," I mutter.

The asphalt is a canvas as I drive. The slashes of painted yellow lines blur the one into the next. The car's shadow flows over it all like an oil spill. It's weirdly hypnotic. I don't pass anyone. No one passes me. The sounds of sirens are distant. There's a car in the ditch, its windows spattered with blood. Birds chirp and crickets whine.

I reach the next intersection.

I stop, staring past the blinking traffic lights, into the quiet street beyond. I've made this trip hundreds of times. This may be my last.

Okay, Marty, I say to myself, *let's do this.*

Out of habit, I signal that I'm turning left, the humble click click of the indicator paradoxically comforting and disquieting in its normalcy. I turn onto a street of freshly planted trees. The townhomes are all new and shiny, built in the last few years. They're small by suburban standards, designed for the compact reality of city living, just a streetcar ride away from the downtown core. An ambulance is crashed into a utility pole. There are two police cars on the far end of the street, angled together as if to form a wall. I don't see any police officers.

I do see a woman in a window, and she hastily pulls the curtain closed. Other than that, I seem to be alone. It's even quieter than my own hood. I drive slowly. The road is an obstacle course. I veer around the empty cop cars. My heart feels like an MMA grudge match, both ventricles drop kicking my rib cage from the inside. I scan for potential threats, living or undead. I pass a car with a half-open window, and a bloody arm reaches for me. I swerve instinctively and unnecessarily; there's no real danger. The car bounces as I hop the curb, and I narrowly avoid a fire hydrant.

Retard, my ex hisses.

I turn the corner, and I allow myself a moment of hope. Stretching ahead of me are three blocks of homes, then another three blocks of condos under construction. At the end of the street are the concrete walls surrounding The Box, the gym I co-own with Gary.

I'm going to make it.

So, why is my ex tensing up inside of my head?

Because you're slowing down, she replies. The edge in her voice is worse than usual. She's scared. And she's right. My foot pushes the accelerator, but, instead of picking up speed, the car is losing it. Three breaths later, Steph's Prius comes to a rolling stop.

I pump the pedal, futilely.

"Come on," I hiss. My shirt is a sponge of sweat. I catch the waft from my armpits. I didn't think to apply deodorant this morning.

I turn the key to restart the car, and the engine releases a pathetic grinding protest.

You're on empty, my ex says with contempt.

I stare at the fuel gauge. The white needle is all the way in the red. I flashback to yesterday. I told Steph not to fill the tank because I had a hunch the price of gas would drop after the long weekend.

"You are such a cheapskate," she rolled her eyes.

"The politically correct term is fiscally strategic," I corrected her. When I left home, I mentally braced myself for white supremacist survivalists setting up a road block to steal supplies; packs of rabid dogs; a school bus full of undead children ready to swarm me. Instead, I'm sabotaged by my own goddamn cheapness.

Loser! my ex hollers at me.

I check my phone. No message from Gary.

I assess the distance to the plain geometric lines of The Box dead ahead. It looks like its namesake, a flat-roofed, concrete cube. A defunct industrial smokestack rises from one corner. The whole place is painted an austere white. The signage is no-nonsense, appearing stamped in black ink on the smokestack as well as the cinder block walls surrounding the front yard. The font is blocky and distressed. Gary and I argued over it for days like it was a china pattern. It's only four streets away.

This is doable, I tell myself. *Just get out and run like hell.*

I grip the door handle at my side.

Stop! my ex begs. I freeze.

The front door of a house is opening ahead of me. The sun's in my eyes, turning the doorway into a rectangular portal of darkness. I slide my short sword free of its scabbard.

My head swivels to the left and bloody hands slap into the driver side window.

"Jesus!" I shriek and jerk away as a mangled face bites at the glass. It's a woman—at least she used to be. I brace myself for her to smash her skull into the window. Except, she doesn't. She looks...confused. She touches the window pane experimentally, like a puppy discovering glass for the first time. It's as if she's thinking *What the what? I can see through it, why can't I go through it?*

I stare at her lesbian haircut and stocky figure, dressed in a blue skirt and matching jacket. Her white blouse is bloody, as is the kerchief wrapped around her neck. She's got a name tag with wings on either side, pinned to her lapel. LYDIA it says. Flight attendant, I'd guess.

Lydia's fingers keep exploring the glass, moving up, down, side to side, then up again, which is when I notice that the window is open half an inch at the top. Lydia's eyes widen with delight as she finds the gap, her fingers sliding through, grasping the edge firmly. Her lips stretch into a maniacal smile, and she pulls. A faint crack fills my ears. She pulls harder and presses her mouth to the opening, her tongue slavering towards me.

I hesitate for a moment, then I shove the sword through the opening, right into Lydia's mouth. Whatever is left of her brain clicks off. Her full weight yanks down on the sword. I hiss as my wrist is twisted into an awkward angle, but I keep a grip. She's caught on the blade, pressing my knuckles to the roof.

"Goddamn it," I mutter, pain running up my forearms.

My frustration spikes, and I angrily jerk my arm back. The sword pops free of her skull, and my elbow hits the horn. Its shriek pierces the air.

Twat! my ex curses.

She's right.

Doors open up and down the street, like a set of toppling dominoes.

Out steps an entire community of mangled, middle-class monstrosities.

CHAPTER 8

A woman in head-to-toe yoga gear, soaked in blood, staggers out of the house to my right. Her hair is up in a bun. Her lips are gone, baring her clenched teeth.

She's joined by a coterie of corpses.

Coming from the house on the opposite side of the street is Business Guy With Toupée; one door down is Acne-Prone Teen; next house over are Sexy Librarian and her husband—Not So Sexy Librarian; they're kiddie corner to Guy With '70s Porn Mustache. They all have bloodshot eyes and portions of their bodies gnawed off.

The nicknames are a buffer between me and this horror show, helping me regain focus.

The infected wander down their front walkways. As one, they stop at the sidewalk. They gaze about, vaguely puzzled. It's as if they know that something drew them out, but they can't quite figure out—or remember —what that was.

The Box taunts me, tantalizingly close.

I tap the steering wheel nervously. A tweaky-looking teen in baggy pants and shirt catches my attention. He's got greasy, shoulder-length hair inside a dirty, red toque. His arm's been gnawed on. His fingers are caked with dried blood. He clutches a skateboard with a skull on it. He staggers into the middle of the street.

What's he up to? I ask myself.

He stands there as if waiting for a pistol fight at high noon. The others watch him. He drops the skateboard, and it rolls down the slight decline, right past my car. Heads turn as it passes. It catches on a sewer grate and stops. One by one the heads angle back to look at Skater Boy. He cocks his ear.

How much of his brain is left? I wonder.

He wanders over to a purple VW bug, and he sniffs at the car. I count to three before he gives up on the VW, straightens, lurches across the street, and does the same thing to a blue minivan. A decal of a smiley-faced stick-figure family is stuck onto the back window. He forgets the minivan, crosses the street again, and slams his nose into the window of a banged up BMW.

He steps away from it, lurching first one way, then another, *seemingly* aimless… I squeeze the hilt of my short sword. His route isn't random.

Dude's walking in a grid.

He's getting closer. He's about six cars away from me. I look to my partially open window. Without power, I can't close it. What happens when he gets a good whiff of me?

Skater Boy stops, standing about ten feet away. He's stock still, staring at me. The others, up and down the row, follow his gaze.

The seconds, then the minutes, tick by. First ten, then twenty. They're in no rush, and why should they be? I carefully remove my cell phone from my pocket. I turn off the ringer so that I don't become a horror movie cliché, where some stupid idiot is about to escape, until someone calls and gives him/her/zir away.

Tweaker Kid lifts his nose to the wind. The others watch him. My grip tightens on the sword.

He stumbles my way, closer and closer. He stops directly behind me. I'm looking over my shoulder. He stares into my eyes. He steps towards me, gaze unwavering. My sword is at the ready. My muscles are a coiled spring. Once I kill him, the others will see. My fight or flight adrenal systems are overloading.

His pace quickens. I face forward, bracing myself against the seat. Sweat beads my forehead. I'm taking quick, shallow breaths. My gaze locks onto the side-view mirror. The reflection of his torn-up limb gets larger and larger, closer and closer. The side of his leg brushes against the bumper. He trails his palm along the rear window, leaving behind thin streaks of blood. He strums his fingers. The taps follow a pattern. It's Nirvana's 'Teen Spirit.'

The closest not-quite-dead people look up, like dogs hearing a can opener; I'm the puppy chow. A few start stumbling toward me. Others follow. Soon, the whole block is on the move. They're advancing, in front of me, behind me, and on either side.

Shit!

I stare at The Box.

Why didn't I run when I had the chance?

Tweaker Skater Kid is right alongside the passenger window. He grasps the door handle and gives it a tug.

It opens.

CHAPTER 9

I lean over and grab the door handle. I pull hard; he pulls harder, grunting. We play tug of war.

Tweaker's grip slips, maybe from all the blood, and the door slams shut. I hit the lock button.

He smiles, unblinking as the others close in. The neighborhood of walking corpses form a ring around the car. They're a wall, blocking everything else from view. They claw and bite at the car. One of them—Pornstache—tries the door, same as Tweaker, and yowls when it fails to open.

Maybe I can fight my way through. I try to channel Rambo, stronger than ever, but macho man is gone. Pornstache pounds his open palm on the window. Tweaker Kid is at his side. A housewife in hair curlers climbs onto the hood. Others press in all around. Blood-caked fingers and tongues reach in through the gap at the top of the window on the driver's side. They push and shove at the car, making it rock. There's a crunch above me; the weight of a foot indents the roof.

Glass cracks. I place the sword to my throat. This time, I can't wait until tomorrow to kill myself because, by then, I'll be dead.

"I can do this," I say. If I'm accurate, I should bleed out in 60 seconds.

For what it's worth, my ex concedes, *you made it further than I expected.* There's grudging admiration in her tone.

Don't think, I tell myself, *just do.*

I steel myself to shove the blade into my throat, and an insanely loud honking blasts the air. I'm so surprised, the blade unexpectedly cuts into me. Warm blood trickles down my neck.

Another honk rends the air. My attackers react like a herd of meerkats. Their heads and bodies pop up, extending to their max heights, freezing as they stare back at the source of the sound. I can't see what they see; too many bodies are in the way.

Tweaker Kid pushes Pornstache and a few others aside. He shuffles towards the source. Others follow. Feet trample on the roof and thud as they hit the ground.

My phone vibrates. I pull it from my pocket. It's a text message. From Gary.

It says: *Put it in neutral.*

I don't understand.

A dull thunk fills my ears. Behind me, a body flies through the air—thunk, thunk, thunk. Bodies are being tossed left and right, like a boat cutting through water. The horn blasts again, and the cab of a freight truck breaks through the wall of undead, barreling right towards me.

"Oh shit!"

I slam the gear shift to N as the truck slams into the car. The Prius is shoved into the nearest undead and sucks the thing under its wheels. Animated bodies stagger towards me. Two are tossed onto the hood and cling to the windshield wipers, their teeth scratching at the front window to get to me.

We leave the rest of their pack behind. The rows of inhabited homes behind us give way to deserted construction sites on either side of the street. There aren't any workers.

The concrete walls and smokestack of The Box are before me. The car's tires pull to the right. The two animated corpses on the hood scrape at the front window. God only knows what's dragging underneath me. I fight the steering wheel to keep the tires pointed towards the thick metal gates barricading the gym's courtyard. I'm convinced they could stop a tank. I'm about to smash into them.

My jaw tightens. In Gary, I trust. My nails dig into my palms, and my faith is rewarded—the gates part. Gary is a modern-day Moses, after all.

I'm pushed inside the walls. Familiar faces—living ones—greet me. Their owners shove the gate closed behind the trucker cab, cutting off a surge of—I'll just say it—zombies. We've dragged in a guy in a business suit. Half of his rib cage is eaten. He turns in time to get an arrow in the face. There's also a zombie grandma with pink hair and a wispy flower-child dress. She takes a kettlebell in the side of the head. She wobbles, then topples. A bloody soccer mom drags herself out from under the car, struggling to her feet. A woman in her 60s wields a sledgehammer and smashes it into the soccer mom's face.

I open the door and stare at the sledgehammer-wielding woman. Her face is sweaty and dusty.

"Laleh," I say.

"Marty," she nods, her smoker's drawl lightly touched by a Persian accent.

She's dressed in head-to-toe Lulu Lemon. Three walking corpses scamper off of the freight truck behind us. Laleh smashes a beer-bellied construction worker across the jaw. My allies also include the pair who opened and closed the gate. There's Devon, one of our trainers. We call him the Natural. He's just turned twenty and was born with the gymnast's body I've always wanted for myself. He shoves a steel bar through a chef's eye socket. Opposite him is Seong, one of our clients. She swings a weighted club bell, smashing the skull of a lumbersexual with a thick beard and a topknot. Her intensity during workouts is intimidating. She's a few years older than Devon. My understanding is she's fucking him whenever she feels like it.

I'm out of the car, blade in hand, panting, looking around to see if there are any more of those things. There's a moment of stillness, of skeptical relief that, for now, we are safe. The door to the trucker's cab opens, and an incredibly handsome man gets out. He's just turned 30 and, as he is fond of saying, he doesn't look a day over fabulous. His white t-shirt hugs a bod that's been featured on the cover of *Natural Physique;* his brain's pumped out a couple of fitness books; and his social media acumen has made him an online sensation, with more than a million followers. I still don't get why a guy like that considers me his friend.

I drop the weapon and wrap my arms around him, crushing him against me. I try to talk. To say thank you. The words come out all mangled.

"That was a close one," he says, hugging me back. After a few moments, he adds with fake machismo, "Okay broseph, get off of me before my husband gets jealous."

I laugh and wipe the tears from my eyes, finally finding my voice.

"Chris, he's okay?" I ask.

"He's right over there," Gary points.

His hubby is shorter and broader than Gary, with the shredded mass of someone who's likely juicing. He's unstrapping containers from the back of the transport cab.

"What about Buddy?" I ask.

"He's fine. He was here with us when it all went to shit," Gary replies.

"Thank God for that," I say.

"Could use a hand here," Chris says.

"Just a sec, babe" Gary replies, his face more serious now. "Where's Steph?"

I shake my head. He squeezes my shoulder.

"Dude..."

I hold up a hand to stop him from saying any more.

"We'll talk about it, later."

I can't, I just can't, or I will shatter into so many pieces that I may never pull myself back together.

I walk over to help Chris. Gary follows.

"So how'd you know where to find me?" I ask.

"Our phones are geo-synced, remember?" Gary says, holding up his smartphone. There's a flashing red dot on a map on the screen, showing my location. "I told you this App was badass." I check my phone. Cell service is back. No message from my dad, though. I try calling him. No answer. Gary watches my face and looks ready to ask. I shake my head. *Later*.

I grab a Rubbermaid bin from the back of the truck's cab—they've been tied down with an intricate webbing of rope—and I'm half-way across the training yard when I hear a woman calling my name.

"Marty? Is that really you?"

Her disquietingly familiar voice sends a chill along my spine. My grip on the bin tightens. This voice is not in my head.

You have got to be kidding me.

I stare and try to convince myself that the woman running towards me, with her bouncing breasts and toned thighs, is a mirage.

But, there's no mistaking her figure or accent—a high-pitched hybrid of Australian (where she grew up) and South African (where she lived for several years). Her name is Heidi. On the 1 to 10 fuckable scale, she's a Miami 11.

She throws her arms around my neck. "Oh, thank God! You're alive! I was so worried."

I almost drop the bin on her foot.

"Marty, you look like you're ready to shit yourself," Laleh says. "Heidi, you gonna help me with this sucker?"

"Sure! Of course," Heidi says, finally unhooking her arms from about me—like I'm a catch and release. "I'm just so glad you're safe!" she says over her shoulder as she quickly and eagerly moves to do her part.

She and Laleh don latex gloves and drag a corpse over to a fire pit made up of cinder blocks. The smell of charred flesh rises with the smoke. It doesn't stop me from staring at Heidi's breasts as she helps Laleh toss the body onto the flames.

Gary comes to stand beside me.

"So," I say to him, "what's my ex from hell doing here?"

CHAPTER 10

"About that," Gary begins, avoiding eye contact as he hands me pink dishwashing gloves. They have the smell of brand-new rubber.

Well, this should be good, only the opposite of that.

"She called here, for you," Gary explains. "Did you know she moved so close?"

"No," I lie as we don our gloves.

"She was trapped in her bathroom," Gary continues. "Her boyfriend was going nuts. 9-1-1 was overloaded. She was begging for you to come save her."

I say nothing. The irony is a bitchslap. Ever since I started learning martial arts, there's a part of me that's been dying to play the hero in front of her. There's also the part of me that's *not* an idiot.

"In a way, *she* saved *us*," he says defensively. "We didn't even know what was happening. That heads up gave us time to steal the truck. Get supplies. Lock the gates."

"Yeah," I say, "lucky."

The psychic scars she left are dull and old. For a second, though, they flare an angry red.

"So, all that stuff you used to say about her, she can't be that bad," Gary says.

"She's dangerous," I reply. It's my truth, and I speak it.

I see the disbelief on his face. Gary's my best friend. Still, he's scared to hear me out. There are serious consequences to what I'm telling him. I have to choose my words carefully, or I run the risk of being dismissed as a whiny, jilted ex.

"She presents well," I admit. In fact, she presents *very* well.

"But?" Gary asks.

I shake my head. I can't not warn him.

"She can't be trusted."

I know immediately that I've been too blunt.

"Dude," he says, "are you asking me to toss her out?"

Yes, Teddy says in my head.

The alternative is to let her stay.

No! Teddy screams.

There lies the dilemma. Obviously, I can't listen to the imaginary persona of a stuffed bear in determining the fate of a person—even if that person is She-Who-Must-Not-Be-Named.

Heidi, I force myself to say. *Her name is Heidi.*

I also can't ignore the alarm bells going off in my head. I made that mistake once before. Then, it was just me and my fragile mental health at risk. Now, it's so much more.

Our undead neighbors claw at the gate. They grunt and moan. It's the sound of hell. To put Heidi out there would be criminal. I also know she's bad news. Wolf in sheep's clothing. Fox in a hen house. Scorpion on the frog's back. Octopussy. There is no animal metaphor to do her justice.

But, how do I convince Gary? I swear to God, if he calls me a drama queen, or some other campy gay trickery, to shame the straight guy so the hot homo can win an argument...I mean, come on! Play fair, man. Granted, I have issues. I talk to my teddy bear for fuck's sake. Weird, but harmless. Heidi, well, I shudder to think who's giving her instructions.

I grab the ankles of the dead cook. Gary grasps his armpits. I grimace as we toss the body onto the fire. For a moment, I'm lost in the sight of it starting to burn.

"I guess we have to figure out what to call these poor schmoes," Gary says. This could easily be us. He's changed the subject. That means he's already made up his mind about Heidi. "Zombies is too weird."

I'm not listening. Heidi called for me. Not on my cell. I changed that number after she dumped me. But, when we opened the gym, there was an article in the local news bulletin. She sent me an email congratulating me. I created a filter to automatically send her messages to trash.

Heidi called for me. I guess she needed me after all.

What would I have done if I'd been here when she called? Would I have hung up on her?

I... Teddy hesitates.

Exactly.

"Sure," I say.

Gary pulls his eyes from the burning bodies.

"Sure, what?" he asks, puzzled.

"Heidi can stay."

What else can I realistically say?

"Great," he says. It's clear by his tone that was never up for debate.

We go over to grab the remains of the business guy. I gag less as we toss him on the flames.

Whatever, I tell myself. *The world's ending. What's the worst Heidi can do now?*

The weak can never forgive;
Forgiveness is the attribute
of the strong.
—*Mahatma Gandhi*

PART 3

CHAPTER 11

Like any good love/hate story, mine and Heidi's starts at the mall. It was four years ago, before I met Gary or Steph.

As Sophia from *The Golden Girls* would say, "Picture it."

I'm at Hallmark, ostensibly to buy a card for my nephew's birthday. In truth, I'm lingering so I can complete my homework challenge from an online pickup artist course. My mission is to ask a random female shopper (preferably hot and single) for her advice on what card to get. If I can drag that out into a conversation, so much the better. If she's engaged in the convo (good luck), and, by some miracle, I get her phone number, then I've gone further than I've ever gone before.

I look for potential targets. I'm alone except for a grandmother-type behind the cash. Her expression makes sour candies look sweet.

I turn my attention back to the Batman card in my hand. I'm smirking at the image of the Joker when I hear the clickety-clack of hooker-esque heels. My gaze bounces up. Outside Hallmark, I see Heidi for the first time. She's a Barbie doll come to life: all legs, hips, and boobs, squeezed into a tight skirt and clingy top. I walk right into a carousel of cards. It sways drunkenly.

I grab the spinning rack and clumsily set it right. Sour Grandma gives me a scolding look. I meekly murmur, "Sorry." She makes shooing motions with her wrinkled hands and rasps, "Go. She's getting away."

I rename her Cool Grandma and mouth the words, "Thank you."

She takes a hit from a flask and dismisses me with a wave of her liver-spotted hand.

My brightly polished dress shoes gleam in the mall lighting as I follow after Heidi.

My brain is on overdrive. For the past five weeks, I've been determined to turn my life around, doggedly completing the online course, which has calls to action like: *Stop Being an Average Frustrated Chump! Quadruple Your Dating! Get the Girl of Your Dreams!*

It's a testimonial to my desperation that I forked out nearly $800 for the internet tutorials.

In the weeks that followed, I filled out visualization sheets about what kind of man I wanted to be (fit, athletic, confident, funny, loved), and what I wanted to move away from (tongue-tied, sweaty, clumsy, lonely).

I learned the theory behind successfully approaching in-demand women *without* creeping them out—or projecting neediness. I'm flooded with a slew of tactics: sneak around her so-called "bitch shield" by employing a time constraint; display higher value; draw her into your world with verbal pebbles, marbles, and engaging storytelling; appeal to her desire for mystery with astrology, palmistry, and the Cube game; project a strong identity with peacocking, banter, and what you stand for; play off her insecurities by employing negs, takeaways, and active disinterest; escalate kinesthetic connections with the Discovery Channel Pattern, the October Man Sequence, and the Tulip Ladder System.

The more I learned, the more I realized how clueless I was. No wonder I always struck out with women and barely had any friends. I never stood a fucking chance. My mind spilled over with theory, but theory meant nothing unless it could be put into practice. I forced myself to make small talk with strangers in elevators and at the grocery checkout. I played around with little bar games with my sister-in-law, amusing her with cold reads and tarot readings—until I told her what I was doing and why.

"Oh Marty, stop with the games already," she said, "Just be yourself!"

Worst advice *ever*.

The mall is where I put it on the line. Have I changed? Can I be that other guy? I make my move. I can't believe I'm doing this. Even if it's a fail, it's also a win, because I'm not at home jerking off to free online porn.

For a moment, I lose sight of her, and I wonder, *where's she gone?* I feel my adrenaline crashing from disappointment. Mixed in is a sense of relief; I don't have to go through with this after all. Until...Yes! Target in sight. 10 o'clock. Browsing through a rack of dresses.

I'm hit with 1000 ccs of paralyzing fear. She's way out of my league. My instinct is to bolt, but I follow the three-second rule: approach within three seconds of seeing a hot woman, so I can't psyche myself out.

Before I know what I'm doing, I'm marching into the store. I pull a dress out at random and hold it up.

"Hey," I say to her, "real quick, would this be a good gift for my sister's birthday? I need a woman's opinion because she always hates what I get her."

My left earlobe throbs. It's freshly pierced and likely infected.

She takes in my pink swoop-neck t-shirt and the silver bullet hanging from a chain against my chest. She bats her Maybelline lashes as if to shoo me away.

Sweat pools in the small of my back. Where did I go wrong? I used a time constraint ("real quick") so she knows this won't take long; I added the word "because," establishing a reason for the interaction; and women love doling out fashion advice.

It's textbook. Still, she says nothing. My bowels feel like they're being rearranged by a Rubik's Cube champion. I want to run away. Paradoxically, I'm tired of running away. I invoke the 1/5 rule and push the interaction.

"Oh, sorry," I say, "You *seemed* well put together, so I thought you might be able to help."

Her face sours. She's caught the subtly backhanded implication that, despite appearances, she is, in fact, *not* put together. Her lips turn pouty. My anti-compliment is having the desired effect. Part of her can't help but want to prove herself. Thank you psychology.

I smile at my cleverness. *This is working!* Until it isn't. She sees my reaction. Her eyes narrow as she figures me out. She shifts her weight from one high heel to the other. I can practically hear the electrostatic vuu-wimzz sound of her Death Star bitch shield going up; it's a beautiful woman's defense in a galaxy where men fancy themselves slick Han Solos, but are, in fact, harassment-prone Jabba the Huts.

"Can I see a picture of her?" she asks.

"A picture?" I ask.

"Yeah, of your sister. You do have a picture of your sister, right?" she asks. There's an *I've got you* raise to her perfectly shaped eyebrow. "Let me guess. You forgot your phone."

She's calling bullshit.

As terrified as I am, this is weirdly fun. She's still talking to me! Fuck staying home alone and pretending not to hate myself. I pull out my cell.

"Got it right here," I say.

She's taken aback. I'm about to walk to her side, but then I get an idea. I gesture for her to come to me. Next thing I know, she's gazing over my shoulder. Her breast is practically touching my elbow.

Holy shit, holy shit, holy shit!

I'm going through a series of shots of me and a real hottie. A Toronto 9 or Los Angeles 7.

"Your sister's very pretty," she says.

"Oh. Sorry," I say, "That's not my sister. Pictures of my ex. I should probably just delete them, but in case I ever have to get a restraining order, I figure it's better to have pics to show the cops," I wink. The pictures are *not* of my ex. I wish. She's gorgeous—if you're into models, which is exactly what she is. I paid her $200 to pose with me in a variety of locations, all taken within the space of two hours, in different outfits, looking like we're the perfect couple. My target now sees me as a guy who is not only worthy of beautiful women but is also willing to leave them, which raises my worth instantly.

From the corner of my eye, I see her brush back her hair. My heart beats faster. She's giving me an IOI—an indicator of interest.

"Here we go," I say, ending on a picture of me and my brother's wife carving a pumpkin together. "Here's my sister."

Heidi smiles. "I haven't carved a pumpkin since I was a kid. My mom used to roast up the pumpkin seeds before Halloween, and we'd eat them while watching *It's the Great Pumpkin, Charlie Brown.*"

I note the unprompted offering of personal information. Her guard is lowering.

"Well, pumpkin seeds are full of phytosterols, so your prostate must be in excellent health," I say with what is intended to be a charming smile. It turns out crooked and creepy. The look on her face screams, *What the fuck, weirdo.*

Shit. I watch helplessly as her bitch shield starts back up. I failed to calibrate properly and jumped way ahead. It's too soon for sexual humor. She doesn't know dick about me—now she doesn't want to. Her jaw juts, and I can see she is starting to close off. Back-pedaling would be a disaster, transforming me into an AFC—an average frustrated chump. She'll see me for the loser that I am—then, I'm done.

My mind spins through my pickup house of cards. She's trumped my prematurely played ace. Time for a Joker.

I mirror her to build rapport. I'm not even subtle about it. I put my hand on my hip, just like she's doing, and I jut my jaw, mimicking her as I pull my head back in an *oh, no you didn't* kind of way. I stay like that as she blinks in surprise. She looks ready to slap me.

Steady, I remind myself, sweat gathering in my armpits. *It's all or nothing.*

She smirks against her will. I look proudly effeminate. A girl like her must have a ton of gay friends and probably loves their bitchy banter. I doubt any straight guy in her life has the balls to play this game. Her posture eases, and though she keeps her hips closed to me (bad sign), her torso opens in my direction (good sign).

She pulls a slinky black gown free of the rack and holds it up. "This is the dress for your sister. And, for your information, my prostate *is* in excellent health. Just ask my gynecologist," she smirks mischievously.

I breathe an inner sigh of relief. I'm in.

CHAPTER 12

I pull myself back to the present. I stand in the training yard of the gym, gazing at the bleak concrete walls that are our savior. The pathetic moans of the undead rise from the other side. It's surreal recalling how I met Heidi, and the person I was back then. Did I really binge-watch every season of *Sex and the City* as part of a pickup-artist online course so that I'd have something engaging to talk about with women? And how is it that out of all the decent, single women out there, I zeroed in on a succubus like Heidi?

Because you were thinking with your dick, Teddy replies. The bear tells it like it is.

I lean into Steph's car and unbuckle the stuffed animal from the passenger seat.

In my defense, that's also how I met Steph, and she was awesome. The memory of her sends a chill through me. Thankfully, a shrill voice snaps me from my inner world.

"Uncle Marty!"

Gary and Chris' son, Buddy, runs out of the concrete building with the words THE BOX painted on it in giant square letters.

The kid's spaghetti arms and legs flail in his blue shorts, Spider-Man t-shirt, and *Cars* rubber boots. How can't I smile? I scoop him into my arms, and he hugs me tight, burying his face into my neck. The kid knows how to hug. I never want to let him go.

"You okay, Buddy?" I ask. His real name is Joseph, but we all call him Buddy so much the nickname's stuck. "You being brave?"

"I get scared sometimes, but Daddy Gary says we're safe in The Box," he says earnestly.

"Daddy Gary's right," I say. *At least, I hope so.* "Hey, look who I brought."

The kid clings to me as I hold up the stuffed bear in my other hand.

"Teddy!" he says taking the raggedy creature into his arms, pushing his face into the fun fur.

From the corner of my eye, I notice Heidi hanging inside the glass doorway to The Box. For a second, I think that she's watching me. As she steps forward, I realize she's actually looking at Buddy. She waves to him. He wriggles for me to put him down. He runs towards her the instant his Lightning McQueen boots touch the ground. She scoops him up and hugs him to her breast.

Seriously? I think. *She's been here for three seconds, and he's picking her over me?*

"She's good with him," Gary says, as if he's asking me to concede that it's a plus having her here.

"This is how it starts," I reply. "She finds a way in and starts spinning her web."

I instantly regret saying it. I'm supposed to be pretending to be cool with her being here. Seeing her with Buddy, it just reminds how she once stole what few friends I had.

"Dramatic much?" Gary asks.

He thinks I'm overreacting. Maybe I am. The moans and scratching nails on the other side of the wall grow louder.

"Sure," I lie. "Just had to get that out of my system."

You're fine, I tell myself. *You're solid. This isn't like last time.*

I force myself to focus my attention on helping to unload the rest of the supplies.

Inside, Chris directs us to pile the bins with dozens of others. Some are marked *canned beans*, others *protein bars*, and more disturbing (and comforting) *weapons*. They've been busy. There's an odd sureness to the survival mode most of us have gone into, but others are not faring so well. Bob, a man in board shorts and a tank top with hair poking out from his chest, is begging with his cell phone, "Please, if you get this, call me back!" He digs his fingers into the tight curls of his closely cropped Afro. Laleh rolls her eyes at him, grabs a clipboard and a pen, and brusquely starts taking inventory.

There's something surreal about all this happening here, at The Box, with its gymnastics rings, Pilates Reformers, and pull-up stations. Six punching bags hang from the overhead beams, looking like alien pod sacks that are ready to hatch. The windows are thankfully high and covered in bars.

"Where's the rest of the early morning class?" I ask.

"Gone," Gary replies. "Got in their cars and went for their families. Hopefully, they made it." His tone tells me what he thinks of their odds.

"Any idea how bad it is out there?" I ask.

"Bad," Gary replies. "Radio reports the outbreak's happening all over the world. The denser the population, the quicker this thing is spreading. Whatever it is, it's already killed more people than the bubonic plague, AIDS, and ebola combined."

The world. The whole fucking world. I remember the newscasts.

"You okay?" Gary asks.

"Yeah," I lie, "I Just need a second."

The last thing I want is Gary babysitting me. I need him to think I'm holding it together, which means I need to hold it together. I head for the washroom. If I can power down, detach, just for a minute, I'll be okay. I'm almost at the door when Laleh steps in front of me.

"Number one or number two?" she asks.

"What?" I say.

"Are you going to piss or are you going to shit?" she asks.

I'm suddenly aware of the pressure in my bladder. With the adrenalin wearing off, my organs are coming back to life.

"Piss. Like a racehorse," I answer.

"Take it outside," she says. "We have to conserve water and take it easy on the septic tank."

She's talking sense—and with such authority—that I climb the stairs, and I'm out on the roof before I realize, *Wait a second, I'm part owner here, shouldn't I be telling her what to do?*

I shake my head. It's petty, but I'm irritated that this old woman is adapting more quickly than I am, in my own house. I walk past the solar panels and rooftop garden, thankful that Gary and I became obsessed with making the place self-sufficient. The cistern and gray water systems are barely two-months old.

I do a quick circuit around the rooftop's periphery, assuring myself that we're clear of any immediate danger. The wall enclosing the former industrial compound is made of concrete and wraps around three sides, with our building comprising the fourth. There are painted targets on the concrete blocks for our clients to throw weighted balls at and metal rings for battle ropes and TRX workouts. The previous owner was going to tear the walls down. When we signed the lease, we asked her to leave them up. A year later, she offered us a great deal to buy her out after we "cured" her debilitating back pain when no else could.

Outside the walls, the swarm of infected sways listlessly. Only two scratch at the gate. Many are wandering back down the street. I see a few going into homes, closing doors behind them.

A notable exception is the three women ripping apart a twitching man in the parking lot in front of the strip mall to my right. I shudder and walk to the opposite side of the roof. The next building over is a warehouse converted into live/work lofts. It rises two stories above me. I unzip. My pee arcs in the air and falls two floors into the alley below. For a moment, the world almost seems normal—until I notice the faces staring out at me.

Some are bloodied, others mangled; a few are disturbingly normal, except for the paleness of their skin. All of them are pressed against the windows across from me. They stare hungrily. My stream of urine slows, then stops. My heart's hammering. I fold my underwear over my junk protectively. Masturbating is going to be a nightmare.

I avoid looking directly into the bloodshot eyes of my dead neighbors. Eye contact can be taken as a challenge. Conversely, I'm leery of taking my gaze off of them, as if they might sneak up on me. I've seen too many horror movies. Steph loved them. Steph is dead. I could join her. Step forward. Off the edge. Feel the rush of air, my spine snapping as I hit the ground. The dark place calls.

You can't do that to Buddy, I hear Teddy say. The kid's innocent face snaps me to reality. I hastily step back onto the roof. I stare at the condo.

My gaze darts from one apartment window to the next, from one lost face to another.

The occupants—what's left of them—look like they're in the stacked tic-tac-toe squares of a D-list celebrity game show. It's a who's who of urban archetypes: top left is Bearded Hipster; bottom right is Chunky Goth Girl; above her is I Can't Believe It's Not Archie; and dead center, Naked Lingerie Model.

She presses her palms and bloody breasts to the window. The others gnash futilely at the panes of glass.

They can't hurt you, I tell myself. It's the same mantra I used to use before high-school gym class. It was a lie then, and it's a lie now.

Bearded Hipster two floors above gets this cunning look in his bloodshot eyes. He takes a few steps back.

That can't be good.

He charges the window and smashes through it. Sometimes it sucks being right. Broken glass flies ahead of him as he sails through the air, towards my side of the alley.

CHAPTER 13

I stumble back as Bearded Hipster barrels towards me. His arms windmill. I turn for the stairs, and he misses our rooftop. I hear a sickening smack.

I clutch sun-heated concrete as I peer over the edge. His frame twitches on top of a closed dumpster. The rest of the Hollywood Squares members are working themselves into a frenzy. Goth Girl runs forward, smashing through her window, yowling as she stretches her arms for me. She almost makes it, smacking into it the side of The Box then landing with a bang next to Bearded Hipster.

The remaining occupants of the building grow still. They stare at Hipster and Goth as if trying to solve a puzzle.

Are their minds still working? I wonder—like the skater kid who followed a grid while sniffing me down. Their shoulders rise and fall—though I doubt they're exchanging carbon dioxide for oxygen. It seems like an autonomic response.

As I back away, a warning goes off in my head. Something's not right. I look back at the Hollywood squares. Naked Lingerie Model is missing.

I hear her howl from the rooftop.

"Oh shit," I swear.

My back is a lake of sweat. I see her rise into the air as she propels herself off the neighboring building. She sails through the sky, lithe legs bicycling, bloody breasts flopping in every direction. The others fell short because they were too low, lacked momentum, and were crashing through a barrier. She's higher up, with a longer running start, and she's not breaking through glass.

Her perfect arms reach for the wall, and—she misses.

"Holy shit," I say, breathing again. I head for the stairs, making a mental note to lock the steel door behind me. The thought is interrupted—I didn't hear a splat. She never hit the ground.

I look over my shoulder as she's pulling herself over the ledge. She's covered in scrapes. She hit and clung to the wall. Only now do I notice her insane forearms.

Rock climber, I think.

She takes a staggering step toward me. Her one knee is busted up. Something's not tracking right. Her pace increases. I'll fight if I have to, but only if I have to. I run for the door. It slams open. Gary and Chris are there; Heidi is right behind them.

"Duck!" Gary shouts, pointing a loaded crossbow at me.

I'm down on the ground as an arrow whizzes above my head. It hits the woman in the shoulder.

"Shit!" Gary shouts.

She charges, fast as hell despite her limp. He jumps over me, ducks under her arms, and smashes the back of her skull in with the butt of the bow. She staggers drunkenly from the blow. Twice more he hits her—there's a cracking sound—and she collapses in a heap of flopping limbs.

"Where the fuck did she come from?" he asks.

I point across the alley at the lofts. Dozens of spectral faces stare out at us. Some press their palms against the glass, but no one else comes crashing through.

"What are they doing?" Heidi asks.

"They're learning," I reply.

Gary helps me up.

"Shit," I say.

"What?" Chris asks, following my gaze to the roof of the loft. We all fall silent.

Half-a-dozen of the building's occupants are up there, dark silhouettes glaring down at us.

"They saw her jump across," I jerk my chin towards the rock climber that Gary took out. "Now they know that from up there, they might make it too."

"They don't know anything," Chris replies.

"Yes," I insist, backing away, "they do. They're about to..."

The first body comes flying over. It's an aging business man. He falls short, and I hear him smack into the wall of our building.

"Holy crap," Chris swears, his grip tightening on a crowbar.

We run over to the side of the building. The man clings to the brick a few feet below. He glares at us and starts to climb.

"Heidi, get back inside," Gary says. "Lock the door in case we don't make it."

"There's just the one," she says.

More of them start jumping off the roof. A petite, athletic Asian woman in Spandex, a young black male football type, and a super-hairy white guy, wearing only boxers.

All three land solidly on our roof. Gary fires an arrow into Ape Man's hirsute chest. He stares at the shaft sticking out of him, and Chris smashes his head in with a crowbar.

The petite woman bowls Chris over as if she were the one to have a 100 pounds on him. Her fingers curl around his throat.

"Chris!" Gary shouts.

"I got this!" I yell. "Man the wall!"

I pull the arrow from Ape Man and stab it into the back of the woman's head. Chris pushes her off. I help him up, and we join Gary. He aims an arrow at the footballer. The first arrow misses—he's only had the crossbow for a week. The second shot hits the guy's collar bone. The third goes through the skull. The kid seizes up and drops.

We wait for more. Another half-dozen of the things stare down from the opposing roof.

"What are they waiting for?" Chris asks.

"They're trying to figure out how best to take us," I guess.

This time, no one argues this time.

CHAPTER 14

"What the hell is going on up there?" Laleh demands when we get downstairs.

"The building next door is infested," Gary replies. "Some of them were jumping over."

"Oh, fuck," Laleh says.

I wince, not at Laleh's swearing—that I'm used to—but at Gary's quick use of the word "infested," and everyone's immediate understanding of what he means. Less than a day ago, they were our neighbors.

"What the mother fucking Christ are we going to do?" Laleh asks.

We all look to Gary.

"We burn the building," he says. "We burn them all inside."

There's a moment of shocked silence.

"We'll need to shut off their water," I say, quick to back him up.

"He's right," Gary agrees. "We don't want the fire sprinklers kicking in."

I feel like I've just aced a test.

"We'll want to block the exits," Heidi adds. "Trap them inside."

She's like that annoying kid in every class who always has to do one better.

"Won't stop them from coming out the windows," I say. "Or the roof."

Ha! I think. I wait for Gary to agree.

"They can't reach us from the windows," Gary says dismissively. "We'll be ready for any roof jumpers."

I might as well be staring at a report card filled with FAILs.

"How do we turn off their water supply?" Heidi asks. "The place is crawling with those things."

Is she challenging me? *Game on, Heidi.*

"We can shut the water off from the outside," I say.

"He's right," Bob says. We call him Bob the Builder because he's a contractor.

Oh, thank Christ, I think. *I mean I was pretty sure, but...*

"I'm not going into the sewers," Chris says.

We all look at his hulking mass, assuming his muscles mean he's up for anything. "What?" he demands. "I hate rats."

If this were a movie, we'd have to go into the tunnels beneath the streets for some contrived reason, and it's not the rats we'd have to fear. A whole crew of zombified city workers would be coming at us; there'd be a chase, some casualties, maybe a surprise rescue by an unexpected waterworks survivor just when we thought all was lost. But this isn't some work of fiction. This is real life.

"No sewers," I say. "No rats. Here's what we need..."

We put down six undead outside our walls. The last one falls.

"Clear," Chris says.

Above, our watchers next door rock back and forth. With the sun behind them, they're dark silhouettes.

Are they the smart ones or the timid ones? I wonder.

Gary, Devon, and I exit the gate, armed respectively with a short sword, a baseball bat, and a crowbar. Gary's strapped the crossbow to his back. Each of us pushes a bike.

To the left is a strip mall with an Indian restaurant. It's quiet, with a large patch of blood where three of the diseased were ripping someone apart.

The street is quiet. The infected are not to be seen.

"Where the hell did they go?" Gary asks.

"Home," I say.

He snorts—until he realizes I'm serious. He looks at where the houses begin, a couple of blocks away, beyond the half-built concrete developments rising from the ground. We picked this location because it was an emerging neighborhood with a nice mix of work/live spaces. It was a perfect fit. We'd get local residents in the evenings. Around lunch, it was the work-nearby crowd. The area projects a very different vibe now that we imagine all those homes as nests for predators hungry to consume us.

"You sure about this?" Gary asks.

"Nope," I say.

"Good enough," he says, and he starts pedaling. I follow close behind, Devon to my right.

Our eyes dart from side to side. We swerve around cars abandoned in the middle of the street. More than one window is streaked with blood. We'll be back to strip them of fuel and anything else useful. Priorities.

We turn a corner and see our target: bright orange pylons around an open sewer hole. A trail of dried blood leads into the dark maw. Next to it is a truck from the city's water department. The back doors are wide open. Gary and Devon stand guard while I look around inside the truck's dim, windowless interior, wishing I'd brought a flashlight.

There are wrenches, pipes, and maps, presumably of the city's sewer system, along with a stack of yellow requisition forms fastened to a clipboard. I'm sweating heavily.

"You okay in there?" Gary asks.

"Never better," I lie, moving a tool box out of the way. My heart's pounding louder than ever. This is my plan. If I don't find what I'm looking for, it falls apart, and I look like an idiot.

I will not let Heidi see me fail. It's a childish thought, especially under the circumstances, but there it is.

I smile as I find what I'm looking for, a metal shaft with a notched circular piece that is a key on one end and a handle on the other.

"Got it," I say, climbing out and holding it up triumphantly. We duct tape the tool to Gary's bike frame. We keep looking around as we do.

"That should do it," Gary says.

Devon and I nod. The look in our eyes is a mix of relief and worry. This is too easy. We look to the open manhole ("utility hole," Steph would correct), at its gaping mouth in a rounded O. We hear a low moan and crunching—snap, crackle, pop— like someone eating Rice

Krispies in front of a megaphone. Gary jerks his head, and we start biking back towards The Box.

As we pedal, I want to say something to Gary. This is too fucking creepy —the empty streets, the stillness amidst abandoned cars, the trail of blood we bike over. It looks as if someone was dragged from the middle of the road to the closed door of a home, knocking over a kid's plastic three-wheeler en route. The lawn is otherwise immaculate.

Our eyebrows raise in unison—as if to say *I know broseph, I know.*

We reach the loft and chain the front doors shut, piling punching bags in front of them. Gary searches the sidewalk and finds a round metal water valve. It's embedded in the ground. He lines up the plumber's tool and gives it a good twist. At first, it won't budge. Devon and I help. We hear a grinding sound and feel a satisfying give. We close it tight, cutting off water to the building.

Next, in the alley adjacent to The Box, we block the loft's side and back entrances with dumpsters filled with weights. We keep an eye on the infected up top. One of them steps forward, a graying sexy Santa. He plummets to the ground, hits, and breaks his spine. He lies there, twitching. The rest contemplate him; they remain put.

We emerge from the alley, grab our bikes and stop.

A partially dressed man is walking towards us. He wears a dress shirt with a tie, a blazer, dress shoes and socks, but no pants or underwear.

His legs are ghostly pale, the veins sticking out like neon blue. His cock is shrivelled and scrotum mangled. He carries a briefcase. In the other hand, he holds a severed forearm; the hand is attached. Every few steps, he lifts the limb to his mouth and takes a bite out of it like it's a drumstick from KFC.

Gary and I exchange a *what the fuck?* look. We cautiously pedal to the front of The Box. We look back. The businessman ignores us. He chews on the arm and keeps on walking.

"I think he's on his way to work," I whisper to Gary.

The business guy is worse than dead, and he's still heading to the office. This truly is hell.

CHAPTER 15

We join the others on the roof. Heidi waves at me. I nod my head.

You can't trust a person like her, Teddy reminds me.

Devon comes up, his biceps jacked as he carries a rubber bin loaded with Molotov cocktails. I stare at the recycled juice bottles filled with fuel, rags shoved into the holes punched into their lids. Laleh, Bob, Heidi, and Seong have been busy while we were gone.

"We've still got gas left in one car," Laleh says as she hands us plastic lighters, "but that's it."

She lights a cigarette.

"Not even pretending to quit?" I ask.

She shrugs. "I'll be lucky if I get to die of cancer."

She's got a point.

We line up along the wall. Heidi's at the furthest edge, a few feet away from me. Gary's to my other side, then Chris, Devon, and Seong. Buddy's downstairs with Bob. It's terrible to say, but I draw comfort from knowing that as long as Bob and Laleh are around, I'm not the weakest link.

I glance over at Heidi and can't help but notice her shapely silhouette. There's a weird look on her face.

"You okay?" I ask.

Her head jerks as if I've pulled her from a texting session with her gay bestie—who bears an oddly strong resemblance to me. "Fine," she says. There's a tightness about her lips, and she won't look me in the eye.

"Let's get this over with," she says.

She picks up a loose brick, pilfered from one of the nearby construction sites, and throws it through a window in the neighboring loft. We hear the piercing crash. The things on the roof and in their apartments sway and moan. Next, Heidi lights the rag stuffed into one of the fuel-filled juice bottles.

She throws it with absolute precision—what sport didn't she play growing up?—and her flaming bottle arcs through the air, landing inside the broken window pane. A moment later, a glimmer of flame rises inside. There's an old man in the unit, half of his face ripped off. He stares at the flames as they draw closer and closer to him. He remains unmoving as his pajama pants catch fire, crawling up him. Even as his flesh burns, he just stares, gnashing his jaw.

"Nice aim," Gary says, throwing the next brick, and the next bottle.

One by one, we follow suit, until the floor directly across from us looks like a giant fireplace from one end of the building to the other. The fire-warning system blares and we see flashing blue lights within.

"Disco inferno," Heidi and I say at the same time. I refuse to acknowledge the jinx.

A chunky woman in a burning bathrobe seeks out the sound, wandering into the hall and inadvertently taking a trail of fire with her, helping it spread. Another woman with curlers in her hair, sees the flames and calmly turns to her kitchen. She returns with a fire extinguisher—and then she stands with it as the flames creep up her nylons, making no move to discharge the fire suppressant. I wish they were all like that. But there is one who is sure to give me nightmares.

He's directly across from me. It's eerie how well I can see him, like we're two love-lorn neighboring teenagers in a music video, who just need the right ballad to realize they are more than friends. The guy's face is a mess of scar tissue running down one cheek and neck. He's a burn victim.

His black hair is pulled into a topknot. He's in a leather jacket and jeans. His t-shirt's ripped down the front, and his stomach's been chewed on, revealing the bottom of his ribs.

I throw a brick, and it smashes through his window.

"Good shot," Heidi says.

"Thanks," I force myself to reply. She's making me nervous. I don't want to fuck up in front of her. *Don't let her turn you back into that guy,*

Teddy councils. I light my cocktail and throw it through the hole in the window.

"Nailed it," I say with relief as it smashes on the guy's hardwood floor and spreads fire across it.

His reaction is utterly unlike the others. He doesn't stand there as if suffering from statue syndrome. He jumps back and hisses at the flames. He growls. The flames spread. His shoulders rise and fall as if in a panic. He retreats, giving the spreading pool of fire a wide berth. He whines and backs into his front door. The contact startles him. He stares at the door handle as if he can't quite remember what it is. He grasps the knob tentatively, then gives it a decisive turn.

For just a second, I'm rooting for him. I can't help it. I like the underdog. He pulls on the handle, but the door doesn't budge. It rattles as he yanks more desperately. The deadbolt is still firmly in place. I wait for him to figure it out. He doesn't. He turns around as the fire closes in. He howls at it futilely, lowering himself to the floor, cowering as he wraps his arms around his head.

The flames lick at his pant legs. They smoke and catch fire. He doesn't try to beat the flames away; he keeps rocking himself as the fire spreads all over him. He burns, howling. I'm not sure that he's in pain, not physically, but a primal part of him must remember how he got those scars. I wipe a tear from my eye.

Poor fucking bastard, I think.

"You okay?" Gary asks.

"It's the smoke," I lie.

The fire is spreading, lighting curtains, furniture, and bedding. More of the occupants—the ones who can figure out how to open their doors —manage to stagger out of their apartments, spreading the fire into the hallway. A couple even makes it to the roof. They bump into some of the watchers who have been waiting up there, and they catch on fire too. We see them wobbling drunkenly, the flames eating away at their connective tissues, and they collapse. One attempts the jump over but doesn't even get half-way before plummeting to the ground. Two others fare better, landing on our ledge. We're ready, shoving them over the side of the building with rakes and shovels.

It's macabre, but as if this a pickup basketball game, we high five each other with relief. Heidi forces a smile as our palms slap together overhead. The fingers of her other hand clench and unclench.

I recognize the tell. She's being shady.

"Heidi, what are you up to?" I demand.

"Nothing," she insists with pouty lips.

"Something's up," I insist. "Spill."

She gets cagey—but only for a second.

"It's the end of the world, Marty, so yeah, that's what's up. Come on. Let's go join the others."

She grabs my arm and pushes me towards Gary. That's when I see the woman in the window. Heidi pushes harder, but I disentangle myself and side step her to get a better look. I hope to hell my eyes are playing tricks on me. They are not.

"Oh, shit," I say in horror. "Guys!"

"What's the matter," Heidi asks with forced innocence.

"That!" I say, pointing.

She turns her head and seems unable to follow my finger's trajectory. Everyone else sees immediately.

"Oh, dear lord," she finally says, hand to her heaving breasts.

We stare at a young woman in a unit at the end of the burning building. She's sobbing and pressing a sign to her window. The sign says, 'HELP!!! PLEASE!!!'

Flames explode out from the windows of the unit below hers, and she crouches down. She still holds the sign for us to see. She's mouthing the words, *Please, save me!*

"We can use the ladder," I say. "We can get her out."

Gary puts his hand on my shoulder.

"It's too late," he says.

We watch as two burning children come at the woman. I can't hear her screams, but I see her lips open wide, desperate and sobbing. The two kids grab her with their smoking fingers and tear into her with their teeth. She pulls on a curtain as she struggles to break free, and it falls on top of them. There are flames behind them, creeping forward. Blood soaks through the curtain, and it, too, catches aflame.

No one is hi-fiving now.

I turn to Heidi. "You knew she was in there, and you said nothing."

"What?" she says with practiced shock. "Of course not!"

No one says anything, looking from her to me. Me they know. She is a stranger—until Chris steps forward and puts his hands on her shoulders, his muscled frame hovering over her protectively. "Of course, you didn't."

She starts to cry, and he hugs her. I look to Gary as if to say, *I told you so*. He won't meet my eyes.

"We had to do what we had to do," Gary says.

"We could've saved her," I say, though I wonder if I'm right, and I think each of us is partly relieved that Heidi has taken the burden of guilt from our shoulders.

She'd just as soon do the same to any one of you, Teddy warns.

"Marty," Gary says, his palm on my chest, redirecting my gaze out to the street. As the flames rise higher, and the sun starts to set, we watch as hundreds of undead come out of their homes and stagger towards us.

Heidi is forgotten, for now. Once again, the danger without is taking precedence over the one within. The undead stand there in the streets, like hypnotized masses, staring at the fire. They sway in the gentle breeze as the fire alarm blares, blue emergency lights flash, and heat-resistant windows grow black with smoke.

CHAPTER 16

None of us sleep much that night, lying on thin exercise mats and using rolled-up towels as pillows; our blankets are jackets and fleeces pilfered from the lost and found. Dinner is protein bars and coconut water. The fire alarm from next door cuts has, thankfully, cut out.

I stare at Teddy in a sliver of moonlight from one of the windows up above. Buddy clasps the bear tightly in his arms.

Tomorrow will be a better day. It's what I tell myself when I feel the dark place closing in. It usually works. Tonight, I know I'm lying. Tomorrow's going to suck. I will be haunted by killing Steph—and by the unused pregnancy tester she left behind. I will be haunted by that woman we killed in the burning building across the way. I will even be haunted by that not-quite-alive burn victim reliving the worst trauma of his life.

I'm breathing—but at what cost?

I wish that Steph were in my arms, so I could tell her that everything is going to be all right—because those are the words I need to hear. There were times with her when I needed to let myself feel weak, and others when I needed to feel strong. She always seemed to know which time was which. Without her, I feel hollow and brittle.

I stare at Teddy, clasped by Buddy's little fingers. He, in turn, is held in Gary's arms, who is folded into Chris' muscled frame. They remind me of those Russian nesting dolls, one inside the other. I'm happy for them, yet their togetherness makes the void of the dark place all the stronger—because I'm on the outside. Because now I am alone without my Steph.

Tomorrow will be a better day, I tell myself. I repeat it over and over. This ache for Steph and my family will dim. And yet, as I hear the undead shuffling and grunting and sniffing outside, what exactly do I think the future holds?

Heidi stares at me from her mat. She gives me a wave. I close my eyes, pretending not to have seen her.

Tomorrow will be a better day, I say one more time. I try to believe it, but the words ring hollow. The hours upon hours of self-help videos, books, and seminars that helped lift me higher than that high-school loser with bacne are sucked into a void. This is the actual end of the fucking world.

No, Teddy's voice corrects me in that sobering way of his. *The world goes on. So will you.*

Are you sure? I ask.

His answer is oddly comforting.

You can always kill yourself tomorrow. Or the day after that.

The next thing I know, I hear people talking, and it's daylight out. I get up. I splash my face and hand-wash my underarms with water drawn up from the cistern. I put on a fresh shirt and shorts from our promotional stock. We have a washer, originally just for towels, but now there's a communal load spinning in it, with extra bleach for the blood stains.

I head for the toilet. There's a sign on the door. Laleh's neat calligraphy now adorns multiple parts of the compound. This one says: *Need to Pee? In the bucket or over the wall.*

I open the washroom door, and I'm hit by the smell of urine from the metal pail on the floor. We have to use the toilet sparingly; we don't want to max out the septic system. With the boom in condo construction under new zoning laws, we could've hooked up to the city sewer, but we wanted to remain autonomous.

Devon is in the kitchenette, shirtless, smooth-skinned muscles busting out from the apron he's wearing. He pours gluten-free pancake mix onto an electric skillet, leftover from one of our member events. The batter hisses and bubbles. He turns down the heat.

"Hey, boss," he says, handing me a plate with a couple of pancakes on it. "There's not much syrup."

"Thanks," I say.

I take the plate and a mug of coffee up to the roof. The building next to us is still smoldering. The roof is partially caved in. I see bits of flame in some of the units, but compartmentation from the fireproof material the building is largely made of has helped the blaze burn out and has kept the structure intact. My nose twitches at the smell of ash. In the window in the far corner sits the singed sign: HELP!!! PLEASE!!! I look away, pancakes catching in my throat.

Gary is in a lawn chair next to the solar panels, licking his plate of what little syrup is on it. Laleh hovers by his side, smoking a cigarette. The bags under her eyes are pronounced. I see charred corpses inside the loft, muscle and ligaments so damaged they can't walk, but they still twitch. Down in the alley, burnt hands poke out from the door we wedged shut with the dumpster, fried fingers clasping at nothing.

Some of them tried to get out, I realize. *Were they afraid?* They could've crashed through their windows, but didn't. They went for the emergency exit. *Like we've all been taught.*

I store this in the mental folder I'm keeping on how they operate, just like I used to do as a kid at recess, tracking the various physical and social threats on the playground. I shift my gaze, looking for more clues, anything that might give us an edge. I scan the periphery of the compound. Last night, the burning building drew out hundreds of these once-people. Now there's not a soul to be seen—damned or otherwise. The undead are gone.

They've gone home, I think, *or to work.*

"Here," Gary says, handing me a pair of binoculars. "Check this out."

I cough a bit on Laleh's cigarette smoke.

"Sorry," she says, exhaling it the other way.

I scan the area through the lenses.

"You have got to be shitting me," I say.

I recognize the people walking our way. They wear a variety of sweat clothes, tank tops, workout tights, headbands, and runners. Some are muscled meatheads. Others are desperate wannabes. They're all former clients of ours. They're partially eaten. And they're coming here.

CHAPTER 17

"Is that what this thing turns people into?" Gary asks, staring through the binoculars as our most loyal devotees draw closer. "Flesh-eating courier pigeons, automatically returning to the places that consumed them when they were alive?"

"I wonder where I'd go," Laleh says, taking a deep drag from her cigarette.

"They're creatures of habit," I say as Gary lowers the binoculars. "Anything on the radio?"

Gary shakes his head. "Just an emergency broadcast that keeps cutting in and out."

"There must be other survivors," I say.

"Fair to say," Laleh replies.

"So what's the plan? Hole up 'til help comes?" I ask.

"*If* help comes," Laleh replies.

"We could be here a while," Gary says.

"Well, we've got enough food for a few weeks," Laleh says. "This will be our last pancake breakfast for a while, though—looks like I'll be losing that weight I always wanted to."

Her tone is stale. She stubs out her cigarette. She takes the binoculars and stares out at the gang of not-quite-alive muscle aficionados striding towards us.

"How did this even happen?" I ask.

Laleh shrugs. "Viruses mutate."

"And they're genetically engineered," Gary adds.

"You think this is germ warfare?" I ask.

Gary shrugs. "It would make sense, the way it spread so fast."

"I don't think so," Laleh replies. "Maybe some terrorist would be crazy enough to use something like this, but we'd be talking about a *really* crazy terrorist, and they wouldn't have the resources or know-how to make a bug that does this, let alone deploy it. No, this wasn't Al Qaeda or some other group with more balls than brains. We could've seen this coming. We were too cozy to pay attention."

"What do you mean?" I ask.

"I'm a social worker," she says. "Do you want to know what these victims look like?"

It's the first time I've heard any of us call them victims.

"They look like tweaked-out homeless people," Laleh observes. "I used to do drop-in work at a city shelter, on a sketchy street with abandoned buildings. On a hot summer day, that block was like a scene from *Dawn of the Dead*. Have you been to a psychiatric hospital?"

I shift uncomfortably, unsure where this is going.

"Many of the patients are so drugged up they're practically catatonic," Laleh snorts. "Just a bunch of zombies, not alive, but still not dead, wandering around in hospital gowns."

She lights another cigarette. From the way she closes her eyes and basks in the feeling from the nicotine, it's like she's on ecstasy. "What I'm saying is, we ignored the warning signs, dismissed the earliest cases as mentally ill or addicts, locked them up or drugged them into submission, and who would care? They're the most marginalized people in our society. Out of sight, out of mind. But all the while, they were incubators."

"That's..." I start.

"Crazy?" she finishes for me. "Do you remember how the AIDS pandemic started?"

She looks pointedly at Gary.

"What?" he asks. "Just because I'm gay doesn't mean I'm an AIDS vector expert."

"No," she agrees, "but you've seen *The Normal Heart*. AIDS started with just a few misdiagnosed cases. Gay cancer they were calling it. Then it spreads, enough to get a bit of attention, but it's still isolated to a few dozen sex-crazed queers. Who's going to miss a handful of that lot in that era? It starts popping up in more cities, New York, San Francisco,

Chicago...But so what? Proportionally, the numbers are small, and it's a *gay* cancer, seemingly spread by butt sex. Journalists even made jokes about it in White House press briefings, if it got discussed at all. The straight white men in power didn't give a shit. Their closet-case peers were too cowardly to act, refusing to risk their careers, their reputation, their political power, even when it was people they knew who were dying. They kept the status quo, and a few hundred cases became millions, all around the world."

"And you think that's what happened here?" Gary asks.

She shrugs. "You come up with a better theory, you let me know."

"So this...this pathogen, maybe it can lie dormant, like HIV," I say, picking up her train of thought as some familiar faces (or what's left of them) stagger down the street towards the front gate.

"That would be my guess," she agrees. "And, like any virus, there could be different strains—some fast acting, some slow. Your body might be naturally more resistant than mine."

"Maybe even immune," Gary says.

"I haven't seen any hint of that in this case," Laleh says, "but it's possible. That's biology for you. It's relentlessly variable. It changes. It mutates. I doubt you can set a timer on how quickly a person will change after exposure or how long they'll go on as a carrier."

I think of Steph. Of her bizarre behavior the night she was bitten, screaming at herself in the mirror like she was talking to her mother. That was less than 24 hours after that kid attacked her. This virus, or whatever, it definitely didn't lie dormant in her.

"This thing, it somehow keeps parts of the central nervous system firing," Gary says, thankfully breaking my train of thought.

"But not all," Laleh agrees. "Maybe it even supercharges sections of the brain. Amping up some aspects, like hunger, dulling others, even killing off certain regions of the mind and central nervous system over time. If someone came into hospital with early symptoms—anxiety, depression, schizoaffective disorder—want to bet the doctors pulled out their prescription pads?"

"No pun intended," I say, "but that's insane. Isn't it?"

"Maybe not," Gary says. "This generation of kids became the most medicated in all of history. ADHD wasn't even a thing when I was in school. Then, at some point, it became normal for kids to take Prozac naps in the middle of class."

I think of my nephew and nieces. I think of Buddy. I wipe my eyes.

"And, what if all those medications slowed the pathogen down. Maybe that's what kept it dormant," Gary postulates.

"Trapped the genie in the bottle," Laleh agrees. "Ish. It would've still been transmittable; early symptoms would be suppressed or camouflaged by well-meaning doctors throwing prescriptions at it, until..."

"Until this," I conclude.

"Who knows how else we might have been fueling this outbreak," Laleh says. "Designer club drugs. Genetically modified food. So many hormones in meat and dairy that we piss them into our drinking water. PrEP. In my social work, I saw reports. Weird instances of sudden violence. People eating people and blaming it on bath salts or some other street drug. Ebola victims rising from the dead."

"There were those incidents on the news over the last few months, in Africa and the Middle East," I add. "Entire towns gone crazy."

"Other than a travel ban, most westerners dismissed them because, let's face it, they are racist as fuck," Laleh says.

The group of athletic enthusiasts, splattered with blood, is only a couple of blocks away.

"I'm not an epidemiologist," I challenge, playing devil's advocate, "but there's a pretty glaring hole in your theory. A bite seems like a tough way of transmitting whatever this thing is on such a large scale, unnoticed, for so long."

"I don't think it's the bite you have to worry about," Laleh says. "It's the saliva."

She lets that sink in.

"So...sharing a drink..." Gary says.

"Or a cigarette," she adds, holding up the one in her fingers.

"Or a kiss," I conclude.

"Could all potentially lead to infection," Laleh says. "*If* my theory is true."

"But if that's the case, *and* this thing can lie dormant..." I say, my eyes growing in horror.

She nods. "It means any one of us could be infected; we just don't know it yet."

CHAPTER 18

As we digest breakfast—and Laleh's words—she stubs out her cigarette, flicks it towards the smoldering building, takes our syrupy plates, and walks away. Over her shoulder, she shouts, "I won't say anything to the others, but someone should." She disappears through the door that leads into the building.

"She can't be right," I say to Gary. "Can she?"

He shrugs. "Fucked if I know." He gets up as if something's occurred to him. "Buddy's down there."

I put a hand on his chest. "If one of us were infected, there'd be warning signs. There were with Steph. I just...I didn't know."

The tears come. I wipe them away and, by some miracle, keep them at bay.

"What if I could've saved her? Gotten her on anti-psychotics?"

"Dude," Gary says. "Who knows how this thing works. Laleh's guessing. There's nothing you could've done."

"Yeah, I know," I reply. But, of course, I don't. It's like the woman we burned alive. We *didn't* save her, so we tell ourselves we *couldn't* save her.

"So... question," he says, "and I hate to ask, but you said Steph had symptoms. Like what?"

I take a deep breath. Thinking of Steph, of those final moments, it stirs up another storm of feelings. *Later*, I tell myself. *You can fall apart later.* I have to be clinical; people's lives depend on it. I feel myself drifting far away, and there's a click of a switch in my mind, turning the emotions off. Dissociation, my therapist called it. Sweet bliss, I say.

"When Steph...changed, her breath was...I can't even tell you. Her teeth were falling out. And before that, she was emotional, erratic. She tore the kitchen apart. She ate a dog."

"Jesus," Gary says.

"And then I ..."

He puts his hand on my shoulder. I'm shaking.

"Listen," I say. "If I'm a carrier, if she gave it to me, you know I can't stay."

"Marty, you don't have it," he says.

"You don't know that. After she was bitten, did she and I share a glass of water? Eat off the same plate? Kiss? I don't know. If I'm infected, you have to think of Buddy first."

Gary doesn't say anything. I see it in his eyes. He'll do what's necessary to protect his son. So will I. We don't discuss what that is.

When we get downstairs, Gary's looking at everyone like they might have rabies. I'm doing the same. I'm also trying to figure out an internal checklist, to self-monitor, in case I start going off the rails: dark moods, *check;* reckless behavior, *check.* I see Heidi talking with the others, and I wonder what she's up to. Paranoia, *to be determined.*

Which raises disturbing questions.

What if you are infected? I ask myself. *Will you be able to think clearly enough to do something about it?*

I hope so. I *pray* so. If it falls to Gary, I'm not convinced he has it in him to do what needs to be done.

I tell myself sternly, *You need to be ready to handle this yourself. He's got a kid. That's enough to worry about without adding you to his plate.*

I can see the veins sticking out on Gary's neck, betraying his fear that at any moment someone in the room might turn into a flesh-eating maniac. His breathing grows easier when he spots Buddy. The kid's helping Devon and Seong wash dishes. Chris is shirtless and sweaty, chopping clumsily at the air as he practices with a short sword. Martial arts was never his thing, but give him a sledgehammer and watch out.

Laleh's talking in hushed tones with the others. I can tell from the looks on their faces exactly what she's saying. Heidi's with them. She's looking at me.

"Is it true?" Bob demands from the edge of the cluster they've formed. "Could any one of us be infected?"

Devon and Seong exit the kitchen, wiping their hands dry. Buddy runs out as soon as he sees Gary and wraps his scrawny arms around his dad's muscled leg. Chris pauses as he's about to chop the head off some unseen attacker.

I put on a big, fake smile and come over to Laleh's side. As discretely as I can, I say, "I thought you weren't going to say anything."

"Yeah, well," she shrugs, lighting up another cigarette.

Chris stomps over to her and yanks the smoke from her mouth; he throws it on the rubberized floor and stomps it out.

"My kid's breathing that air," he says. The look she gives him could hard-boil an egg—while it's still inside the chicken.

"You're right," she says to me, holding her hands up for peace. "I'm sorry. It didn't seem right for them not to know."

"You weren't going to tell us?" Bob demands.

Gary does his *settle down* hand gesture. "It's just a theory."

"What are you talking about?" Chris demands.

"We might all be infected," I blurt out.

Chris looks like I've slapped him.

"Hopefully Laleh's wrong," Gary says, "but we're going to have to take some precautions. Spit seems to be the carrier agent, so we'll need to make sure everyone has their own cup, plate, and utensils. No sharing."

"That's not going to stop someone from ripping our throats out in the middle of the night if they've already got it," Seong says.

"There are warning signs," I say. "Right, Laleh?" As if she knows.

"Should be," she replies.

"Should be?" Bob sputters. "We are so fucked."

"Hey!" Chris says, indicating Buddy. "Language."

"The world's fucking ending," Bob shouts. "If your kid can't handle a few eff bombs, then he's even more fucked than the rest of us!"

It's the fastest I've ever seen Chris move, and I barely get between him and Bob in time.

"You want to get out of my way," Chris warns me.

I stand my ground. Heidi's watching me with surprise. That's right, I can be alpha.

"Bob," I say. "Outside. Now."

"Or what?" he demands.

I don't know if it's because Heidi's here, and I feel like I have to prove to her that I'm not a wimp, or because Bob, the guy whose body I helped fix, is yelling at me in my house, but my fingers are curled into a fist, ready to clock him one.

I catch myself, thinking of my mental stability checklist. *Inability to control anger...* I relax my hand. As long as I'm in control, I'm not infected. I may still slap him, though.

"Or," I reply with a deep exhale, "I let Chris do whatever he wants to you."

Bob's glaring, but he knows Chris could beat the crap out of him. He grumbles and heads outside. Chris is still in my face. Everybody's staring.

"You need to watch yourself, Marty," Chris says.

"Are you kidding me?" I demand, taken aback.

"Come on, baby," Gary says, putting a hand on his husband's shoulder. Chris jerks it off.

"I am so sick of you coming to his defense," Chris says. "Maybe you could take my side once in a while."

I look to Laleh. *Am I hearing this?*

Yikes! her face projects.

"We are not doing this right now," Gary says.

"Of course we're not," Chris snorts, "because it's never a good time for this conversation."

"I'm just saying that you need to keep your cool," Gary snaps back. "Marty thinks that rage might be an early warning sign of being infected. Tell him, Marty."

He did not just bring me back into this.

"Marty thinks?" Chris rounds on me. "Well, that's just swell. So now, if I have emotions, that means I'm infected? Is that it, Marty? Do you have any other theories to help you get between my husband and me?"

"I...what?" I reply.

Gary is blushing profusely.

"Let me be clear," Chris says, addressing the group. "Anybody swears at my kid, ever, I will lose it on them, and it's not because of a virus."

"I'm pretty sure that's not going to happen again," Heidi says.

He rounds on her. He looks ready to rip her throat out.

I wait for her to crumble before his mammoth frame, but this is Heidi. She's a Jedi of manipulation. She does her patented big-eyed, pouty-lipped *I'm-just-a-silly-girl* face. As if she's Obi-Wan saying, "these are not the droids you're looking for," Chris falls for it—just like I used to.

"Sorry," he says.

"It's okay," she replies, giving his biceps a squeeze. He puts his hand on her shoulder like a trained bear. Her eyes glow with delight.

My stomach feels like a sailor's using it to practice a new knot.

Fuck me, I think. They're becoming allies.

"Well," Laleh says, pulling out a cigarette; she thinks better of it and puts it away, "now that everybody's best friends, we still need to keep our spit to ourselves. We're going to need more plates."

I look at our pile of supplies, which seemed so ample yesterday.

I exhale loudly.

"We're going to need more of everything."

CHAPTER 19

I kneel in the dusty training yard. Steph's Prius is behind me, facing a concrete wall. I'm drilling planks of wood into the front door to The Box to cover up the glass. Laleh holds the wood in place. Heidi's shrill laughter rises from the kitchenette, where she's counting the plates and glasses with Chris. Their hag-fag connection is electric. With her GBF Kevin presumed dead, she's auditioning for a replacement.

"You worried about their budding alliance?" Laleh asks me.

"What?" I say, snapping from my reverie. "No," I lie. "Alliance? What is this, *Survivor*?"

"Yes," she replies.

I wait for the punchline, but there isn't one. Laleh apparently went to the Social Work School of In Yo' Face.

"People like them," she says, "they turn on you."

"Agreed," I say. Heidi is what we in the social artistry world call "a natural." She lives and breathes the nuances of interpersonal relations. It helps (a lot) that she's pretty, and Chris has his issues, but it goes beyond that.

As much as Heidi's uncanny ability to manipulate could be my undoing, I can't help but admire her Olympic grace as she wraps Chris around her finger. A well-placed compliment, an inside joke, a bit of pouty-face here and there with her big doe eyes, and voilà. Classic Heidi. He's licking it up like Oreo ice cream on treat day.

Laleh snorts. "Men are stupid for a pair of tits, even the gay ones."

I laugh so hard it comes out a bark. I catch Heidi appraising me from the kitchenette. I can't help a moment of satisfaction. She's got her ally. I've got mine. I still have to be careful, though. As I said, Heidi's a natural.

For me, it's different. I'm the epitome of the four stages of learning. At first, I didn't know just how socially clueless I was, never mind my brain damage when it came to women. As I methodically followed the online social artistry seminars, the vaseline got washed off the lens. I got better, but everything was a conscious effort, every hello, every anecdote, every flirtatious aside. With Gary and Steph, I got to enter the fourth stage, where the games allowed my best me to emerge. That they truly cared for me was also a big help.

You've come a long way, Teddy assures me.

Have I? Whenever Heidi's around, I can't help but feel that all the progress I've made is the thinnest of veneers, that *I'm* the fake.

I'm reminded of how things ended between us. The way the relationship devolved is too clichéd to be anything but true.

On our first date, I pulled a classic *meet me in my lobby* routine, promising that I'd come right down once she buzzed my unit. It was trickery. When her voice came through the intercom, I told her to come up to my place "real quick," because I had to "finish an email." Lies, all lies.

The purpose was to familiarize her with my apartment so that it was no longer foreign territory. That way, when I invited her back to my place later, she'd be more likely to say yes. As she stood in heels in my front hall, wearing a short skirt and a silky blouse, I couldn't believe she was there.

"Cool art," she said of the framed funky *Star Wars* prints I got on Etsy.com.

"What's that famous Yoda quote?" she asked.

"There is only do, or do not," I said with a smile.

"There is no try," she finished for me with a wink.

I never stood a chance.

I took her to a retro Greek restaurant. I knew all the staff by name (she was suitably impressed), followed by fourth-row center at the musical *Wicked* (it was her "fav-seys"—her word, not mine, though I made sure to use it that night to create a sense of rapport.)

I followed my online course's instructions, "bouncing" from one place to another. With each new location, the sense that we'd known each other for longer than we had grew stronger—for both of us. As we drove towards a new frozen yogurt shop that was getting rave reviews, I realized I wasn't just working to get her to fall for me. I was having a good time, and I was genuinely falling for her.

As we sped down a near-empty city street, I winked at her.

"You were such a Galinda in high school, weren't you?" I said, referring to *Wicked*'s socially elite character who would grow up to be one of Dorothy's saviors in *The Wizard of Oz*.

"It's Glinda, now," Heidi winked back, quoting the play. "The *Ga* is silent."

We laughed. The best part of it all? I was having fun. Somehow, by using game, I planted the seeds for a great time, and those seeds grew organically, like magic beans. She was laughing at my jokes. I laughed at hers. I thought, *I'm not sure who this me is that I am right now, but I like him.* For a brief spell, I stopped being that loser from a '90s high-school comedy. I became that other character—the confident one who gets the girl. Heidi put her hand on mine as I shifted gears—goosebumps.

Heidi contemplated me as I drove. Assessing. Weighing. Preparing to strike. "You were an Elphaba in high school, weren't you?"

Bull's-eye. My stomach shriveled.

I thought of Elphaba, the musical's green-skinned reject, who would evolve into the Wicked Witch of the West. Her backstory was one of ridicule and social isolation. Despite my hocus pocus, I'd been made. My hands tightened on the steering wheel. Heidi was cold reading me, turning my tricks against me. My larynx squeezed, and my mind went blank. She'd found and sank my battleship.

In retrospect, I should've laughed and made a joke, turning this into another bonding moment. Foolishly, I was silent. I couldn't speak. Vocal chord malfunction. Selective mutism is what it's called according to my therapist.

"I knew it," she smirked. "You were a loser."

There was a weird tone of satisfaction in her voice—as if she were an alien parasite and my discomfort was making her stronger. I didn't know it at the time, but she was cataloging the moment, storing it in her databank, to be used against me later. It was the first time I caught a glimpse of her real mean-girl self. Admittedly, my online course never promised to find me someone nice—just someone hot. An instant later, her persona was back. She batted her eyelids, lips full and hinting of a kiss. That's all it took. I melted and smiled. I drowned in euphoria. Her mask was firmly affixed, and I pretended not to have seen what lay beneath.

CHAPTER 20

The sun beats down on us, and The Box heats up as we process the possibility that any one of us could be carrying whatever is destroying humanity. We need each other, yet we fear each other.

We hear banging on the front gate. Outside, I climb the ladder we've propped against the wall enclosing the yard and look over. The mutilated muscle boys have arrived, along with a few of our other former clients trailing behind. Even in this state, the betas are following the alphas. I can't help but wonder which one I'd be.

The undisputed top dog of this pack is Eric, an asshole elite CrossFit athlete; he's all muscle squeezed into breathable shorts and a spaghetti-string tank top with the word *Aesthetic* on it. His arms hang like a gorilla's, biceps the size of cantaloupes. His right one is half eaten, exposing the bone. He stares at the solid gate before him and yanks on the handle with his good hand. The lock clangs, refusing to open. A part of him seems to realize this isn't working. Without changing expression, he starts slapping his palm on the hard steel. He does this for three beats, drops his arm, stares, and then, like a wind-up toy, repeats.

He's flanked by his workout bros, one with a thick lumbersexual beard and a pec popping shirt that says *Do You Even Lift?*; the other guy has tattoos running down his neck and wears a cut-up shirt with the words *Shut Up and Train*. Hanging out behind them are six clients who were at this morning's fitness class. They range from chunky to hunched. When shit went down, they all took off to get to their families. They never made it. However much they loved their spouses and children, whatever gray matter they have left in their fried brains, it brought them back here.

"No pain, no gain," I sigh.

94

"Do you think if we just leave them they'll eventually go home?" Gary asks me.

"I think for them this is home," I reply.

There's an uncomfortable irony in what we do next.

We each carry the heaviest plate or kettlebell that we can manage and pile them on top of the wall. We're all sweating and breathing hard. A day ago we would've turned on the gym timer.

I look back at how seriously we took ourselves—as if those workouts were a matter of life and death. Catch phrases like "feel the burn, love the burn" are now a pathetic joke.

Gary and I stand on top of the wall. The 45 lbs plates look like a stack of pancakes big enough for an ogre. The kettlebells are like cannon balls with handles, ready to be fired. On the outside of the gate, Eric slams his palm against the unyielding metal. Gary throws a kettlebell and crushes the guy's skull.

On our side of the gate, Seong, Devon, and Bob are headed back into The Box where Buddy is playing. Heidi and Chris talk in the dusty training yard. Something's up. Heidi and Chris are doing their best not to look at us, but their furtive glances betray them.

"We still have to come up with something to call these things," Gary says. "Zombie is just too..."

"Supernatural?" I ask.

"Creepy," he replies.

"How about the departed?" I ask.

"You pay your respects to the departed. We're going to have to smash their faces in," he says.

"Living dead?" I ask.

"Well, they're animated," Gary agrees, "but are they alive? I mean, part of the process seems to be that they do die."

"And yet they're not dead," I counter.

"Dead not dead," Gary muses.

"DNDs," I say.

Gary nods, dropping a weight onto a portly woman. Her name was Sally. She was a pharmacist. Her skull splits like a watermelon. I wince and look away, willing my stomach back under control.

"DNDs," Gary echoes. "That might work."

Shortening catch-phrases to acronyms is one of Heidi's little tricks. The realization puts me on edge. Heidi is watching us closely.

"Gary," Chris says, "can you come down here for a second?"

They're making their play.

"Uhm, can't this wait? I'm a bit busy," Gary replies.

"Oh, no worries," Heidi says, climbing the ladder. "I'll take your place."

I look to Gary with my strongest stink eye, giving him a subtle shake of the head, begging him with my eyes to shut this down, hard and fast. He has his own idea.

"That would be great," he says.

"I will cut you," I say to him.

"Love you, mean it," he replies. He makes the shape of a heart with his hands, which he places over his left pec.

I don't look at Heidi as she reaches the top of the ladder. Gary climbs down.

You could push her off, Teddy suggests.

He's joking; I think. But if she happened to slip and fall...

"I like the tattoo," she says, looking at the outline of a butterfly on my shoulder.

"Thanks," I say curtly.

I drop a kettlebell, and it slams into the shoulder of Gareth, the lumbersexual. The guy's got a killer upper bod and chicken legs that refused to grow. He falls to the ground, and Heidi releases a 45 lbs plate that cracks Gareth's skull.

"Looks like we make a good team," she says.

I ignore her. *Is this fun for her?*

The fear of screwing up in front of her has me sweating profusely. It's like every minute of every moment, I feel like I have to prove myself to her or she'll find a way—directly or indirectly—to start tearing me down. I hate this feeling, I hate her for stirring it up, and I hate myself for being such a pussy.

I wipe my sweaty palms on my shorts, lift another kettlebell, aim it like Wile E. Coyote with an anvil, and throw it down. It smashes an old woman in a track suit in the face, and she crumbles to the ground.

"Good shot. You're a lot stronger than you used to be," Heidi says.

Her compliments are barbed darts in my neck. *Is she trying to get me to lower my guard?*

I remember on one of our first dates she said, "Struggle is the father of all things. It is not by the principles of humanity that man lives or is able to preserve himself above the animal word, but solely by means of the most brutal struggle."

At first, I was impressed. I told her how much I, too, liked Darwin. She smirked. "Darwin's not the only one into survival of the fittest."

It was Hitler who said it. What more of a red flag did I need?

I keep that in mind as I watch her lift a 45 lbs plate overhead and whip it down at Trevor, a muscled dude in his 20s. It hits with such force he's thrown off his feet. He twitches in the dirt, his *Shut Up and Train* t-shirt soaking up his tar-like blood. Heidi's not weak, never has been.

Even now, since I've become a trainer, I wonder if she's got more explosive strength than me. Quicker and more agile to be sure. I've grown a lot in the last few years, but it's tough for someone like me to compete with someone like her. She grew up doing pole vaulting, gymnastics, ballet, diving, swimming—the latter at a national level. Her body moves like she's weaving a grand tapestry. I've only just learned to cross stitch.

Now, I stand on a wall dropping weights on people I once knew, whose identities have been stripped away, leaving behind the husks of their humanity.

"Did you know them?" Heidi asks.

"The fit ones in their 30s, that's Ed and Claire." I drop a kettlebell, and it smashes Ed's skull in. Heidi takes out Claire.

"Who's the fatty?" she asks.

Fatty is an understatement. The guy is obese. I can't help but wonder what the heck we'll do with his body. Moving him won't be an option. Burn his remains on the spot, I guess.

"That's Sam," I say.

"Not exactly one of your success stories," Heidi says.

Her words take a chip out of me. It's a familiar feeling. This is how it starts. She finds the slightest insecurity and starts tapping away at it, widening it little by little. Over time, her seemingly off-hand remarks turn the merest fracture into full-on fault lines. When the final blow comes…

Don't let her get away with it, Teddy tells me. *Don't let her do this to you again.*

"So, I'm a failure, is that it?" I demand.

She's caught off guard, and the weight she's holding slips from her hand; it smashes Sam in the face. He teeters, like a dancing Disney hippo, and then goes down.

"That's not what I was…" she starts to reply.

"He was a person, Heidi," I shout. I don't mean to yell, but there it is. "I knew him, okay? He lost twenty pounds in two months, thank you very much, and you want to know what the biggest reason was for his success? Because he stopped listening to people like you. He was terrified to come here, but he did. He was brave for facing his fears and showing up in an environment where he felt he didn't belong. He didn't want to wake up in five years and realize he still hadn't done anything to change his life. You show some respect, do you understand?"

"Sure," she says. "No problem. Sorry."

I wait for her to ask the obvious question: *are you sure you're talking about Sam? Or are you talking about yourself?*

She does not. Chris and Devon come out.

"Marty, what the fuck are you going on about?" Chris demands. To Heidi, he says, "You okay?"

"Everything's fine," Heidi says with her false cheer.

Chris grunts something; it makes Devon blush. Chris glares at me and doesn't go back inside. Devon keeps glancing at the door but doesn't dare leave Chris' side. I want to yell at them to fuck off. A couple of blocks away, a few DNDs come out of their houses, unblinking as they gaze straight ahead. My yelling must've drawn them out. They make no move toward us.

"You're right," Heidi says, lowering her voice. She sees them too. "We should pay our respects. Who's that one?"

She points at a woman in her 70s, in designer track pants and an exercise top that's pretty much a sports bra. Makeup is slathered on her face, and pink earrings stretch her earlobes. Her skin's been fried by endless fake-and-bake sessions, and her hair's a bouffant of chemical curls.

"That," I say, forcing the words out calmly as Chris glances at us every so often, "is Margery."

"Tell me about Margery," Heidi says.

Margery spent most of her time complaining about her various aches and pains. She then ignored our advice on how to get better. Hardly seems like the epitaph she'd want, accurate as it might be.

"Margery was a dreamer," I say instead. "She was drawn to shiny things and sought out beauty. She never wanted children. She was in her prime and wanted to enjoy it. But as she put it, what choice did she have? It was a different time. All the parties she wanted to keep going to, her husband attended without her, leaving her to raise the kids he insisted they have, meanwhile cheating on her left and right. She drank herself to sleep each night. On the day she buried him, she poured a bottle of gin over his grave and never drank again."

"Goodbye Margery," Heidi chirps.

"Goodbye Margery," I agree, but with sadness and regret as I drop a weight on her head.

She's the last of them.

"You okay?" Heidi asks.

I'm shaking.

"What fucking hole did we fill in their lives that they came back here?" I ask angrily.

"OCD?" she wonders out loud. "A sense of community, maybe. Or who knows, could be that's just what was randomly left after everything else was gone." She reaches a hand for my butterfly tattoo.

"Don't," I warn.

"Okay," she rolls her eyes, "are we going to talk about this or what?"

"This?" I ask. "We're not Chris and Gary. There is no *this* for us to talk about." I look at Margery. "We'll need to burn the bodies."

"Or bury them," she says. "PS, you need to grow up."

It doesn't matter what I do, stay quiet or speak up, I can't win.

"We're trapped here together," she says. "So, yes, I ended things with you. It happens. I'm sorry. Get over it."

"Is that what you think this is about? Our breakup?" I feel my fingers clenching. With an effort, I force them to release. "No, Heidi, this is not about you leaving me. You did me a favor. After you dumped me, I met the love of my life." Heidi flinches at that. Thinking of Steph stretches my seams. I can't.

I force myself to say to Heidi, "*This* is about the nightmare I went through during the time that we were together."

She pinches her brow as if dealing with a petulant child. Amidst the emotions, I wonder, *Is she right? Am I being a big baby?*

"Marty, it's the end of the world. How can anything that's happened in the past even matter?" she asks. "We're fighting for our survival here!"

Her words are a laser beam of clarity.

"I agree," I say, "this *is* about survival." I feel like cold stone inside.

"This isn't about what you've done," I say. "This is about what you're going to do."

"Marty, you're talking non..."

"You see those schmucks down there?" I point at the montage of corpses below. "You want to know why they came back here?"

She shakes her head, confused. "I don't see what..."

"Habit," I say. "When they were alive, they came here over and over, and that habit brought them back one last time. At the end of the day, that's what we all are, the sum of the actions we do again and again. For you, that doesn't mean doing what the group needs to survive. You do what *you* need to survive. This time, when you turn on me, I could literally have my heart ripped from my chest, but only *after* you've used me."

"Is that really what you think of me?" she asks, her hand pressed to her breast. It's convincing, I'll give her that. If I hadn't fallen for this very move time and time again…

Remember the pattern, Teddy says.

I do remember. My therapist had me draw it out—more than once.

—>Heidi is verbally and/or emotionally belittling and abusive—>I pull away and stick up for myself—>Heidi acts sweet and kind to draw me back in—> I fall for it, lower my guard, and think I have my girlfriend back—>REPEAT—>

"It's a classic abusive pattern," my therapist explained. "Every time Heidi turns sweet again that needy, rejected part of you gets hit with neurochemicals that have a stronger effect than crack-cocaine. They've done studies on rats. You're addicted to her."

I write the pattern in my mind. Right now, we're at the stage where Heidi acts sweet. *I am not a rat, and I am not a junkie.* The thought works. I laugh; it sounds like a bark. She's taken aback. I've rehearsed this moment too many times to count. Chris and Devon are staring. I don't care. I've just finished smashing in the faces of nine people I knew.

"Do you know what happens to something when you freeze it, then heat it, then freeze it, then heat it, again and again?" I ask.

"Marty, what are you…"

"It grows brittle," I say, "and then it shatters."

She still looks confused, until she doesn't.

"Is this because of when I teased you for using Viagra?" she asks.

"Oh for…It was one time! And you still can't let it go!"

"Marty, I'm kidding!" she insists. "You know what? Fine. I'm a horrible person. All of the things, whatever they are, they're all my fault. Can we *please* move on?"

"That's just it," I reply. "For me to let the past be in the past, I have to take ownership of my bad decisions. The only way I know how to do that is to learn from my mistakes and to make different choices. My mistake, before, was letting you in."

That hits a button.

She snorts. "Let me in? Don't you mean how you pursued me with your manipulative pickup routines?"

I blush guiltily. Steph once forced me to watch a YouTube video, showing how much harassment this one woman got from random guys hitting on her as she walked the streets of New York. Spliced together, it felt incessant. It also highlighted some of my douchey past behavior. And yet, without those skills, I never would've met Steph. Fuck, I miss that woman. Tears spring to my eyes. I'm too tired to hold them back.

Heidi sees. Whatever. Let her. I'm done.

"Marty," she says, her voice softening.

Her fingers touch my shoulder. I flinch and instinctively jerk away, throwing myself off balance. Where I think there should be safe footing is only air. I see the sky above and, over my shoulder, the dead bodies below. I try to find my balance; I fail. This is going to hurt.

Heidi grabs my arm, pulls with just the right amount of force, and with a quick contraction of my abs, I'm safely back on the wall. Our eyes meet. I'm breathing hard. So is she. I don't pull away from her touch, this time, but my whole body goes rigid. She feels it; she lowers her eyes and takes her hands off of me. She holds her palms where I can see them.

"Thanks," I force myself to say. The word is barbed wire in my throat.

I almost wish she'd let me drop to the hard ground below because all I want is to get down from this goddamn wall. Heidi's between me and the ladder. If I were Gary, I could jump off and roll—or some other bullshit-badass-ninja-awesomeness; the kind he effortlessly pulls out of his perfectly hairless asshole.

You're not Gary, a part of me reminds myself. My inner critic is alive and well, but it speaks differently now. With Heidi right in front of me, the saboteur no longer sounds like her. It sounds like me.

CHAPTER 21

After Heidi dumped me—and before I cracked like a southern omelette —I watched an online clip of Oprah and Dr. Maya Angelou. They talked about the importance of forgiveness. It resonated. They said that in forgiving someone, it doesn't mean you have to invite the offending party to your table. What forgiving can mean is "go away."

As I watch Heidi climb down the ladder, I think, *I forgive you, Heidi. Please, just go away.*

When she reaches the ground, she makes a big to do of wiping her eyes in front of Chris and Devon (Chris especially), saying loudly, "I'm fine, I'm fine. All this zombie business is getting the best of me."

She gets a lot of "there theres" from Devon and "I know what you mean, girl" from Chris.

I wait for Heidi to go back inside before I climb down the ladder. Chris and Devon are getting ready to take some animal cages outside. I wonder what raccoon steak and squirrel kabob taste like.

"Everything okay?" Devon asks.

I laugh at the question. They look at me like I'm losing my mind; maybe I am. "The world's ending," I say. "My fiancé and family are dead, and I'm stuck here with my ex. But sure, everything's swell."

Instead of words like "that sucks bro" or "shit, man," I am met with judgmental silence.

You're letting your emotions control you, Teddy's voice warns. *Careful.*

"You guys up for helping me burn some bodies?" I say with forced calm.

"Yeah, let's do it," Devon says, clearly relieved at the change of topic. Chris grunts.

Teddy's right. I have to be more careful.

The day is productive, if surreal. We set traps for urban prey and pile the remains of the dead dead (we now have to be specific) in a ditch. We decide to burn them later in case the fire attracts more DNDs. To protect against climbers, we attach a ring of scavenged barbed wire atop of the wall surrounding The Box.

The loft next door is still smoldering. If there are any DNDs in there, the plan is to make them come to us, on our terms, instead of going into a burned-out building.

We raid a local construction site, where we snag cement and cinder blocks. We use them to block up the mouth and rear of the alley that sits between our building and the loft.

The dumpster filled with weights blocks the loft's emergency exit. Twitching arms dangle from the partially open door. We chop off the hands with axes and use metal poles to stab the heads that we can see. We pull the dumpster back a little, allowing the door to open a bit more.

A few smoldering DNDs try to attack us, but they get jammed in the doorway. We put them out of our misery.

"We could use this to burn bodies in," Heidi suggests, knocking on the dumpster. I hate to admit it, but it's a good idea. There are nods of agreement. She's making herself useful. Am I? Is it enough? In my mind, there's a constant tally of how I'm stacking up against her. If push comes to shove, would they choose her or me?

We roll the dumpster aside and out topples a scene from a Rwandan war crime. We'll deal with the charred human remains later. For now, we've got to get out of the pen we've created.

"Let's move," Gary says.

We prop open the residence's back door and then escape into The Box, locking it tightly behind us. We head for the roof, the sound of our stomping feet echoing up the stairwell. It reminds me of our fitness classes. It's still bizarre how all that we played at before are games no more.

Up on the roof, I scan the potted plants, the solar panels, and the picnic table. *Clear.* We head for the side of our building, overlooking the alley, and dangle a couple of speakers from the edge. I look to Gary. He's sweating through a t-shirt with large ovals cut out of the sides, showing off his flanks. I nod, and he plugs the speaker jack into his phone. He presses play and out comes the *Wicked* soundtrack. The song 'Popular' rings through the air.

I laugh before I can stop myself. The others are smiling. A DND stumbles out of the building, drawn to the sound. The juxtaposition between ditzy, blond Glinda, singing about "proper poise" and how to "talk to boys," and the still smoking DND is wildly inappropriate. What else can we do but laugh awkwardly?

There's a twinkle in Heidi's eyes and an upward curve to the sides of her lips.

"I thought you'd like it, Elphaba," she says as she contemplates me.

My smile dissolves. The song was her idea. She's been colluding— with Gary. I try to assure myself that this is innocent enough, "girl games," Gary calls it, but it rankles.

I grab a kettlebell with dried blood on it and throw it full force at the smoking DND. It crushes his skull.

"...*popular*..." Glinda sings.

A singed DND with a guitar strapped to his back comes staggering out. Glinda wails about the importance of being "good at sports" and joining "the right cohorts." Gary drops a weight on him. The DND's guitar twangs as he smacks to the ground.

"That's the thing about Elphaba," Heidi says, un-phased by my silence. Her eyelashes flutter like a wasp taking off. "She comes into her own in the end. Just like you. You've changed. Not just your body. Not just the tattoo."

The difference between this conversation and the one we had on the wall is striking. She's steering clear of my weaknesses and emphasizing my strengths. Instead of hollowing me out, she's building me up.

The pattern, Teddy warns.

I got this, I assure him.

"I have changed," I say. For a moment, I believe it—cocky Marty is back, and it's as if I can breathe again.

Down below, a woman in a tattered floral dress comes staggering out of the residence. She trips over the guitar man and falls to her stomach. I toss a kettlebell at her. It smashes into her back, cracking her spine. She lies there, twitching. I'm about to throw another weight at her, but Gary waves for me not to bother.

"We can deal with her when we go down there," he says. "Let's save our ammo."

"You're like your butterfly tattoo," Heidi says. "You've come out of your chrysalis. Remember that documentary you made me watch? It said that the butterfly has to struggle out of its cocoon on its own to develop wing strength; if you help it, it won't be able to fly."

I say nothing. I don't have to. She smiles in her *I've got your number* way. "And just so you know, I'm not the same Heidi that you remember," she says. "I know that you think I can't be trusted, but I can. People change, Marty. You did. So have I."

The others are watching us. Watching me. Waiting for my reaction. Glinda's words trail off from the speaker system, ending with a reminder that no matter how popular Elphaba becomes, she'll never be quite as popular as Glinda.

They aren't falling for this, are they?

For me, seeing Heidi in action is like going to a magic show that I've attended too many times. I've figured out all the tricks. I see through the smoke and mirrors. For the others, this is all new. They're oblivious to the strings and misdirection. They're taking her at face value—because they want to. I can't even be angry. I once fell for all this, too.

"Can I help you?" I ask them.

They turn away as a crispy woman comes stumbling out of the loft. They all throw their weights at the same time. She's hit from so many directions, she looks like she's being stoned to death. It reminds me of a Biblical quote. *Ye who has not sinned, cast the first stone.* It's not like I'm an innocent in all of this.

Still, I want to rant at Heidi. She's being so damn reasonable, I'll look like a lunatic if I do. *They'll think you're infected*, Teddy warns. Heidi chose wisely to have this conversation in front of everybody.

I don't care, I reply.

Are you sure? Teddy asks. *Do you want to be kicked out? To be alone? Out there? This isn't the playground. You can't survive by yourself.*

Gary would never do that to me, I reply.

Gary will do what he has to do, to protect Buddy.

The thought stings deeper than any slap in the face. I, too, would do anything for Buddy, even play along with the one person I trust least in all the world.

"You're right," I say. The words don't even pain me. It's like I'm far away. "People *can* change. In the last few days, all of us have evolved. Or devolved." I look at the blackened sign in the window across from us. 'HELP!!! PLEASE!!!'

"Maybe this is our clean slate," I say. If so, it's getting dirty awfully fast.

"I'd like that," Heidi says. She grasps my forearm, and she's got that twinkling in her eye that used to melt my heart because I would think, *she* does *love me*. I know better, now. This is her *I'm getting away with it* face. As much as it kills me, I have to pretend that she is. Sometimes you have to play along to get along.

She offers her hand for to me to shake.

"Friends?" she asks.

Everybody's watching. I grudgingly take her palm in mine.

"Not enemies," I reply. I force myself to smile and wink.

That earns some cautious laughter as the tension breaks. I hope it's enough.

And I, Teddy says nervously, *hope it's not* too *much.*

CHAPTER 22

No more DNDs come out of the residence, so we go to them, methodically making our way through the husk of a building. At its core, the converted warehouse is made of steel, concrete, and bricks, so structurally it's held up despite the fire.

We snag keys from the front desk. We then go floor by floor, apartment by apartment, and room by room. Once an apartment is clear, we spray paint a red X on the door. If the unit is habitable, we spray paint a blue circle. If it's too badly damaged by the fire, but there's still stuff we can salvage, it gets a green circle. If it's a write off, it gets a second red X. We hear growls and banging coming from the elevator, but that's a problem for another day (Gary will ultimately get the honor of climbing down the elevator shaft, opening up a panel in the ceiling, and then stabbing them from above with the sharpened end of a broom handle).

I remind myself again and again, they aren't people—not anymore.

We move quickly and efficiently. In the hallway, I loop my belt around a door handle, plant a foot on the wall, and open the door just enough for a DND in curlers to stick her slavering head out. Heidi ends her with a crowbar.

We scan the apartment—like most of the units on the second floor, it's untouched by fire. Blue circle. The fumes from the spray paint make me light headed. It's not entirely unpleasant, and there's something soothing about the light shhhwitt sound as Heidi presses the nozzle.

"I guess you were right," I say, dragging the woman in curlers into the hall.

"About what?" she asks. "I mean, other than everything." There's that girlish *look at me, I'm so cute* twinkle in her eye.

My laugh sounds contrived—because it is—but she goes with it.

"What you said earlier," I reply. "We do make a good team." Lies, all lies, even if, in this one particular instance, it's true.

"The dynamic duo," she says.

We move onto the next unit, and I wonder if this is what it feels like to be her: fake. We finish one floor, a pile of dead now in the hall, then check in with the others. As a group, we move onto the next level. The higher we go, the more burned out the apartments get, and the fewer DNDs we have to put down. The third-floor apartments are smoldering husks with twitching, smoking DNDs that we easily finish off.

We're putting them out of their misery, I tell myself as we choke on the smell of their charred bodies. *I'd want the same if positions were reversed.*

My stomach still clenches with every skull I stab. At least I'm pulling off my farce with Heidi—until we get to the apartment at the end of the hall. We knock and listen. No answer.

The door is unlocked. I look closer. There's a key broken inside the deadbolt. I imagine someone running here in a panic, trying to escape from DNDs, turning the key so hard that it snapped as they got it open. We go in. The place is rank with the smell of ash, blackened from wall to wall. The door bangs into a couch, a hasty barrier pushed in front of the entry, but easily shoved aside. *Something forced its way in*, I realize. Heidi's shaking the red spray can. *Rattle rattle.* I hold my hand up, and she stops. There's movement by the busted window. A pleasant breeze comes through. Crispy legs stick out from a set of curtains wrapped around three twitching bodies.

Heidi sees the look on my face. "What is it?" she asks.

I don't answer. I walk forward, take a piece of scorched cardboard out of what's left of the window and hold it up for Heidi to see. It says 'HELP!!! PLEASE!!!'

Heidi's eyes water up. She scuttles over to me and wraps her body in mine. I force myself to put my arms around her when what I really want is to shove her away.

I say "there, there," and I assure her, "there was nothing we could do for her." My response is robotic—but holding Heidi is organic.

For a moment, the tension that's been holding me together evaporates. I float, I drift, soaking in her warmth, drawing real comfort from having her in my arms. I kiss her on the top of the head. It's an autonomic response. I don't even realize that my lips are touching her for the first time since we broke up—until she squeezes me. Like a wave that instantly freezes, the tension sweeps back through me. She feels it.

"Marty?" she asks, looking up at me with her big Bambi eyes.

An alarm is wailing in my head.

Abort! Abort! I take her arms and force her off of me.

"What's wrong?" she asks with her two-year-old pouty face.

"Nothing," I lie, followed by the truth. "Everything."

I take the crowbar from her hand and tower over the three twitching DNDs caught in the drapes. They writhe under the curtains. It's haunting. It's tragic. It's grotesque and creepy as all fuck.

The curtain pulls tight around their skulls as they press against it, reacting to the sound of us entering. The fabric outlines their mouths and hollow eye pits. The macabre tableau reminds me of comic books, the panels depicting scenes of tortured souls trapped in purgatory. I lift the crowbar and with three decisive swings—*whack! whack! whack!*—I set them free. Black blood soaks through the curtains.

Panting, without looking at her, I hand the crowbar back to Heidi. I feel the weight disappear from my hand as she takes the tool. I use the curtain to drag the three bodies out into the hall.

"Let me help," Heidi offers.

"I got this," I snap.

"Marty, don't be silly."

"I said, I've got this."

And I do. They're bones and burnt sinew—light as can be. Once I pull them into the hall, I pick up a can of spray paint from the floor. I paint two red Xs on the door then jerk my head for Heidi to follow me back to the stairs.

"We're done, here," I say coldly, as distant as I can be—because a part of me doesn't hate the idea of hugging her again.

CHAPTER 23

Over the next week, we clear out the bodies from the complex and block the building's front entrance and first- and second-floor windows with cement and cinder blocks. Bob makes a list of materials to fix the roof, otherwise we'll be flooded by the first heavy rain.

Throughout, Heidi has decided that she and I are now besties. She can't say "Hello," "Good morning," or "Pass the salt," without touching some part of my body. I remind myself that I don't trust her. In truth, I'm not sure that I trust myself, not after our hug and a kiss moment.

Remember, she saw that woman and said nothing, Teddy warns. *She let us burn her alive.*

I know, Teddy, I reply. *I know.* He's starting to sound less like a wise, old dad and more like a nagging mom with attachment issues.

At dinner, I sneeze loudly and repeatedly into my forearm.

"Hay fever acting up?" Gary asks.

I rub my watery eyes and nod.

"Allergies are for the weak," Heidi often said with disgust when we were dating. Tonight, she's handing me a paper napkin and rubbing my back.

"Thank you," I say as I blow my nose.

"No worries," she replies. "I don't suppose anyone's got any anti-histamines they can spare?"

It's as if she genuinely cares about me.

"Or Advil?" Laleh adds, rubbing her temples.

"Or condoms?" Devon pipes in.

We all look at him. Seong punches his muscular shoulder.

"What?" he says to Seong. "You said you were off the pill and didn't want to get pregnant."

"What are condoms?" Buddy asks.

"I think we need to start making a list," Heidi says.

"Toilet paper," I say.

"Toys!" Buddy chirps.

"Lube," Devon adds.

This time, Chris punches him.

"What?" Devon demands. He's got a hot bod and runs a killer boot camp, but the guy is a bit dense.

"Not in front of the K-I-D," Chris says, covering Buddy's ears as he spells it out.

Heidi is writing away in her bubbly calligraphy on a notepad. "Don't worry," she winks at Devon. "I've got you covered."

He mouths the words, "Thank you."

She's bribing him onto Team Heidi, Teddy says.

To my surprise, I'm not sure that I care.

The next day, we set forth to raid the neighborhood.

At our first house, we knock on the door, quietly enough to avoid rousing any of the neighbors, but loudly enough to draw any DNDs occupying the building in question. A woman in an apron comes lurching to the door. Her face is pulled plastic-surgery-tight by the bun atop her head. Dried blood cakes her apron. She pulls on the door handle, but the deadbolt catches. She rattles the knob a few times before stopping and staring. Hesitantly, as if she doesn't know why she's doing it, she lifts her hand, grasps the deadbolt, and gives it a twist. She seems startled by what she's done. We force the door open, and Gary does the gruesome but necessary deed of taking her out with a baseball bat.

We leave Devon and Seong to loot the place.

The next house over, the door is ajar.

A balding man with a combover sits on the couch, staring at the static on his television. There's a thick rubber band wrapped around one arm. On the coffee table, there are a bunch of cigarette stubs, overflowing ashtrays, and syringes. In one hand he holds his converter. His other wrist ends in a bloody stump.

I'm right behind him. I raise my crowbar. I step on a squeaky floorboard. We all wince. The DND's eyes light up. His gaze meets mine in the reflection of the TV. He whips around, jumps over the back of the couch and tackles me to the ground. His teeth go right for my throat.

Chris and Gary grab him from behind and yank him off. They press him against the wall. Heidi stabs him through with a hunting knife. They drop him to the ground. I'm shaking and panting.

How the hell did I manage to fuck that up? I had the drop on him for fuck's sake!

"Thanks," I say. My voice is shaking.

"No worries," Heidi says, offering her hand. As much as it galls me, I allow her to help me up.

The rest of the house is free of people, alive, dead, or not quite dead. The recycling bin overflows with instant-dinner trays, a half-empty bottle of scotch sits on the coffee table, and a pile of porn magazines lounge on the sofa. The place screams bachelor-pad-in-need-of-an-intervention.

"To be safe, let's clear out any DNDs from next door together, then two of us can come back here to take what we need," Gary says.

No one argues. Safety in numbers.

The owners of the next house could not be more different than their heroine-addict neighbor. There's a woman in a floral print dress on the porch face up, a steak knife in her eyeball. There's a man half on top of her. There's a nasty bite on his forearm. His blond hair is perfectly coiffed.

They look like a couple, based on the similarity in age, about mid-30s, same brand of jeans, in matching T-shirts; both are fit. It makes me think of a game Heidi used to play. She called it "Rate that Mate!"

The rules were simple. She'd give a couple a numerical ranking out of 5 for how good they looked together. Anything below a 3, and she'd declare, "Mismatch!"

I look at the blond pair before us, then at Heidi. I can tell she wants to say 4.5. Back in the day, she gave us a 2. The pain on my face was like soul food to her. Before I can stop myself, I wonder how that rating might have changed. I kick the bottom of the blond guy's sneaker. He trembles, pushing himself up grudgingly. He gets to his feet and stumbles, reaching wide of me as if he's drunk. I stab him in the face.

"Heidi and I can take this house," Chris says. "You and Gary go back to the last one."

I arch an eyebrow. It's weird for Chris to offer up Marty and Gary time like this.

"No," Gary replies. "Marty, Heidi, you two ransack this place. Chris and I will take next door."

I open my mouth to argue, or at the very least question, but there's a tenseness to Gary's voice.

Are they having problems? I wonder. If so, I'm not about to make things worse, even if it means more fake bonding with Heidi.

"Sure," I say. "We got this. Let's go."

There's an odd distance between Gary and Chris as they cross the lawn. I'll ask Gary about it, later. For now, I fish out the keys from the blond guy's pocket. They jingle in my hand, attached to a lucky rabbit's foot. I step over the bodies, unlock the door, and let it swing open. Only now does it occur to me that we haven't determined if the place is empty.

Sloppy, I think. I knock and wait. I am met with motionless silence.

"I think we're clear," I say.

Heidi doesn't respond. She's staring at the face-down couple on the veranda.

"Do you think they were happy?" she asks. "You know, before?"

"I don't know," I reply. "But he stayed with her, even after..."

"After stabbing her through the eye?" she asks. "Even after his brain was fried from the inside out? Even after..."

Before she can finish her sentence, she shudders, like a dog shaking itself dry after jumping in a lake, and the weird look on her face passes. I feel a pang in my chest. All of this, it's a lot, for anyone.

"Let's get this over with," she says.

I offer her my hand. She takes it to step over the corpses.

We enter the front hall. She snakes her fingers into mine.

"Do you think they had kids?" she asks.

I jerk my head at the framed photos on the wall, full of the couple's beaming faces.

"Doesn't look like it," I say.

"It's kind of weird, isn't it?" she says, rifling through their mail. "Going through people's houses like this—with all their secrets on display."

She's getting off on this, Teddy whispers.

Is she? I wonder. How do I know for sure?

We void the home of toilet paper, soap, paper towels, Javex, and Kleenex. We dump it all into a hockey bag.

Heidi opens a medicine cabinet and lets go a low whistle at its contents—row upon row of prescription bottles.

"Looks like Matthew Mendrick," she reads the name on the bottle, "had a thing for pain pills and anti-depressants."

"Do you think that's why he was stumbling?" I ask. "He almost seemed high on something. Do you think narcotics still affect them?"

Heidi shrugs. "Fucked if I know."

She pops a Xanax from a blister pack and downs it.

"Momma needs to take off the edge," she admits.

She offers the packet to me.

"I'm good," I say.

She shrugs, slipping the remainders into her pocket. I let it slide. We also score a shelf-full of designer soaps and shampoos.

"Leave the conditioner," I say.

"Why?" Heidi demands.

"It's not on the list, and it'll just weigh us down."

"I suppose I can survive split ends," she concedes.

I zip up the bag and follow her out. I pass a bookshelf in the hall. I stare at the shelves full of books and board games. We'll need stuff like this for our mental health, but that's not our priority right now. Considering Laleh's theory on how the pathogen works, maybe it should be—maybe it should've been all along.

I touch the game *Settlers of Catan*. There's a contemplative look on Heidi's face

I shake my head. "It's not on the list."

I shove the box back into place. She assesses me in that way that she does, always gauging, rating, and ranking. When she's spit out the report, only rarely have I measured up.

"I won't tell," she says.

"We should get going," I reply brusquely. "Bag's full."

"Your call," she says, shrugging again, followed by another hair toss. "Just remember, you only live once."

"If only that were true," I joke.

For a moment, I'm less concerned with surviving and more concerned with living. Heidi, for all her faults, has that effect on people.

"One second," I say.

I go back into the bathroom and grab a travel-sized tube of conditioner. She smiles when I hand it to her.

"Put it in your pocket," I say. "If it's not taking up space in the bag, it doesn't count."

Outside, Devon and Seong are waiting for us on the sidewalk. Chris and Gary are crossing the lawn to join them. We compare our checklists, marking off what we've got so we can prioritize as we move down the street.

It's going smoothly—until Heidi and I get to our fourth house. That's when shit gets real.

CHAPTER 24

We're raiding a set of modern townhouses. Seong and Devon are in the first one. We've cleared the second of DNDs. At the third, Gary, Chris, Heidi and I are on the front terrace battling it out with a burly guy with a thick beard and black curly hair sprouting from every part of his body —except his bald scalp. He's dressed in jeans, black leather boots, and a white tank top. His shoulder is half eaten.

He instinctively protects his head with his thick arms. We break them with hard cracks of Gary's baseball bat, my crowbar, and Chris' mallet. The guy's limbs drop useless to his sides, and Heidi finishes this ugly business. The man falls with a thunk. We hear the door of the house next to ours rattle, and we duck into the townhome. The neighbor stumbles out. He looks like an aging Justin Timberlake. He peers about with bloodshot eyes.

The rest of the doors on the block remain closed. *Are they becoming less sensitive to sound? Do they only respond to certain kinds of noise?* More questions, not enough answers. After a few minutes, geriatric Justin heads back inside.

"See you guys in half an hour," Gary says.

Heidi and I nod. Sweat covers us. The hairy DND lies there like a slain wooly mammoth. The guy's name is Philip, according to a cheesy tourist plate that has a picture of him and an even bigger guy with a salt and pepper goatee. The souvenir says *Philip and Stan, Puerto Vallarta, 10-year Anniversary*. They're wearing goofy straw hats and huge grins.

A grand piano dominates the living room. I'm tempted to play 'Chopsticks,' but I've seen enough horror movies to know how moments like that end under circumstances like this. I pick up some fallen sheet music. It's marked with hand-written edits—and splattered with blood.

There are music degrees and diplomas on the wall. A shelf is full of awards.

"We should get moving," Heidi says.

I drop the sheet music, but my mind stays far away.

Upstairs, I'm mindlessly throwing a box of rubber gloves (was Stan a nurse or something?) into a shopping bag when Heidi screams.

"Marty!" she shrieks.

I'm moving before I know it, crowbar clenched in hand, but I don't know where to go. Heidi's nowhere in sight.

Where is she?

"Heidi!" I call.

I vaguely remember her saying she was going to check downstairs.

"Shit!" *Why did I let her do that on her own?*

I'm taking the stairs two at a time. I raise my crowbar, but still no Heidi, just bloodied sheet music on the main floor.

"Maaaarrrty!!!!" she howls.

It's coming from an open door leading to the basement. I charge, feet rattling down the steps. I emerge into a fully-stocked S&M dungeon. Light filters in through a series of frosted, sunken windows.

A black leather sling hangs from the beams in the ceiling. In a glass display case are an assortment of dildos, nipple clamps, butt plugs, paddles, and an electroshock device. There are a couple of mannequins in the room, dressed in vintage military wear. Dominating the scene is a huge guy in head-to-toe latex, including a mask that's zipped right over his face. Two tiny holes for his nostrils allow him to breathe—not that he needs to breathe. His neck's ripped out. It drips black tar.

That must be Stan.

What's left of him is staggering around, blindly swinging a chain attached to his right wrist. His left arm pulls another chain along the floor behind him. Heidi is cowering on the ground, backing away from him, crying.

"I can't see Marty! I can't see!"

Blood gushes from a gash in her forehead, flowing over her face and blurring her vision. The guy in latex stumbles towards the sound of her voice, arms reaching, metal links dragging behind him. I grab the chain attached to his left wrist and use the climber's clamp at the end to hook him to one of the many eyebolts in the wall. He takes another step, and the anchored binding yanks him back as he tries to reach forward.

He grunts in surprise and futilely pulls harder. His growls of frustration intensify. Like a kid having a hissy fit, he starts thrashing his free arm around. The chain manacled to his wrist smashes the head off one of the military dummies and shatters the glass case. Dildos fly everywhere, bouncing and quivering like toppled Jello towers.

I crouch and skitter forward. Stan the Man slams the chain down in front of me. I let out a surprised yelp and hop back. I lunge for the chain. Stan yanks it out of reach. He draws his arm back and unleashes the glinting metal with uncanny precision. The deadly links whisper along my back, slamming into the floor behind me with an angry thwack, cracking the marble tiles. That could've been my skull. I push off my back heel like a sprinter hearing the starter pistol.

I reach Heidi and kneel beside her, placing my hands comfortingly on her shoulders. She screams at my touch. Stan's head whips blindly towards us, and he tries to lurch in our direction. His bound arm jerks him back.

"It's me," I say, and Heidi wraps her arms around me. I hold her without a second thought.

The mask muffles Stan's growls, but his actions say it all. Like an angry baby tossing all his toys from his playpen, he starts smacking the chain anywhere and everywhere—busting up the floor, bursting designer lightbulbs into a spray of glass, and scattering a tray of stainless-steel nipple clamps. We cringe every time the metal links get close to us. He's between us and the stairs. The windows are too small; we can't climb out. We're trapped.

Stan pulls sharply on the arm that's keeping him from reaching us. The eyebolt shudders where it's screwed into the wall. He pulls again, and the bolt wiggles. He yanks harder; there's a sickening pop as he dislocates his arm, and the bolt pops free.

He staggers forward, grunting and half-tripping in surprise. I hop to my feet and swing my crowbar, smashing him across the jaw.

I hear the *ka-wack* of breaking bone, and he twirls almost comically, tripping on the chains and falling to his knees—just as quickly, he's getting up. He's a spry fucker, that's for sure. His one arm dangles uselessly, but the other whips the chain in a random pattern, disemboweling the second dummy and taking a slice out of my forearm.

The pain sears into me, and bright red anger flares to life. It blots out my reason.

"Enough!" I shout.

The challenge either excites or infuriates Stan the Man. He swings, and I drop to my knees, bending at the hips Matrix-style. His weapon sails above my chest and face, dangerously close. With a twist of my obliques and legs, I'm back on my feet, shooting my arm after the sailing chain. I grab it and yank it towards me, jerking him off his feet. He slams hard to his knees

Now that I've broken his jaw, his growl comes out a gargled whimper. He tries to get to his feet; I kick his leg out from under him. He squeals, and I almost feel sorry for him as I take the massive blade from the holster at my side and shove it through his hooded skull.

Blinded as she is, Heidi sees none of my heroism. I assure myself, I don't care.

"Marty," Heidi calls, "Marty, are you okay?"

"I'm fine," I pant. "Hold still."

I grab a first aid kit prominently displayed on the wall. These guys played hard, but safety first. I put on latex gloves as I lift a flap of skin on Heidi's forehead back into place. She hisses as I disinfect it, but she doesn't whine or struggle.

"This will need stitches," I say.

For now, I fix gauze into place with a butterfly bandage around her forehead, pulling the knot tight. She looks like a wounded extra in a

World War 2 movie. If Steph were here, she could fix this no problem. God, I miss her.

Really? Teddy challenges. *Because you and Heidi seem to be getting awfully cozy.* I ignore him.

"We'll need to find some needle and thread," I say, wiping the blood from her eyes with a paper towel. She opens them and sees Stan on the floor, the chain splayed around him.

"You did that," she says. It's a statement. Mixed in with the surprise, I detect a hint of respect.

"Gotta' be honest," I say, "I was pretty bad ass."

She looks up at me gratefully. Cocky Marty is killing it.

"Thank you," she says, her lips closing in on mine like a stealth torpedo.

Evasive maneuvers! Teddy cries. Whether it's instinct, or my continued loyalty to Steph, at the last second, I jerk my chin to the left, and her kiss lands on my cheek. She doesn't acknowledge the dodge, simply hugging me tightly. I take in the warmth of her breasts against me, the smoothness of her skin, and the earthy scent of her unwashed hair.

I awkwardly try to disentangle myself. She holds on for a second more as if saying, *No, not yet.* Truth be told, I'm not trying that hard to escape. When she lets me go, I'm relieved—and disappointed.

"I'm sorry," I say. "This is my fault. I shouldn't have let you come down here alone."

"We work better as a team," is her reply. She looks around the room and picks up a hood with pointed ears and a snout. It vaguely reminds me of a doberman. She slides it over her face without doing up the zipper, wincing as it grazes the bandage on her forehead.

"It's not on the list," I tease.

"Woof," she replies through the snout.

"What is that even for?" I ask as she takes it off and tosses it onto Stan the Man.

"Puppy play," Heidi explains.

"What's that now?" There's a limit to the gay speak Gary's taught me.

"It's a thing where grownups pretend to be baby dogs. Kevin dated a guy who was into it. Well, as much as Kevin dated anybody."

Her tone is wistful.

"You must miss him," I say.

"I'd like to think he's still alive, and that, somehow, we'll find each other," she admits. "Don't take this the wrong way, but I sometimes wonder if that's why it's such a relief that I'm in this with you."

I look at her quizzically.

"Well, you know," she says. "You two always looked like brothers. Now that you've beefed up, you're practically twins. It's…comforting."

It's a classic neg, pure game, combining a compliment and an insult all into one. My heart squeezes. Part of me is flattered—because Kevin's hot. Another part of me is hurt. She's not drawn to me; she's missing him. I just happen to be here. I shouldn't give a rat's ass, and yet…

Don't let her play you, Teddy warns. *The pattern. Remember the…*

"We should go," I say.

"Hold on," she says. She walks over to a trio of gym-style lockers that are attached to the wall. She opens all three. One is piled high with jockstraps, the second has a wrestling singlet hanging in it, and the last one causes Heidi to squeal with delight. She pulls out a Costco-sized box of condoms and a gallon of lube with a push pump. She says triumphantly, "They're on the list."

CHAPTER 25

Outside, we rejoin the others. The bandage around Heidi's head makes her the instant center of attention—girl is loving it.

"Are you okay?" Chris asks, immediately hugging her.

He gives me an accusing look, either because he suspects I did this, or I didn't do enough to prevent it.

"I'm fine," Heidi says. "I was with Marty. He saved me. You've never seen such a hero."

Heidi gives me a wink, wraps her arm in mine and kisses me on the cheek.

"Down girl," I say, blushing.

There's a part of me that wants to egg her on.

And that's the part that's going to get you killed, Teddy warns.

Hush, I reply. *I've been dying for this moment. Just let me enjoy it.*

We're loading our bags into a hybrid car. It's quiet enough not to rouse the undead. Chris has the keys. Blood spatters the front of his shirt. We load up our hockey bags in the back and tie a couple to the roof.

We're about to get into the car when I spot a house that's caught my imagination ever since we set up The Box. It's ultra-modern and huge. The owner—some international DJ or something—had two houses torn down to put this one up. It looks like a fortress, now. Drop-down slats of steel cover all the windows and doors. There's a round security cam glaring at us with its red light. Solar panels line the roof.

"What about that place?" I ask.

Gary shakes his head. "Chris and I tried. It's sealed tight."

"Someone might still be alive in there," I say. "Maybe even the whole family."

Gary contemplates it. "It's possible."

He grabs a pad and pen from inside the car. He quickly writes: *If there's anybody in there, you're not alone. We're at The Box.* He rips the paper off and catches it in the mailbox, half sticking out. The sun is starting to set, and none of us fancy being out after dark. We squeeze into the car. Gary's at the wheel. Devon's in the passenger seat, Seong on his lap. I'm in the back with Chris, Heidi between us. A couple of DNDs shamble towards us. One jumps in front of the car. Gary runs him down. The DND thunks onto the hood and bounces off the windshield. The sound carries. The doors to the homes we've cleared stay shut. Others open. By then we are back at The Box, its gates closing behind us.

Safe in the training yard, we unpack the loot. It feels like Christmas. I pop antihistamines, Laleh gets her codeine, and we all tease the hell out of Devon when we hand him the jug of lube and the box of condoms.

"You have to share!" Bob insists.

It quickly becomes apparent that I was the only one anal enough to stick to the list. Seong is ecstatic that she'll finally get to read *The Hunger Games* (before, "there was just never enough time!"); someone filched a poker set (and whiskey); and when a trio of porn magazines (*Hot Hooters, Big Jugs*, and *Milk 'Em*) fall out of one bag, I have to ask, "Really?"

Bob grabs them from my hands. "Thank you, merciful God!"

We all look at him.

"In case we run out of toilet paper," he lies.

We won't have to worry about that for a while. We've got piles of TP, along with ladies' sanitary pads, a plunger, and cans of air freshener, not to mention plastic utensils and plates. Our medication supply includes antipsychotics and antivirals. We also found several guns, ammo, and a hunting rifle with a scope.

We organize most of it on the shelves behind the front desk. The guns and bullets, we lock up. I lie down on my mat on the gym floor. Tomorrow, we will divide up the residence next door, deciding who will stay where, but everyone's cooperative about spending one more night together in The Box. I get the sense we all feel a bit safer this way, and there's something to be said for the show of unity. We've snagged a few pillows and blankets from the lofts that didn't get burned in the fire, along with some sleeping bags.

I'm about to settle in when I feel something hard under my pillow. I pull it out. It's the board game *Settlers of Catan*. There's a birthday card, for Stan, the guy in the full-body PVC suit. His name's been crossed out, and in Heidi's bubblegum handwriting:

Because I know you like to keep score. Thanks for the conditioner. And my life. I owe you.

I smile despite myself. Weirdly, I feel tears in my eyes, which is fucked up and weak. It's just a stupid board game, why do I even care?

Because it makes you feel loved and appreciated, Teddy answers. *Idiot.*

He's right, and I know he's right; the pattern, and all that. So what do I do? Throw it away? That seems petty.

Thankfully, Buddy comes to my rescue.

"What's that?" he asks, waddling over. He's in Lightning McQueen PJs and carries Teddy under his arm. Buddy spies Heidi's gift, and his eyes light up. "Oh cool! *Settlers of Catan!*"

Gary comes over and sees the game in my hand.

"Holding out on us?" he asks.

Heidi's sitting cross-legged on her mat, combing her hair and watching us.

"It was going to be a surprise," I say.

"Can we play, Daddy? *Please?*" Buddy begs, rubbing the box with his little thumb like he's trying to free a genie.

"Maybe tomorrow," Gary says. "Give the game back to Uncle Marty."

"Awe," Buddy says, obediently returning it. I wish he'd save me from myself by taking it with him, but I don't want to get him in trouble.

Gary scoops him up, and Buddy collapses with exhaustion into his dad's body, heaving a big sigh. I watch Gary and Chris tuck in the kid. Candles glimmer around Chris. He reads a picture book to Buddy—*The Adventures of Philippe and the Outside World*—about a Christmas ornament who accidentally gets thrown out with the tree and has to find his way home. It's Buddy's favorite. Chris finishes, and the kid's eyes flutter shut.

I wish it were that easy for me. Chris blows out the candles. In the moonlight filtering in from the upper windows, I see the outline of the game box. How much of Heidi's voice, that's been stuck in my head all these years, can I blame on her? This is *my* saboteur, after all, fueled by *my* childhood inferiority complex and a male ego that's so easily bruised it's practically hemophiliac.

I flash back to Heidi in my arms as we escaped near-death in the S/M love nest. For just a moment, I indulge in the fantasy that I'd let her kiss me for real and that I'm truly a hero to her at last. My dick is hard as I doze off.

That's when my night terrors start.

A strong man doesn't have to be
dominant toward a woman.
He doesn't match his strength
against a woman weak
with love for him.
He matches it
against the world.
—*Marilyn Monroe*

PART 4

CHAPTER 26

I'm dreaming of Steph. We're in our house. It's dark and full of shadows. She's hunting me. I can't see her, but I know she's there, coming for me. I trip down the staircase. She appears with a serpentine grace. Her face is rotting, buzzing with flies, hair stuck to her scalp in clumps. She pants as she gets closer. I smell the fetid wave of her breath. She crawls on top of me. Acidic saliva drips from her mouth, *Alien*-style, burning holes into my skin. She nuzzles me, her lipless mouth pressed to my ear, scraping my lobe with blood-covered teeth, and she says, "I love you so much, Marty. Come be with me."

I wake, screaming in the middle of the gym.

Flashlights flare to life, their jerky dance disorienting and blinding me. I shake and thrash in my sleeping bag. Sweat mops me. Someone at my side grabs my arm and opposite shoulder.

"Marty, it's me, Gary. You're okay," he says.

I'm hyperventilating, but at the sound of his voice, my breathing is coming back under control. I feel more foolish than afraid. In the darkness, Chris watches us. Is he scowling?

Another hand comes to rest on the nape of my neck, landing like a leaf escaping a breeze. It brushes my sweaty hair over one ear. I assume it must be Laleh, smoker's drawl ready with a sarcastic remark, but she's several feet away. She blinks like a stoned owl, her beauty mask pushed up to her forehead.

Heidi kneels next to me, her hand on my cheek.

"You're safe," she says—the one thing I never felt with her.

My post-Heidi stress disorder should be kicking in. The Heidi I know doesn't believe in vulnerability, only lack of strength. I can't let her see me like this—can I?

129

She hands me a bottle of water and says, "It's okay, Marty. I'm here for you. We're all here for you."

Am I hearing this? From Heidi? Teddy's persona crashes, replaced by a robotic OS that repeats over and over, *Cannot compute. Terminal failure.*

Everyone stares at me.

"Sorry," I blurt out. "It was just a nightmare."

"Okay, back to bed everyone," Gary says. "Marty's fine, and we've got a lot to do tomorrow."

Heidi's hand is on top of my own. She gives it a squeeze. "If you want me to stay with you, I wouldn't say no." She brushes her hand through her hair, momentarily revealing the bandage covering the stitches in her forehead.

Before I have a chance to answer, Buddy comes to my rescue. He hands Teddy to me. Out of everyone, this simple gesture is what makes me feel the safest. I hand the stuffed animal back.

"It's okay, Buddy, you can hold onto him," I say.

He shrugs and then nestles into my arms, way better than any Teddy bear. He's so small and warm I can't help but feel big and strong. His even breathing helps mine slow down. Heidi glances over her shoulder as she heads back to her cot. In the moonlight streaming through the window, I see her watching us. I've seen this look on her face before—when her cat would jump onto my lap instead of hers. A few weeks later she developed a sudden allergy and gave Miss Puss to a shelter.

I wait for Teddy's program to reboot in my head. Instead, I doze, Buddy's warm back against my chest.

The next day, we finalize who will live where in the residence. I remind myself the move away from communal living has nothing to do with me waking everyone up in the middle of the night. Most of the units are burnt-out wrecks forever imbued with the stench of the bodies the fire consumed, but a few apartments on the second floor are salvageable. We all agree to give the biggest one to Gary, Chris, and Buddy. Devon and Seong, not surprisingly, decide to share a one bedroom. Laleh and Heidi get to be roommates in a two bedroom. Bob and I each get a studio unit.

We've been working on them, tossing out burnt furniture and décor, scrubbing down the walls, ceilings, and floors, and spraying them with room deodorizer to kill the smell of ash. Gary comes by with a bowl of burning sage, cedar, tobacco, and sweetgrass, presumably to clear away any bad mojo. He always claimed "not to believe in that stuff" and only kept the traditional Ojibwe medicines in a ziplock bag in his pocket to honor his birth parents.

"It can't hurt," he says as he walks through, not that I was challenging him on it. I press my hands together. "Namaste." If we had some holy water, I think we'd use that too.

He carries his smoking bowl to cleanse Bob's unit. I gaze at what's left of my place. It's pretty bare and desolate. I gave the bed to Gary and Chris.

Heating, plumbing, and electricity are shot, and the windows are now walls of cinder blocks. The guy who lived here didn't have much. My main furnishings are a couch where I will sleep and a metal bookshelf that survived the fire in another unit, with the scorch marks to prove it. I have almost nothing to put on it—some tattered clothes and shoes, *Settlers of Catan*, and an empty picture frame where I place a photo of Steph and myself, the one that I grabbed from the fridge at home. That seems a lifetime ago.

A can of baby-blue paint, a paint tray, and a roller are on the floor. I have enough to coat one wall. I've scrubbed the former occupant's brain off of it. I work by candlelight. When I'm done, I step back to admire my artistry. The one pristine wall makes the rest of the place all the more depressing.

A knock at the door breaks my Debbie Downer thoughts. Laleh lets herself in. She carries a pair of beers, opening them using the countertop. She hands me one.

"Nice wall," she says.

"Thanks," I say as we clink bottles. I take a sip of the lukewarm brew. "You can't even tell that a guy put a gun to his head right over there."

"Maybe he had the right idea," she says.

I can't tell if she's joking, and I don't have the energy to ask.

"How's your place coming?"

"Pink," she replies. "Very, very pink."

"How girly of you," I say.

"I'd tell you to go fuck yourself, but, given your options, my guess is you're way ahead of me," she snorts.

I laugh. With that mouth and smokers rasp, I swear she's a drag queen.

"Please, tell me you and Heidi are not doing it," she says.

"We are not," I assure her.

"But you're thinking about it," she says. It's not a question.

"I learned my lesson the first time," I reply.

"Men never learn their lesson," Laleh replies.

"So I take it she hasn't won you over," I say.

"I'm like that kid from *The Sixth Sense*, except I don't see dead people. I smell bullshit. All the time. It's everywhere. Especially with her," Laleh says.

"Everyone else loves her," I say.

"Everyone else is a blind idiot," Laleh replies. "We need to go out and find you a nice girl, one who's not going to eat your brains for breakfast."

"Cheers to that," I say. Once again, we clink our beer bottles together.

We're laughing and joking about starting a reality show called *Dating in the Apocalypse* when there's a knock at the door. Heidi lets herself in. She's dressed in overalls smudged with pink paint, a bra, and a bandana to hold back her hair.

"There you are," she says, talking to Laleh, though her eyes keep shifting from her roommate to me as if we're a math problem she's trying to solve. "Well, look at you two having a party behind my back."

She smiles, giggles, and toss-tosses her hair.

"This is for you," Heidi says to me.

She dangles a key tied to a pink ribbon. I accept it in my palm, looking at it with confusion.

"You know what I'm like with keys," she explains, "so if I...I mean, we," she winks at Laleh, "ever get locked out of our apartment, I'll know you're always there to let us back in."

I look to Laleh.

"Good idea," she says.

Sarcasm much? It's not lost on Heidi.

"Or we could just leave our door unlocked," Heidi says to her, a note of challenge under her flighty facade. "What's the worst that could happen?"

We hear the moans and scratching of the dead not dead outside our walls.

"Touché," Laleh concedes in a cloud of her own cigarette smoke.

I think of the previous inhabitants of this building. Locks didn't save them. Still, I know I'll sleep better with the deadbolt in place. I'm guessing Laleh feels the same.

"Maybe I should get *your* spare key," Heidi says to me, casually touching her breast.

"I already gave mine to Gary," I say.

If I'm infected—*you're not*, I assure myself—but if I am, and I turn DND in the middle of the night, whatever's left of my brain hopefully won't figure out how to get out of the apartment. In that case, it will fall to Gary to unlock my door to finish me off. The reverse is also true. I have Gary's spare key. If he's infected or Chris is or, heaven forbid, Buddy...*He's not*, I insist. *They're not*. But if one is, they likely all are—or will be. They're sharing the same space. They've accepted their fate as a package deal. Same with Devon and Seong. Those two exchanged enough saliva leading up to this mess that they figure what's done is done. Heidi and Laleh at least have separate bedrooms with their own locks.

Heidi stares at the key in my hand as if she's thinking of taking it back.

"Well, lucky Gary," Heidi says at last. Her expression is the same as when, on the rare occasion, I would say no to her while we were dating. It's like she's tasting something unexpectedly sour. Her eyes flick towards the exit.

Am *I* chipping away at *her*? Weird.

She forces a smile, in her lips if not her eyes. She takes the beer bottle from my hand—a total alpha move—and is about to drink from it. I grab it back before it can touch her lips. It's like she's got Bell's Palsy the way half her mouth collapses. An invisible crank and pulley system struggles to jerk her lips back into place. She snaps into girly mode, giggling at our little game.

"Oh Marty, such a tease."

She smacks my chest hard enough for it to sting, her teeth glinting in the candlelight.

"Didn't your mother teach you to share?" Heidi asks, putting on her best two-year-old pouty face routine as she reaches for the bottle once more. I hold the beer way from her, using my body as a shield.

"We're not supposed to," I say. "Saliva, remember?"

She nods. "Right—because anyone of us might be infected. That was your theory, wasn't it Laleh?"

"It still is," Laleh answers, sipping her beer.

There's an awkward silence.

"Well," Heidi says with the smile of a Disney Queen, "thank goodness for you. Whatever would we do without you, Roomie?"

CHAPTER 27

That night, I stare at my wall of blue in the light of a single candle. A framed vintage *Star Wars: A New Hope* print hangs there. Laleh salvaged it for me from another unit. Darth Vader and the Deathstar loom ominously in the background. In the foreground is Luke Skywalker, his karate-esque top billowing artistically in an unseen wind, revealing a beach-ready bod that actor Mark Hamill never actually possessed. His arms stretch overhead, lightsaber ablaze. Crouched at his feet is the regal Princess Leia, shoulders turned at a jaunty angle to flaunt her porn-worthy cleavage, showcased in a nighty inspired by a Victoria's Secret catalog. It's not as hot as Leia's slave girl outfit in *Return of the Jedi*, but I still jerked off to it as a teen.

I fall asleep. To my relief, it's a sound slumber. If I dream, I'm too deep to realize it. All the same, for the second night in a row, I wake to screams.

I jerk upright on the couch. I'm groggy, disoriented, making out only shadows in the darkness. The screams fill my world. I automatically slap my hand over my mouth, assuming that, once more, the sound is emanating from me. It is not. Another horrible howl bloats my eardrums. I try to get up; my sleeping bag encases me like a ravenous worm. I fall to my knees onto the floor.

"Goddamn it!" I swear, jerking my legs free.

I grab the flashlight from under the couch; it beams to life. I swing it towards the *Star Wars* poster, then the kitchen counter, coming to rest on the metal shelf. I'm alone. The screams grow more frantic.

I stagger to the door and yank it open. I look up and down the hall. Other doors are opening. Beams from other flashlights come to life, moving in an erratic dance as we search for the source of the cries. I'm holding a crowbar in my other hand. I don't remember picking it up.

I look to Gary and Chris in the doorway next to mine. Buddy's rubbing his eyes sleepily. He's hugging Teddy to his chest.

"Now what?" the kid asks.

"Stay with him," Gary says to Chris.

"What's happening?" Heidi asks, baseball bat in hand. "Where's Laleh?"

"She's not with you?" I ask.

Heidi shakes her head.

Devon and Seong are also notably absent. Gary gets to their door first. It's wide open. Did they forget to lock it? I'm a step behind. His light shines inside the loft, finding first the bathroom, then the kitchen, finally landing on Seong in the corner, arms wrapped around her knees, sobbing. My beam finds the back of Laleh's head—she's hunched over Devon. He's splayed on the bed, eyes wide and unseeing, shadows artfully highlighting the definition of the gym-built bod that made him an Instagram sensation. His once fine abs are ripped out.

Laleh half turns. Devon's guts dangle from her mouth. She blinks in the light, like a raccoon who's been caught with its paws in a garbage can, a *who, me?* expression on her face. She contemplates us, jaws working soundlessly on Devon's insides, bloodshot eyes watching as Gary and I step closer. Heidi slips in behind us. She sticks close to the wall and skitters over to Seong, kneeling down beside her.

"It's all right, we're here," I hear Heidi murmur.

Laleh returns to her feast, then looks up at me as I lift my crowbar. I hesitate.

Oh, Laleh. My breathing stiffens, and tears burn my eyes.

"Dude, I know you two were close," Gary says. "Let me."

I shake my head. "Wait a second," I force myself to say. I push the emotions down.

Laleh goes back to eating. Gary lifts his short sword, and I put a hand on his chest to restrain him. "Something's not right here."

"What?" Gary asks.

"I don't see any bites," I say.

136

I almost wish I hadn't said anything because there's a sudden hush in the room.

"We'll need to be sure," I say. "Which means we need to keep her as intact as possible." Cold. Logical. Mr. Spock. *She was your friend*, part of me chastises. I ignore it.

I circle Laleh, who is keeping one bloodshot eye on me as I pick up a steak knife from Devon's bedside table. He was prepared, and yet unready. I approach slowly. There's something odd about Laleh's movements, even for a DND. She's almost lethargic. I've seen dogs like that, completely tranced out as they munch on a bone like it's their smack. Maybe that's what this is, a feeding induced sloth, but I haven't seen it on the other DNDs when they're eating.

"Is it just me, or does she look high?" I ask. Her pupils are dilated, but so what if they are?

No one responds. I take a deep breath.

"Laleh," I say.

The reflex of looking when hearing one's name is so deeply ingrained she automatically turns towards me, and I stab the knife through her eye socket. I yank the blade free and catch her as she falls, easing her to the ground. I'll cry for her—later.

Devon's hand starts to twitch. Gary takes the knife from my listless fingers, glides past me, and shoves the blade under Devon's jaw, up into what's left of the dude's brain. Seong's weeping is the only sound we hear.

I kneel next to Heidi.

"Seong, we're going to get you out of here, okay?" I say. "Seong?"

"It's not that simple," Heidi says.

Seong won't look at us. Heidi takes the other woman's forearm and turns it gently. In the flashlight's beam, I see a deep red bite mark, piercing the skin.

I say the only thing I can.

"Shit."

Seong has always struck me as one of those people who is strong to a fault, possibly with ice in her veins. There was always a focused matter-of-factness in her workout style, a let's get 'er done attitude with maximum intensity, otherwise what's the point? As her shock at what's happened wears off, I see this persona reassert itself. Her tears dry as if a valve were turned off.

She gets up, shooing away Heidi's offer to help.

"Can you cover him up?" Seong asks, looking away from the body.

Gary pulls the bloody blankets and sheets over what's left of Devon.

"Thank you," she says—as if someone's been thoughtful enough to hold the door for her. "Does anyone have the time?"

Gary looks at the watch on his wrist. "A little after 5:00 in the morning."

"In that case," she says, "I'd like to see one last sunrise."

Nobody objects—although the question in our eyes is, *does she have that long?*

"Also," she says, "I'll need a gun."

We form a procession line in the training yard. Seong emerges, nodding as she walks by us. Heidi takes a step towards her, arms open to give her a hug. Seong holds her hand up to fend her off. Heidi steps back.

Seong reaches the end of the line, literally and figuratively, and stares into my eyes. My hand's on the lever to open the gate.

"It doesn't have to be like this," I say.

She smiles sadly. "The alternative is you tie me to a chair, and we wait for the inevitable. That's not how I lived. It's not how I'm going to die."

"We could try our stockpile of antivirals and antipsychotics," I say.

She rolls her eyes like an executioner swings an axe. "At best, they'll delay the inevitable, if they work at all. Those odds suck."

"But…"

She cuts me off. "I won't risk doing to any of you what Laleh did to Devon—and to me."

She extends her open palm. I hand her a pistol. She tucks it in her belt and kisses me on the cheek. I smell a wave of rot on her breath. The pathogen is acting fast on her. I stiffen involuntarily. If she notices, she doesn't show it.

"Take good care of them," she says.

I want to say, *That's Gary's job*.

"I will," I promise.

"And no watching," she says. "If I know I'm alone, I can do what needs to be done."

"If that's what you want," I say.

"It's what I need," she replies.

I lock the gate behind her. The others stay on the main floor. I go up to the roof. I crouch out of sight, and I break my promise. I watch. The reality is we've given her a gun. If she loses her nerve and runs off, we need to know where she's gone. We need to get the gun back.

There are a few DNDs about 20 feet away. One of them is a surfer type with scraggly blond hair and board shorts. He spots Seong and starts walking towards her. She points the gun at him. He gets closer. When he's a few feet away from her, he stops. He contemplates Seong, sniffing madly at the air. The other DNDs watch.

Seong is trembling. The gun shakes like crazy. Tears roll casually from Seong's eyes, but her nerves hold. The surfer hiccups, bites at the air, and then he turns and walks away. The other DNDs seem to accept his assessment and go back to listlessly wandering.

Seong's icy composure breaks. She sobs, sticking the gun into her mouth. I look to the sky, wincing as the gunshot blasts in my ears.

Seong's suicide shot has drawn more of the DNDs. None of them seem interested in her remains, but some linger, so we have to wait a full day before we can recover her body—and the pistol.

We use the time to examine Laleh's remains. We bring her sheet-wrapped form into the training yard—it's where we've got the best light. Buddy's inside, playing Tic-Tac-Toe with Bob the Builder.

I pull back the sheet. Heidi cuts Laleh's pajamas away. We search her body, front and back, then front again. She would've been furious to be exposed like this. She refused even to be seen in a bathing suit. There are no bites.

We look at each other grimly.

"What about these?" I ask, holding up one of Laleh's arms. There's a trio of red dots about her veins.

"They look like needle marks," Chris says.

There's a long silence. We look from one to the other. Nobody bothers to suggest she might have had blood work recently. They're that fresh.

"Any idea what she was injecting herself with?" Gary asks Heidi.

"I found these in her drawer." Heidi holds a used syringe, a lighter (Laleh always had one on hand), and a burnt spoon.

I look at the injection marks in the old woman's arm.

What the hell Laleh, I think. She always struck me as being tough as nails, but then I think of her chain smoking and her adamant refusal to quit no matter how much it might help with her fitness goals. She clung to her addiction as if her life depended on it. Maybe it did. Maybe the smokes kept her away from something much worse—until they didn't.

We all have a past, I remind myself. I never knew this was part of hers.

"So she overdosed," Chris concludes.

"And turned into a DND," Heidi finishes for him. "She warned us that any one of us might already be infected. She was right."

Heidi cries and wraps herself into me. I hold her and caress her hair. I think of Laleh's other warning, *I smell bullshit.* It's tough to take advice from a dead junkie who killed herself and two of our friends.

We wrap Laleh up in the sheet, and the next day we carry her to the empty piece of land behind our compound, along with Devon and Seong. The vacant lot used to be home to a derelict warehouse that was condemned by the city. It was torn down and filled with dirt. We dig three graves in the lot. It's sweaty work. The ground is hard. The graves are shallow. Our hearts are heavy.

We'd fallen into complacency, thinking we'd figured out the rules of this new world. Despite Laleh's warning, we'd convinced ourselves that the danger only lay outside of our walls. Now, three of us are dead.

We bury Seong and Devon first. Laleh is last.

Chris reads a passage from the Bible—it was on Devon's shelf. Devon was an atheist, largely because of an overly religious upbringing. That was before the end of humanity. My guess is he stole the holy book during our neighborhood raid. It was not on the list.

The passage Chris reads has something to do with the valley of the shadows of death and not fearing evil and such. I know I've heard it before. It's a popular one. It doesn't fit with the Devon I knew, but neither does the way he died. Laleh would've hated it. She was no fan of the Quran, either. She was more into inspiring memes plastered on top of images of guys with pecs and six packs. It was only weeks ago that she was showing me a jacked physique model, rasping, "I'd tap that."

We each share a few memories of the departed. When it's my turn, I talk about Devon always pushing his limits, even after he face-planted doing box jumps taller than himself. He embodied the idea that failure was a milestone en route to achievement. I admit that Seong intimidated the hell out of me. There's a bit of laughter, and a few "amens." I also confess that I slept a bit easier knowing she had my back.

"And then there's Laleh," I say. I think of the needle marks in her arms. Relapsed injectable-drug addict does not fit with the Laleh I knew.

For the first time in the years that I've been her trainer, I wonder what got her into social work and what demons drove her to help others in that caustic way of hers. I never thought to ask while she was alive.

"Everyone has a past," I say. "Laleh used to say that. Sometimes the past gives us strength. Sometimes it catches up to us. Sometimes it wears us down or holds us back. Laleh was pushy, bull-headed, and a pain in the ass. She also cared more than anyone I know. And I will miss her."

I wait for Bob to say that she was a druggie killer and that we should've burned her body along with all the other DNDs. Instead, he says, "here here," and lifts a can of beer. If I didn't know better, I'd say he was crying. *Did he and Laleh have a thing?* I ponder this possibility. *I have got to start paying more attention.*

Not that there's many of us left to pay attention to.

CHAPTER 28

The days that follow are solemn. Heidi does her usual theatrical antics in an attempt to lighten the mood, but it comes across as forced, as do our smiles. Ever the social barometer—the woman can read a room—she changes tact; her eyes tear up instead of trolling for laughs. I swear Bob and Chris are getting off on comforting her, and even Gary and Buddy. I catch her looking at me, gauging my reaction.

Now that Devon and Seong are gone, I realize how they brought a youthful energy to the group that reminded us that we were more alive than dead. Laleh, with her gruff chain smoking and what-the-fuck attitude, slapped us out of self-diagnosing ourselves with critical cases of ennui, while her tough love pushed us forward.

We still have Buddy, but I find myself wondering, *What kind of future will this kid have?*, instead of, *I have to protect him at all cost.*

Gary catches me staring at his son as the kid plays frisbee with Bob the Builder in the training yard. I'm sharpening a branch into a spear.

"Protein bar for your thoughts?" Gary says.

"Just worried," I say. "What happens to Buddy if none of us are left?"

It's clear from the look on Gary's face that this has yet to occur to him.

"The thought of him alone, in this world, surrounded by death, that's no way for a kid to grow up," I say.

Gary taps the point of a spear into my chest, right above my heart.

"He's my son," he says with barely repressed fury. "You let me worry about him."

He stabs the spear into the ground between my feet and stalks off. My mouth gapes. I look for Laleh to share this what-the-fuck moment with, but she is gone. Instead, I see Heidi.

She glides over and sits next to me on a concrete planter. She puts a hand on my knee.

"Give him time," she says. "He's grieving. Probably feels like he let us all down."

"Maybe," I say.

"You don't think he's infected, do you?" she asks.

"What? No!" But, now that she's put the thought in my head, it's impossible not to consider the possibility.

She leans her head on my shoulder.

"Well, at least you still have me," she says, "and I have you."

Over the following weeks, more and more packs of DNDs drift out of the city center. Some just wander past our area, but others, whether they catch our scent or distribute at random, find our streets. It's getting harder to keep our neighborhood clear, cutting off our access to supplies.

We start rolling cars and positioning them at various intersections, creating barricades across the most obvious access points. We also pile tires, filling them with concrete at a few alleys and lane ways. It's not a perfect solution, some of the DNDs climb over, and that inevitably draws a few followers, but, for the most part, they choose the path of least resistance and pass us by.

It's harder to deal with the impact on our psyches. The walls around The Box that keep them out are feeling more confining as they keep us in. The occasional climber gets tangled in the barbed wire cresting the wall, and we have to take gruesome measures to get them out. We've stopped thinking of the DNDs as former human beings.

The growing hordes trekking down the nearby highways emphasize our frailty and insignificance. If they ever decided to jump our feeble barriers en masse, their sheer numbers would keep us trapped inside the walls of our compound. We have to take greater care to stay out of their sight lines and to keep the noise we make in check. This is toughest on Buddy. The kid's squealing laugh is a siren.

He's been spanked, I don't know how many times, for just enjoying himself. If he cries, he's locked in a basement room where the DNDs can't hear him. Ever since Laleh and the others died, I swear he cries louder on purpose.

Today is the worst. "I can't find Teddy," he says to Gary. There are tears in the kid's eyes. He looks on the verge of a full-on meltdown.

"That's what happens when you're careless," Gary snaps.

The kid loses it, unleashing a piercing wail.

"Oh, shit," Bob says.

I hear the ka-thud of pounding feet on the street, running towards The Box, followed by the slam of bodies smashing into the gate. I don't know if there's some latent instinct to hearing a kid cry, but Buddy drives the DNDs wild like nothing else. It's going to be hell clearing them away, but that doesn't deter the kid.

"No!" he wails. "I want Teddy! We have to find Teddy!"

"Why did you have to bring that fucking bear here in the first place," Gary snaps at me.

I've got open-mouth-shocked-face. Gary grabs his son and drags him to the stairs that lead to the basement. This upsets Buddy even more. He wails at the top of his lungs. I almost admire him, letting rip with his raw emotions as if he's daring the world to fucking come and get him. Gary gives his bottom a hard smack. Buddy smacks back.

Honey badger don't give a shit, I think, recollecting Steph's and my favorite YouTube hit. I burst out laughing. Gary shoots daggers my way as he yanks the basement door closed behind him and Buddy.

I take the hint and lock myself in the supply closet. I can't stop the convulsing in my chest. It's wild and unchecked. It hurts, it makes me cry, and after five minutes of it, I hear Teddy's worried voice, *Are you going insane?*

That makes me laugh even more. Maybe I am.

It takes a while to let it all out. My sides ache, and my shirt is moist from wiping away the tears from my eyes.

When I come out, Gary is standing there, watching me, a strange look on his face, as if he doesn't recognize me.

"You okay?" he asks. He's holding a spear.

"Fine," I lie.

He nods in a way that says, *I don't believe you.*

"I said I'm fine!" I shout.

He points the spear at me.

"You want to say that a little louder?" he asks. "A couple of flesh-eating zombies in China didn't quite hear you."

"Sorry," I say.

"Yeah," he agrees, "you are."

I've seen that look on his face—when he fires an asshole client. My eyes dart about, searching for a weapon.

Heidi comes and stands between us. I want to shove her out of my way; I want to cower behind her. Gary lowers the spear, and says, "We have work to do."

The whole group of us spends the rest of the day dropping weights on the DNDs outside and then assembling a fence of sharpened spears in a perimeter around the walls of The Box. The stakes are set at an angle that will skewer the average person through the chest. Gary and I work as far from each other as we can get. We're half-way done when Bob gives a whistle from the compound. There's another hoard of DNDs coming. We fall back.

That night, I'm alone in my room. There's a single candle to fight off the darkness. I'm in my pajama pants, throwing a tennis ball against the wall. The repetitive ka-thunk sound is doing a piss-poor job of calming me down. I'm sucking on the arrowhead Steph gave me.

I catch the ball as someone knocks at my door. The arrowhead falls from my mouth and slaps against my chest. I throw the ball and yell, "Come in."

It's Gary. I catch the ball and consider holding onto it, apologizing for making noise. Instead, I throw it again. I'm like Buddy, asserting myself in stupid ways where and when I can. The ball ka-thunks against the wall and then slaps into my palm. I wait for Gary to go all alpha on me. Instead, he says, "Sorry about earlier. I'm a little tense lately. We cool?"

I roll the ball in my hand, then throw it again—ca-thunk. I consider his apology.

"Sure," I say.

"Great. See you tomorrow," he says.

The door clicks behind him, and I keep throwing the ball. It's going to take a few days of normalcy for us to be cool, and I can't help but test him a little. There's another knock at the door.

Here it comes, I think, expecting him to barge in to chew me out for the tennis ball throwing.

The door opens and in walks Heidi. I miss the ball, and it bounces along the floor, stopping at her foot. She's dressed in a tank top, short shorts, no bra. She carries a steaming mug in one hand. She places it on the coffee table in front of me.

"It's chamomile," she says.

I breathe in the soothing aroma.

"Thanks," I say.

She stands there, waiting for an invitation, and I could sure as shit use the company. I don't trust myself to be alone.

"Want to sit?" I ask.

"Sure. Just for a bit," she says.

"Just for a bit," I agree.

"Do you want some?" I ask, holding up the mug. "I've got an extra cup."

"No," she says, "I hate getting up in the middle of the night to go pee. Now more than ever."

I smirk. "Chamber pots over there if you need it," I point to a large mason jar in the corner.

"Gross," she smacks me. I pull my eyes from the tiny scar on her forehead, a reminder of our encounter with the S/M DND.

We sit on the couch and stare at the framed *Star Wars* print. Candlelight shadows dance over R2D2 and C3PO. In days gone by, a passerby would think we were watching TV. I sip the tea. She takes my hand. I let her. She squeezes it. I squeeze back. I drink more tea. It doesn't take long for me to drain it.

"You tired?" she asks.

"Yes and no," I say, both exhausted and wired.

"Let's lie down," she says.

"Okay," I agree.

I spoon her. The warmth of her back settles into my bare chest. I don't know what this means or if it's even what I want, but it's a break from what lies out there. Even Teddy says nothing.

She wriggles her ass into my crotch. All I can say is, "Sleepy."

"I know you are," she pats my arm, hugging it into her breasts. "You just rest."

Somehow, I do.

CHAPTER 29

Tonight's nightmare is the worst of my life. I'm in a mental fog. I catch glimpses of things, familiar yet distorted beyond recognition. My brain hurts.

I walk as if enshrouded in a glob of molasses that follows wherever I go. I wrench myself forward in an attempt to escape. Instead, everything spins in a kaleidoscope.

A dog barks.

What happened to all the pets? I wonder.

I remember the fish in tanks, floating belly up, budgies we've set free —almost guaranteed to perish. The dogs and cats have mostly been eaten.

There's a yelp, and the canine is silent. Shouting takes its place. The sound is muffled, absorbed into a layer of dreams and distorted into YARs and TEEs, over and over, a record skipping. But, like a struggling camera lens, the shouts come into focus.

The YARs become MARs and the TEEs become ARTEEs. There are new shapes, too, reflected in the moonlight—a rectangle and a hovering ball of light. The glare hurts my eyes. It's hard work to lift my hand to shield my brow. It's easier to stare at the ground, which is a gentle haze of dots and yellow stripes in a sea of tar lapping over my feet.

My heart beats faster, filling my larynx. Something is wrong. I am in danger.

I thrash my arms. It's working. I'm waking up.

The shouting intensifies. There are several voices, familiar, yet terrifying for their overlying desperation. Their calls yank at me and fill me with panic.

"MAAAARRRR-TEEEEE! MAAAARRRR-TEEEEE!"

It's my name, over and over. The rectangle is a sign on a chain link fence. The dots and yellow stripes are lines on the road, done with reflective paint. The glowing globes are street lamps that still miraculously function. But it's the moving objects that fill me with terror —outlines of men and women with stumbling steps, the whites of their eyes seeming to glow.

"Oh my God!" I hear Heidi. "He's outside the gate!"

I swing before I even realize that there's a baseball bat in my hand. The skull of a white business woman explodes.

Heidi's words echo over and over like a siren in my mind. *He's outside the gate*. She's right. This isn't a dream. I'm standing in the street.

How did I get here? The words are loud in my brain, hurting my head.

I stagger back, trying to orient myself. The Box is behind me, a silhouette of squares. I trip towards it, moving like the undead. *Am I infected?*

I hear a DND behind me. I plant, turn, and swing, smashing its wrist with the bat. My movements are clumsy; I'm using too much muscle, and my grip is like a baby trying to open a jar. The bat goes flying into the dark, clattering out of sight.

Shit!

I'm in pajama pants and nothing else. I wince as gravel bites into the bottoms of my feet, but that's nothing compared to what's about to rip into my throat.

The DND—an old Asian woman in a bathrobe—looks at her useless hand, which I've just broken, then lunges at me. Her face is alight, all teeth and gaping eyeballs. Her one good hand claws at the air an inch from my face.

"Get down!" I hear Gary shout. That voice, which I've become programmed to obey, sends a message direct to my trembling knees. I'm crouched and hugging myself before I know it. There's a boom that rattles me to the core, and I feel a wet splatter on my bare skin as the thing goes down.

There are more booms in the night; gunfire is all around. I'm shaking. I feel hands—warm hands—on my shoulders.

"Come on, come on." It's Heidi speaking in my ear. She takes my hand, pulling at me. I follow like a lost puppy, my steps staggering as if the ground were made from melting silly puttee. There are more shots, each one making me wince.

I make it through the gate. I hear it clang behind me.

*We're safe; we're safe; we're safe...*Teddy says over and over, but I can tell he's as freaked as I am.

"What the fucking hell!" Chris says.

"Easy," Gary says to his husband.

"Don't easy me," Chris snaps back. "I'm tired of you defending him. He wanders out there in the middle of the night and leaves the fucking gate open? He could've gotten us all killed! If Heidi hadn't noticed he was missing, those things would've walked right in."

"He was sleepwalking," Heidi says. "He does that sometimes."

No, I don't, I want to say. Not for years and years anyway, not unless I'm on certain medications.

I want to explain this to them, but my mouth is dry. I can't unstick my lips. It's as if I'm smothered in a Saran Wrap layer of shame. My throat tightens. My selective mutism is back.

No!

I force my mouth to work, but all I can say is, "I'm sorry...I don't know what happened."

"It's going to be okay," Heidi says, taking my hand. I get the feeling that she's the only thing stopping Chris from tossing me out right now. He turns to Gary.

"I have to go check on Buddy, our son," he says with emphasis, storming off.

The first hints of dawn are lighting the sky. Bob goes back to bed, giving me a look mixed with pity and loathing.

"Come on," Gary says. "We need to make sure you weren't bitten."

Not *are you all right?* or *broseph, that was way too close.* I can see the strain on his face. *He's losing patience with me.* I'm no longer a project to show off to potential clients. I'm a liability.

150

We sequester ourselves in the kitchenette, and I strip without prompting. I think my volunteerism will make this less humiliating or terrifying. It does not. It's still dark, so he uses a flashlight, moving it over my body in a grid.

"Testicles left," he says.

I can't look at him as I move my junk to one side...

"Testicles right," he says.

...and then the other.

"Turn," he says.

I wonder if he's going to make me bend over. He does not.

"You've been slacking on the sit ups. Otherwise, you're good, broseph," he says.

I laugh nervously. His joke was forced but a relief. I put my clothes on, and he hugs me. It's taking me a moment to accept he hasn't frozen me out.

"Please, don't do that again," he says. "You scared the shit out of me."

"I'll keep that in mind," I say, hugging him tightly.

That day, I make a big show of reversing the deadbolt on the door to my unit so that it will lock from the outside, locking me in. I feel responsible and sensible when I do it, a martyr making a necessary sacrifice for the good of the group. I expect people to console me, to say it's tough but necessary, to show their appreciation. Expectation turns to neediness, neediness culminates in disappointment. No one says it, but instead of the *what a good guy* vibe I'd wanted, I get a silent *well, it's the least he can do* attitude with a dollop of *loser* and a smidgen of *deadweight*. Bob is no longer the weakest link.

The closest I get to validation is Gary's "good idea," which does not reassure me that our friendship is on solid ground, hug or no hug. Chris keeps Buddy away from me the entire day.

I miss Laleh.

That night, I knock on Gary's door. Chris opens it. Before I can say a word, he grunts, "I'll get him," and closes the door in my face. Gary appears a moment later.

"Ready?" he asks.

"Yup," I say.

I go into my apartment alone and close the door behind me. Gary's on the other side. My only light is from a candle on a plate in my hand. I hear the lock turn and click in place. It's my idea, and yet I feel like something's been taken away from me. I can no longer choose to come and go at will. If nobody opens that door, I will die in here. A disquieting chill spreads over me. I've felt this way before.

This is different, Teddy tries to assure me.

Sure, I pretend to agree.

I turn around and stare at the couch. I wonder how long I will lie there, awake, praying for sleep to take me. I'm answered by a light knock on the door. It unlocks, and Heidi squeezes past Gary to come in. She's carrying a mug of steaming tea.

"I thought this might help," she says.

She hands it to me.

"Thanks," I say.

I set the candle on the counter. I wait for her to leave. Instead, I hear the deadbolt click into place. I flinch. She notices.

She makes a mock grimace, "I guess now we're locked in here together."

I turn away from her.

"You don't need to do this," I say, though I'm relieved to have her company.

I can't meet her gaze. I stare at the book *Fire in the Belly* on the coffee table.

She squeezes my biceps.

"You're doing that thing you do," she says.

"What thing is that?" I ask.

"Where you get all quiet." She lifts my chin. "What's wrong? And, don't say 'nothing.' That always drove me crazy."

"What's wrong?" I echo. "Besides the obvious?"

She shrugs. "Including the obvious."

I shake my head. "You won't understand."

"Maybe," she says. "Maybe not. But, I promise to listen, like, actually listen, the way I should have when we were together."

I consider her words. I'm worn out enough to give it a try.

"I'm slipping," I say. "Day by day, I'm losing the person I thought I'd built myself into, right when I need him the most. I'm regressing back into a needy, insecure…loser." The last word comes out like a coughed-up pill.

"Marty, that's not true," she says.

"It's funny," I shake my head. "I used to blame so much stuff on you —some of which was your fault, FYI—but, I can't blame you for dumping me. By the end, I was so pathetic and hollowed out, not only did you not want to be with me, I didn't want to be with myself. It's a scary feeling."

She looks to the door. She's thinking of bolting. Shit just got too real.

"This is about being locked in here, isn't it?" she asks.

I blink. She *is* paying attention.

"It's not the greatest," I admit. "But it is what it is."

"Yeah, but it must remind you of…" her words trail off. She hesitates. She doesn't know, does she?

"The hospital," she forces herself to say. "After you tried to hurt yourself."

Her words make my gut constrict. She knows.

"How did you…Did Gary tell you?" I ask. There's an edge in my voice.

"No," she says. "Kevin. He was banging an orderly who worked there. He said something about a guy who looked like him being admitted. Didn't take much to put it together."

"Well, thanks for visiting," I say.

"Marty…"

"It's fine," I say. "I'm sure you two got a good laugh out of it."

She doesn't deny it.

"Marty, I'm sorry. I was knowingly cruel; I strung you along when I needed your money more than I needed you, and the way that I left you…"

"That was not a great birthday," I agree. "And I got fired. You just had to go for my boss' barely legal son?"

She winces. "Pool parties do bring out the worst in me, and he was quite the specimen. It was a *challenge accepted* moment. At least, that's what went through my drunken head at the time. I think part of me wanted to see how much I could get away with. I feel so ashamed about it all now. What I did. Who I was."

"Well, I never wanted to be an accountant, anyway," I admit.

"Did you just make a joke about it?" she asks. She sounds impressed.

"I'm hilarious," I shrug.

Something lifts from me when I say it. As much as this conversation sucks, it's probably the most honest one we've ever had. Are we communicating in a mature and authentic way? All it took was the end of the world.

"Drink your tea," she says.

We sit at the counter. I sip the warm liquid. She watches me. I stop drinking. I'm not sure why. On an impulse, I offer her the mug.

"No, no," she says. "We're not supposed to share, remember?"

"Right," I say. "No kissing, either."

We share a laugh. Ha ha. I set the mug down.

"You don't want it to get cold," she says, picking it up and putting it back in my hands.

My paranoid subconscious throws a thought into my forehead.

"Last night was pretty scary," I say.

"I thought my heart was going to jump out of my throat," she says, pressing her palms to her breasts.

I move the mug away from my lips to test a theory. Her eyes follow it. I hold the mug off to the side. She catches herself gazing at it, and she forces herself to look me in the eyes.

"How's the tea?" she asks.

"Delicious," I reply, although I've barely taken a sip.

"Well then, drink up!"

I hear Laleh's warning. *I smell bullshit.*

I set the mug down. All that bonding we just did...

154

"You said something that stuck with me when you guys were bringing me back in from outside the gate after my little sleepwalking incident," I say.

"I wouldn't call that little," she says. "My God, Marty, you could've died. You could've killed us all."

It's a good ploy, trying to distract me with fear for my life and guilt for putting everyone in danger.

"You mentioned something interesting," I continue, undeterred.

"Did I?" she asks, coy as she sits on a stool at the counter, pushing the mug towards me.

"About how I sleepwalk sometimes," I say.

"You gave us such a fright," she replies.

"My only adult sleepwalking incident was with you," I say. "When you gave me that Ambien because you were sick and tired of me tossing and turning at night."

"Marty," she sighs, like a mother with a petulant child. "I'm trying to help. If you prefer to spend the night alone…"

She gets up, taking a few steps towards the door. It's a familiar play, threatening to leave to get her own way. She pauses, waiting for me to change my mind.

"What's in the tea, Heidi?" I ask.

She blinks at the question.

"What a silly thing to ask. It's plain, just the way you like it," she says.

I hurl the mug at her.

I don't know what's gotten into me. Maybe it's the lack of sleep, the daily grinding stress, the rising need for violence as a solution to daily problems beyond the gate, or my fear of being reduced to the guy I was.

At the last moment, I force myself to throw wide. The cup smashes against the doorframe. The smell of chamomile fills the room, and hot water splatters all over the *Star Wars* poster. The tea bag slaps against the floor.

"Jesus Christ, Marty, what the hell are you doing?" she shouts.

"What the fuck are *you* doing Heidi?" I demand. "Drugging me?"

"No!" she shouts.

"You put a sleeping pill in my tea last night!" I yell.

"I would never!" she insists.

"I could've been killed!" I shout. "We all could've. And for what?"

"I didn't!" she cries.

"You're fucking with me," I say, "And I will not let you turn me back into that broken chump!"

Chris throws open the door and rushes in, Gary behind him.

"What the hell is going on in here?" Chris demands.

"He's paranoid!" Heidi says, throwing herself into Chris' arms. "You warned me. I should've listened." She's crying where moments ago her eyes were drier than the Sahara.

"She drugged me," I say. "That's why I was sleepwalking. She put Ambien in the tea."

I look around for the evidence in the candlelight and see it splattered all over the wall. There's broken porcelain on the floor. *Shit.*

"Back the fuck off," Chris warns me.

"Okay, let's all just take it easy," Gary says, coming over to me.

I clench my fist. I try to step past him.

"Tell them what you did Heidi," I demand.

"I didn't do anything!" she cries.

I lunge towards her and Gary's arms wrap around me, the crook of his elbow digging into my neck.

"What the fuck are you..." I start to say, but my air supply is cut off.

I struggle, trying to remember the appropriate defensive counter, but his sleeper hold is already taking effect. The candlelight is growing dimmer. My thrashing arms flop like noodles. My legs wobble, and Gary is dragging me towards the couch.

My hearing's going in and out, along with my vision, but Chris' words come through, "...he's unstable...he's dangerous...he's sick."

The last thing I see before I pass out is Heidi's satisfied smile as she clings to Chris' muscular frame.

CHAPTER 30

I wake with a gasping breath, sitting up on my couch. The last thing I remember is Gary's choke hold and my lungs burning for air. I inhale deeply to prove I can. It's dark. I'm fully dressed. They didn't even take off my shoes.

I stare at the nothingness, blinking, thinking, remembering. One thought blots out the rest.

Heidi.

I reach under the couch, tapping around on the floor until I find a flashlight.

It blazes to life. I'm hoping that I was just having a nightmare, but I see the water stain on the *Star Wars* poster. On the floor is a tea bag amidst the shards of a broken mug. I look at my watch. It's the middle of the night.

I pace and mutter to myself, insisting that "she won't get away with this" and "they can't do this to me." I stop. This is what crazy people do. They called me paranoid and sick.

Am I?

I raise my fist to bang on the door.

That'll just make it worse.

I lower my hand. I want to throw something.

You have to keep your cool. It's Teddy's voice. Buddy lost the bear, but I carry him with me, always. As usual, he's right.

"So, what the fuck am I supposed to do?" I rage. "She's fucking me over, again, and getting away with it, *again.*"

Talking to myself. Not good.

I yank the door handle. The deadbolt holds. I'm about to kick it.

No, Teddy says. *This is how you prove that you're still sane.*

"Fuck you," I say, and I beat the door with my foot, the blows echoing up all around.

This lasts a minute, maybe two. I pant, leaning on my knees. Tears build in my eyes.

"You are not going to cry, you fucking baby," I tell myself. I push the tears away and use the flashlight to search my place. The crowbar is gone —no knives or baseball bat, either.

"She did this," I mutter. "She set you up. I knew this would happen. I knew it, I knew it, I knew it! I…"

I stop talking and stand up straight. I hear the familiar sound of the deadbolt clicking open.

I hurry over to the door. I freeze as I grasp the handle. I'm terrified to turn it, to find out that it's still locked. I'm terrified to turn it, to find out that it's open—because what then? Are they waiting for me on the other side? To hurt me? To throw me out?

Fuck it. I yank the door open, putting me face-to-face with.nobody… No one is there. Who let me out and why? Was it Gary? Is he hoping I'll sneak off in the night and spare him the bother of kicking me out?

Gary wouldn't do that, I assure myself.

Which is why you should save him the trouble. You don't belong here. You've never belonged here. Go! The voice of the she-devil is back in my head.

"No," I say. "I'm not listening to you."

More talking to myself. This is bad.

Maybe you're infected, Heidi's voice changes tactics. *Do you want to infect Buddy?*

I hesitate. Anything to protect Buddy. That's my pledge. The thought is interrupted by the sound of creaking hinges. I poke my head into the hall as Heidi's silhouette slips through one of the emergency exits.

What the hell is she up to? I wonder. *Why is she letting me out?* Maybe it's anger, ego, or madness, but against all logic, I follow her, determined to beat her at her own game. In the stairwell, I hear the fire exit below open and close.

Heidi, what are you up to? I wonder. I take the steps two at a time, determined to find out.

I leave the lofts on the side of the building facing Seong, Devon's, and Laleh's graves. Heidi's flashlight is rounding the corner of the building.

"Fuck," I whisper.

I've become that stupid idiot from a horror movie. I'm unarmed, it's dark, and this screams trap.

Turn back, Teddy begs.

I'm already chasing after her.

My eyes adjust to the moonlight and there are still some streetlights on here and there.

I trip over a DND, what's left of it. Fresh, tar-like blood oozes out of its eye socket. I pick up my pace.

Heidi stops. I hide behind a car. Obviously she wants me following her, but let her guess if I actually am. My heart's pounding. I hear snapping, grinding teeth, shuffling steps, and low growls. I see the outlines of a dozen DNDs. She waits as they close in on her.

What the hell is she doing? I wonder.

The DNDs surround her. They pull her hair and poke her flesh. One of them sniffs her all over, nostrils sucking hungrily. In moments, the DNDs lose interest and start to disperse.

Fuck me.

She scans the area, eyes drifting over my hiding spot. I hunker down.

Did she see me?

Apparently not, as she casually strolls to a house. It's the modern monstrosity with the slats of steel covering all the doors and windows. We've yet to see anyone go in or out of it. Gary's note sticks out from the mailbox. I angle the car mirror to watch her.

She takes a key from under the welcome mat and lets herself in. There wasn't a key there before. We checked. She got ahold of it somehow and left it there recently. The moment the door closes, I sprint to the neighbor's driveway and hide behind their mini-van. Fifteen minutes later, Heidi's coming out, locking up behind her. She slides the key under the mat.

She's smirking.

We'll see who's the joke, I promise myself.

Except you're exactly where she wants you to be, Teddy warns. Yeah, there's that.

She fixes her hair and strides purposefully back towards The Box. I wait a few moments, sure that she'll turn around. She doesn't, disappearing around a bend.

I run to the house she just left and find the key under the mat.

Trap, Teddy reminds me.

I slide the key into the lock and take three sharps breaths.

Obviously, I reply, pushing the door open.

CHAPTER 31

I jump aside, expecting a gun or crossbow to fire. All I hear is the early morning chirping of birds.

I peer inside. The place is, in a word, magnificent. Ultra modern lines, hardwood floors in a stain of gray that must have cost a fortune back when money mattered, fireplace in the center of the living room with the exhaust overtop, designer this, that and the other, including limited-edition Haida prints on the wall, softly lit from above. The place has power.

Bands of metal cover the floor-to-ceiling windows. The front door could guard a vault. The security pad requires a thumb print. It's not armed.

I search for signs of Heidi's presence here, clues to tell me what she's up to. The kitchen is beyond bad ass. There are two dishwashers, an oversized fridge and freezer, an island with its own sink, in addition to the double sink under another window that's blocked by bands of metal.

I can see why Heidi likes the place. It beats the shit hole we're living in. I head upstairs. There's a series of closed doors—and one open one. It's the master suite.

It's a designer's wet dream, with a low-to-the-floor bed (it's crisply made, with three rows of decorative pillows), sleek dressers, and built-in nightstands. The shower and tub are open concept, all glass, marble, and steel. Puffed-up towels are neatly folded on the vanity.

It's very I-would-never-shop-at-Ikea. I've seen the inside of this place before, in a magazine. Its owner was an international DJ. Steph and I loved referring to it when we were talking about the renos we would do in our pad. This room cost more than our entire house.

I don't know what to make of it. Was the place vacant when everything went to hell? People like this have at least one vacation home or yacht. Were they there? How did Heidi get access?

My flashlight illuminates something out of place. Amidst the fon-fon perfection, a *Star Wars* poster is tacked onto the wall.

Has Heidi been redecorating? I move the flashlight. A row of priceless paintings leans against a dresser. Squares of unfaded paint show where they used to hang. They've been replaced by more posters, of the X-Men, Batman, and one of Linda Carter's Wonder Woman. It's campy nerdy—like me.

This isn't for her, I realize. *It's for me.* She's dumping me here. It's a sweet crib, but that doesn't matter—because I'll be alone.

A lump sinks in my stomach. This isn't what I was expecting (*what were you expecting?* I rage at myself) but it's still a trap.

"Idiot," I whisper.

I've got to get out of here. I make it as far as the hallway when a loud siren erupts from the house, coming from every possible angle as if there were bugles hidden in every nook and cranny.

Burglar alarm? I wonder.

I run down the stairs, yanking open the front door. My pounding feet carry me as far as the front lawn when the siren dies out. I stop. Doors are opening in houses up and down the block.

You'll never make it.

I look back at the house. A dizzying light show erupts all across it, in sync with the audio blasting from external speakers, of a high-energy remix of the song 'Gangnam Style.'

"Fuck me." I'd forgotten how the DJ owner bragged about the sound and light system, which he put in for his kids. I watched it on YouTube. At the time, amazing. Now, not so much.

This was Heidi's plan. Turn the others against me. Lure me here. And then trap me with the sounds and lights that are zombie crack.

DNDs step from the homes around me. They come from left and right, ragged remnants of humanity. Some take twitching, staggering steps, others—the younger ones, the athletic—are sprinting with terrifying ferocity.

A group of women who all look like they belonged to the same early-morning jogging group are shoving other DNDs aside, growling as they charge for me, closing the distance between us at superhuman speed. One of them trips with such force that, even over the music, I hear her ankle snap. She goes down, but the others are undeterred.

I turn to escape back into the house—my prison—when a neighbor bursts through the bushes and lands between me and the door. Just my luck, it's a bloody jock, and I want to scream, *When the hell did everyone start getting so damn fit?*

He reaches for me. I control center line, just like Gary taught me, blocking one forearm, then the other. I grasp his wrist, yanking it taunt while hitting rugby jock's chin with my open palm. I hear a satisfying snap. He looks dazed as the electric current to and from his brain is short circuited. I clench my abs and throw him aside.

The pack of runners is closing on me. I jump inside the house and slam the door shut, quickly turning the locks. I hear the DNDs banging against the metal barriers all around, filling the front and sides of the house with the echoing clatter of a Caribbean street festival. I run into the kitchen, grab a knife and pull open the back door. A DND—a short girl wearing a green hijab—lunges for me. I kick her back. More DNDs are pouring over the fence. The light show is back here as well.

I slam the kitchen door shut, locking it. More DNDs pound on the covered windows. I run upstairs. The Korean pop hit is still blaring away. I go up another flight of stairs, emerging onto a rooftop deck that is hella swank, with a hot tub, enormous BBQ, and even a retro camper trailer, cause what kid doesn't need one of those on his/her/zirs rooftop deck?

I watch the wave of ragged DNDs surrounding the house at street level.

I need to cut the power, I realize. *Basement.*

I'm about to head back down when I see Heidi. I catch glimpses of her in the pools of the streetlights that are still working. There's a solar powered construction road sign that blinks on and off, casting an orange tint to her face as she strides the street. A few of the DNDs at the back of the mob notice her. They break off from the group and run towards her, ready to tear her to pieces. She doesn't blink. As they get close to her, they stop. They stare at her, they touch her, they smell her, and then they lose interest, rushing back to the house, where they push against each other. A few try to climb on top of each other to get higher up, but it's like drunks at a rock show. They just fall back down.

Heidi reaches the back of their mass.

I wait for them to part for her, like Moses and the Red Sea, but they don't. She shoves her way through them. Again they smell her, touch her, get right in her face. A beefy, bearded hipster grabs her breasts. Heidi stabs him in the face with her orc-inspired dagger. A teen girl's bevy of rings catches in Heidi's hair. Heidi grabs the teen's scrawny arm for leverage and slices the fingers off. In this way Heidi forces her way forward, cutting, stabbing, shoving, stepping. She reaches the front door and looks directly up at me. Our eyes meet, and she gives me a wink.

With quick darting motions, she stabs the DNDs pounding on the door. Her knife goes in and out of the backs of their heads with cold precision. They fall like marionettes free of their strings. She pushes them aside. Others fill the space. Again her knife slices and dices. More of them fall. The ones around her start to figure it out. They step back and stare at her, waiting. She pulls out a ring of keys. I hear the locks opening. I wince at each click. She opens the door and slips inside. The door closes, followed by each of the locks latching back into place—click, click, click.

The grip on my knife tightens.

CHAPTER 32

I barely hear 'Gangnam Style' as I walk downstairs. The pounding of fists against the metal barriers seems distant. By the time I reach the first floor, Heidi's waiting in the living room, sitting on the custom circular couch that surrounds the fireplace. Several logs crackle and burn under the metal hood. Candles flicker around her. She sips on a glass of cognac. Her blade is in her lap. She's covered in blood the color of tar. I don't bother hiding the knife in my hand. It's puny compared to hers.

I stop in the double doorway between the front hall and the living room.

"You must have a lot of questions," she says.

"Fewer and fewer," I reply. "You drugged me the other night because you wanted me to sleepwalk. You were going to lead me here."

"I slept right through you getting up," she confesses. "My bad."

"So you tried again, the following night. But I figured you out."

She lifts her glass. "Two for two."

"So tonight, after the others went to bed, you unlocked my door and lured me here."

"Gold star," she says, swirling the liqueur and taking a sip.

"And now you've trapped me here," I continue, "surrounded by those things. Do you have a final monologue to rub my face in how you outsmarted me, stole my friends, and turned me back into the loser I used to be?"

She rolls her eyes. "You read too many comic books."

I stop myself from arguing. It doesn't matter. "I'm impressed by your whole walking among the dead trick," I say. "How are you doing it? A repellant?"

She smirks. "Oh you know," she says mysteriously.

I'm pretty sure I do.

"You're infected, aren't you?"

She avoids the question, mouth puckering as if tasting something sour.

"Have you seen the upstairs?" she asks.

I play her game—for now.

For now? Teddy asks. *She's been playing you all along.*

"The bedroom's impressive," I say. "I'm sure I'll be very comfortable here."

"I'm sure we will," she replies.

I freeze. *Did she just say* we?

I notice a framed image on the shelf.

I pick it up. It's of Heidi and me, playing a round of *Settlers of Catan* in The Box just a week ago. She clearly found a printer. We're making asinine faces.

"I love that picture of us," she says. "It's like, it doesn't matter that the world is falling apart, you still know how to make me laugh. I've always loved that about you."

It's not the only photo of us. There's a selfie of her on a bike in the foreground, and me on a bike in the background—I'm blurred and out of focus, like when we dated. The one that my gaze lingers on is of her, me, and her gay bestie, Kevin.

She gets up from the couch and comes towards me. I hold my knife menacingly. The whiff of cognac from the glass in her hand burns my nostrils.

She looks at the pic of the three of us.

"It still amazes me how much you two look alike," she says. "Even back when you were scrawny, you could pass for brothers."

She strikes with speed and grace, disarming me before I can react. My knife clatters to the floor. She's behind me, her arms wrapping around my waist. I've got counter moves and…

Is she hugging me?

She rests her head on my back.

"This time we'll get it right," she says, nuzzling into me. I'm in a house surrounded by flesh-eating zombies, and I'm fairly certain I'm safer out there.

She kisses my neck. The cognac is ripe on her breath, along with peppermint mouthwash, but underneath is the slightest whiff of rot. How did I not notice it before?

Heidi's infected, yet she's holding it together. How?

Steph lasted less than a day after she was bitten, but who knows how this thing works. Infinite variety, à la Darwin. That's what Laleh hypothesized. No two of us are alike. Maybe Heidi's immune system is able to slow it down. Maybe there are different strains. Too many maybes.

Could be I'm delusional, but when Steph began losing her hold on reality, I'm convinced she battled her illness in an attempt to protect me. Even as her mind disintegrated, and her hunger for warm flesh consumed her, her love for me prompted her to go outside, disemboweling the neighbor's dog instead of her fiancé. That's what I believe. I have no such hope for Heidi. For Heidi, I was always something to feed on—spitting out the parts she didn't like.

I feel her teeth on my skin. I grab and uncoil her arms from about my waist. I spin away and push her back, more roughly than I intend—and nowhere near as roughly as I'd like. I touch my neck. No blood. She didn't break the skin.

"What's the matter?" she asks, genuinely confused. She caresses my cheek with the back of her hand. Scabs cover her knuckles.

"You're trembling," she says. "You always were a nervous goose. Remember how you couldn't even get it up our first time together?"

I grab a solid glass DJ award from the shelf and swing it at her. She catches my wrist. She's preternaturally fast and strong. She squeezes. I gasp at the pain radiating up my arm, and I drop the trophy. She presses the palm of my hand onto her breast. Her shirt is clammy with DND blood.

"We're going to be so happy together," she says.

Something crashes upstairs. She looks up. There's shuffling movement.

My guess is that a DND's made it to the roof and broken in. Heidi smiles maniacally.

"Sounds like someone misses his daddy," she says.

"What's that now?" I say.

She slides her palm into mine. Her grip is a vice. I grimace, sure that she's about to break my hand. "Come," she says, "I'll show you."

She drags me into the hall. I'm twice her size, but I might as well be Teddy the way she's manhandling me. I gaze longingly at the knife on the floor. She drags me up the stairs, stopping in front of a closed door.

"I have a surprise for you," she says, eyes twinkling.

She opens the door, revealing the room beyond. My mind takes snapshots of the *Spider-Man* poster on the wall, a broken lamp on the floor, the bed in the shape of a car, and the toy cement mixer truck on a shelf next to a pile of comic books. The name ANDY is in big letters above a dresser, and a massive Space Lego world sits on a table by one shuttered window.

Heidi and I are not alone.

There's a kid, around Buddy's age, dressed in brand new smiley-face pajamas. A leather collar is locked around his neck, attached to a chain fastened to his headboard. He growls at the sight of me, reaching with his thin six-year-old arms. His face is a mask of hunger and fury.

Heidi beams with pride. She coils her arms around mine, leaning her head on my shoulder.

"You see?" Heidi says. "It's everything you've ever wanted—house, home, children…and me as your wife."

I'd scream if I thought it would help.

She comes to stand in front of me, and she holds my cheeks in her hands.

"There's something I want to say to you," she begins, "something I should've said a long time ago. I'm sorry for leaving you. I'm sorry for the way I failed to appreciate you. I'm sorry for everything. And I'm going to make it all up to you, I swear."

It's everything I longed to hear from her during the suicidal depression after she dumped me, and all I can think is, *How am I going to kill her?*

The little boy in the PJs is growling, reaching for me ravenously. He pulls so hard on the bed that it drags forward by half an inch, bumping into the nightstand.

Heidi pushes me deeper into the room, keeping herself between me and the doorway as she wraps her arms around the DND child. She kisses his chubby-cheeked face. He ignores her, reaching for me. I don't see any bites on him. He looks like a regular kid with bloodshot eyes and unusually pale skin.

"Hello, sweetie," she says, smoothing back his hair. She hugs him again. "Did you miss Daddy? Did you? Oh, you love your daddy, don't you?"

The right sleeve of his pajama top is pulled up, revealing the crook of his elbow. I pick up the knocked-over light and tighten the bulb. It springs to life; I aim it at his arm. He's either an injectable drug addict or someone's been shooting him up. The track marks on his pale skin are just like...

"Laleh," I say. "You killed Laleh. You injected her with contaminated saliva to infect her and street drugs to kill her."

"Laleh was a cunt who was filling your mind with poison to turn you against me," Heidi says.

"You killed her!" I shout. "And she killed Devon and Seong."

"You should've heard the things Devon said about you behind your back. And Seong, well, that little slut couldn't wait to get into your pants. I protected our family."

I look at Andy—what's left of the little boy.

"He was alive when you found him," I say, thinking out loud. "This whole family was alive. They were safe here, as safe as anyone could be until you weaseled your way in—like you always do. You played off their better natures before revealing what a monster you are."

She ignores me. Andy is trying to shove her away to get to me.

"What?" she says to the kid. "No hugs for Mommy?"

I search for a weapon. That's when I spot Teddy on the bed, beady black eyes seeming to plead for rescue behind wisps of ragged yellow fur.

Fuck me, I think. She took him, too.

I'm so floored, I almost don't see the baseball bat. It's leaning against the wall in the corner.

"Come on," she says to him, "give Mommy a hug."

She grabs his arms roughly, trying to force them around her neck. He struggles against her, inadvertently elbowing her in the face. She jerks back and touches her finger to her nose. It comes away bloody.

"You ungrateful little asshole!" she yells at him. She smacks his cheek so hard he falls to the ground. "I'm the one who feeds you. I'm the one who cleans and deoderizes you. *I* take care of you, but all you want is Daddy, Daddy, Daddy. Well, fuck you, you ungrateful little bastard."

The kid gets up like nothing's happened, jaws growling and snapping the air, fingers clawing to get to me. I'm edging myself towards the bat, deeper into the room. Heidi's head swivels towards me.

"I think he's hungry," I say, hoping to distract her.

"Oh you do, do you? Because you're the one who's here at home with him all day?" she demands. She looks ready to charge me. I hold my hands up for peace, eyeing the bat, which seems further away than ever.

She gets up and pushes me aside—closer to the bat. She yanks open a cupboard door. To my horror, inside is a laundry basket of human body parts—arms and legs sticking out, each of them in an individually vacuum-sealed see-through baggie—including the head of the international DJ.

"That's all I am to you, isn't it?" she demands of Andy. "A goddamn cookie jar!"

She grabs an arm, rips it free of the bag and tosses it at the kid.

"You want to eat, eat!" she shouts.

The limb smacks zombie Andy in the face and falls to the floor, ignored. He's still reaching for me. A dead, rotting limb can't compare to the fresh feast before him. My hand wraps around the bat. I turn, ready to lift and strike at Heidi, but she's crept up on me, standing right in my face. Faster than Gary, she grabs the bat and easily yanks it from my grasp. She stares at me, tapping the bat in her palm. I say nothing. She says nothing. The seconds tick by, dragging on endlessly. And then, she wheels about, bat overhead. She smashes it into the DND kid's skull, crushing it over and over.

She stops, hunching. Her panting weighs down the room. She wipes sweat and the kid's blood from her face. Andy stands there for a moment —until his knees fold under him, and he crumples to the ground.

"I guess this is going to be one of those days," she says with a nervous laugh. She pulls a bottle of Xanax from her pocket. She pops it open and pours half-a-dozen blue pills into her mouth. She crunches on them loudly, chewing them, swallowing them little by little. She takes a few deep yoga breaths, and her shoulders fall as the anger drains out of her.

Her body spasms, as if she's waking up from a deep sleep. She stares uncomprehendingly at Andy's headless remains. The leather collar is still fastened around the kid's neck.

"Andy?" she says. Her listless fingers drop the bat. It clatters on the floor and rolls under the bed, out of reach. My heart sinks.

"Andy!"

Tears brim in her eyes.

"No," she says. Her voice is pure motherly anguish. "No, no, no."

She scoops him up in her arms, cradling and rocking him.

"Mommy's sorry," she says. "Mommy didn't mean it. It's going to be okay. Mommy loves you very much. You just make her so mad sometimes!"

I'm stepping away from her, backing up towards the door. Teddy stares at me accusingly as I prepare to leave him behind.

I have to, I tell him.

I know, he replies.

I turn the knob and pull the door open, wincing as it whines. Heidi sobs as she rocks the kid back and forth.

"Hush little baby, don't say a word..." she sings.

I step into the hall. The floor creaks, but she doesn't look.

"Momma's gonna buy you a mockingbird..."

I turn, and her head snaps up.

"Where the fuck do you think you're going?" she demands, dropping Andy from her arms. He clunks to the floor. She stands, fingers flexing in and out.

"I..." I begin to say. I meet Teddy's glassy eyes.

Run, he says.

And I do.

CHAPTER 33

"Honey?" Heidi calls after me, her voice suddenly sweet again. "Honey, where are you going?"

I have no fucking clue. I can't leave (surrounded by flesh-eating zombies). I can't stay (trapped with psycho, infected ex). Either way, I get consumed. It's the perfect metaphor for Heidi's and my failed relationship.

I push open the door one room over, hoping I can lock myself in to buy some time. Instead, I trip on a flowered and pink Barbie camper, complete with fold-down hot tub for her and the girls. I land on my hands and knees, just out of reach of a little girl who could pass for Andy's twin. She's collared and chained to a bed painted with fuchsia stars. Her parents were definitely into gender binaries.

Her pigtails quiver, head shaking as she growls and reaches for me. Her name's on the wall in big, pink, bubbly letters. Annie. The song from the musical of the same name comes to mind, about the sun, and tomorrow, and other such bullshit.

I kick her hard in the chest, and she flies onto the bed, smacking the back of her head against a purple star. Her skull leaves behind a bloody print the color of tar. She starts crawling towards me.

"Fuck me," I say, escaping back into the corridor. I yank Annie's bedroom door shut. Heidi stands at the end of the hall, staring at me.

"What's the matter baby?" she asks. "This is what you always wanted. A home that we built together. A family. Me."

What Monkey's Paw did I use to wish this hell into existence? I stumble into a bathroom, locking the door.

"Honey?" she says, tapping on the painted wood. "Knock, knock, who's there?"

She Geisha-giggles. I search for weapons.

"You can't hide in there forever," she says. "Remember, we promised never to go to bed mad."

We never promised any such thing.

"I said, come out!" she shouts with her full fury. "Open the goddamn fucking door! Fucking men! You're all the same. Give them what they say they want, and they run and hide. Well, you can't hide from this, and you can't hide from me. You have responsibilities."

I smash the mirror with my elbow and wrap a towel around the biggest shard of broken glass.

"I know what you're doing in there," she laughs—as if this were all one big joke. She always was a sucker for a punch line. "You're afraid of me, aren't you, you fucking coward? You think I'm sick. You think I'm *infected*."

The word is like venom from a viper's tongue.

"Heidi, please don't do this," I beg. "You need to stop."

"You said that this is what you wanted! You said so! When we broke up, your exact words were 'all I wanted was for you to love me.' You were *sobbing*. Well, I'm here, loving you. Now open the goddamn fucking door!"

It's terrifying to hear my own words thrown against me like this, the very ones that echoed over and over in my mind as I spiraled down into the dark place.

She pounds on the wooden barrier so hard it cracks.

"Maybe we can help you," I say. "Maybe we can slow it down. Use anti-psychotics or..." my words trail off. Her mind is rotting minute by minute, second by second, and the more it rots, the less she can judge her growing demented state. Steph, I think, had some insight that something was wrong, enough to take her out into the yard. Maybe Heidi does too, in her way, popping Xanax to give her a measure of control. But, unlike Steph, Heidi inhabits a delusional world of her narcissistic making, one in which she is the star around which all else revolves.

Now, everything that I knew about her, everything she kept hidden from the rest of the world, is manifesting bit by bit for all to see. It's what I wanted, for everyone else to witness her true nature, and I can't help but think, *I should've been more specific.*

She speaks with a frightening coldness.

"It's him, isn't it?" she asks.

Prolonged silence is my reply. *What's she talking about?*

She pounds on the door, and the crack widens.

"Answer me!" she shouts.

"Who do you mean?" I ask, genuinely confused.

"Who?" she mimics, using her best I'm-a-dumb-bro voice. "There is only one *him*. Gary, and that monster child of his. You're so fucking in love with them, you haven't got any love left for your own family. Well, I'm your wife, Martin, and I'm the mother of your children, and I will not let some bloody cocksucker get between us."

The veins in my temples are ready to explode. *Buddy. Gary.* She wouldn't dare hurt them. *Of course she would!* I rage. Something snaps in me.

"You leave them the hell out of this!" I yell, slamming my palm against the door. "I am not your goddamn fucking husband, and you are not my goddamn fucking wife, and we don't have any fucking children, you fucking psycho bitch!"

I wait for her to lose it, the way I just have, for her to come smashing through the door so I can stab her through the eye or ear or the base of the skull. I grip the glass with the cloth wrapped around it. I sway on my heels.

Steady, Teddy says.

"I don't like it when you talk to me that way," she sulks. "It's disrespectful."

Shit. I've calmed her down.

Okay, I think, *use that to your advantage.* Not that I have a clue how. My mind races faster than my heart.

"It crushes me to see you like this," she says. "It's sad watching you pine after that man, worshipping him like he's God's gift. You think if you're in his presence long enough, you'll absorb a fraction of his bro-ness and stop being the loser that you hate so much."

"Heidi," I say, "this is between you and me. Nobody else."

"I wish that were true," she says. "You can lie to yourself, but not to me. I know you too well. I'm your wife. You tell yourself that you're a part of their family, but you're not. You're a part of *this* family. Do you have any idea how much it hurts knowing that's not enough? That *I'm* not enough?"

It's like she's playing back some twisted reverse-world transcript of my therapy sessions.

"Let's be honest," she says. "You'll never see yourself as enough, either, not as long as Gary's around to be better than you at everything."

"Heidi, please..." I beg.

"Just remember," she says, "I didn't want to hurt them. "

"Heidi, you don't have to hurt anybody!" I say.

"You made me do this," she replies. "I'm yours, and you're mine, you've always been mine. Marty and Heidi, that's what people say. I love you so much, and I *will* protect the ones I love!" She slams her hand hard on the door for emphasis.

No, no, no, no, you stupid idiot! I curse myself. *You've put Buddy and Gary in danger.*

"Wait," I say. "Heidi..."

"Yes, Marty?" she asks hopefully. *My God, is that what I used to sound like every time she threw me an emotional crumb? No wonder she dumped me.*

"Heidi, honey, you're right. I've been a fool. I've been selfish, and blind. *You* are my family. *This* is where I belong. Just you and me."

"And the kids," she says.

"Yes," I agree. "And the kids." I'm nodding at my words, projecting that I believe this. Gary's always saying, *Marty, my man, you gotta own it before you can sell it.*

"Does that mean you're coming out?" she asks.

"Yes," I say. "I'm coming out."

I slowly and carefully drag the broken glass across my left forearm. I hiss. Blood wells up from the shallow cut and drips onto the floor. I take a deep breath, set the piece of mirror on the sink and unlock the door. I open it and step back.

She doesn't come in immediately. She's suspicious.

"I'm hurt," I say, showing her the cut on my arm.

Her eyes widen in alarm.

"Serves me right for freaking out like that," I say. "Can you forgive me?"

She rushes forward and drops to her knees, taking hold of my left hand.

"Of course, I forgive you my love! You're my forever." She looks ready to kiss the cut. I quickly yank it free of her grip. She looks like I've slapped her.

"We need to disinfect it," I say.

She nods vigorously. "Yes!"

"Here's some peroxide," I say, grabbing a bottle from the medicine cabinet, "and some wraps."

She unscrews the bottle and balances it over the wound. I wince as the peroxide flows over the self-inflicted gash. She uses a liberal amount of gauze, binding the cut carefully, taping it in place.

"There," Heidi says, "All bet...

My fingers close around the shard of mirror on the edge of the sink, and I bring it down, aiming for her neck. She blocks it with her arm. The makeshift weapon jams into her wrist, catching on bone. She lurches back and takes the shard with her.

She growls. "I will not be treated this way!"

She's faster and stronger than ever as her rotting mind forgets any pre-imposed limits. She crashes into me. I get her in a headlock; my forearm catches under her chin, jamming her diseased mouth shut. Her heels dig into the tile floor. With a grunt, she launches us backward. I trip over the tub, ripping the curtain down and slamming into the wall. I hit my head and see stars.

She wraps the see-through curtain around my face, pinning me in a vinyl web. I gasp, sucking in what little air was caught inside the membrane. I see more stars; the room's going dark.

At the last moment, she jerks the curtain free. I collapse to my elbows and knees, coughing but able to breathe.

"I am a human being," she says. "You can't just use me, lead me on, and then throw me away like a piece of garbage."

Honest to God, is post-breakup me writing this stuff for her?

"Baby, listen," I say, trying to use her own two-year-old pouty face routine against her. "I love you, baby. I want to be with you."

I get up, and she kicks me back down. It's her turn to get me in a headlock. Her muscles are a vice. I might as well be an infant the way she yanks me out of the tub and drags me down the hall.

She opens the door of the room with the chained little girl in it. Annie growls and reaches for me hungrily.

"Your daddy's been a very naughty boy. You know what I do with naughty boys," she says.

I think of how she smashed Andy's head. Heidi slams Annie's door shut and drags me down the stairs. My body bounces on each step. I claw at her to no avail. She cuts off my breath, and the world grows hazy. She's too fucking strong. We reach the front hall, she yanks open the door leading to the basement and pushes me down the stairs. The sound of my tumbling rings through my ears.

"You need to think about this relationship!" she yells. "I deserve to be appreciated, and I *will* get what I deserve!"

She slams the door. There's an audible click of a deadbolt sliding into place. I hear her footsteps above me and the sound of the front door's multiple locks being undone. The door opens, closes, followed by click, click, click as she seals the place tight. I'm alone with the DNDs pounding on the metal covered windows and the looping tune of 'Gangnam Style.'

178

CHAPTER 34

I run up the stairs to test the door. I yank, I push, I rattle. It's locked tight. I take stock, hoping to find tools that can get me out of here. Instead, I stare at a kid's playroom. It's full of mini-sized furniture in bright colors, dimly lit by a plastic table lamp in the shape of a wilting mushroom. There's a Fischer Price table with crayons, markers, and coloring books; a bead station for making jewelry out of gaudy plastic baubles; a row of coat hooks with painter's smocks hanging at little person height; a copy of *The Adventures of Philippe and the Swirling Vortex* on a rocking chair in the reading corner; and a giant stuffed bear that would rightly make Teddy jealous.

Who puts a lock on a kid's playroom?

Heidi, that's who. God only knows how long she's been planning this. There are empty cans of beans with used plastic forks at the kids' table. I pick up a picture, drawn in crayon, of a little girl crying over the mangled bodies of what I assume are her parents. *Is this where Heidi locked those poor kids before turning them into DNDs? Did they see her kill their parents?*

The thought is too dark.

Focus, I order myself. I have to freeze my heart if I'm to get out of this. I can thaw out later.

At the back of the playroom, I discover a narrow closet. There are boxes marked X-mas decorations, a pile of folded towels and sheets, and, *thank you, God*, a cordless electric drill. I squeeze the button and nearly cum at the sound and sight of it whirling.

I rush up the stairs. I saw this on Vimeo when we locked ourselves out of the gym and were too cheap (and poor) to hire a locksmith. I press the drill bit directly above where the key would go, and I drill into it. It takes a few tries to snap all the pins inside. At last, I feel and hear the last one pop. With a flat-head screwdriver, I twist the lock. The door opens.

I did it!

As far as I can tell, the house is empty. The DNDs outside bang frenetically on the metal-covered windows. No sign of Heidi.

I go to Andy's room, stepping over his tiny body. I reach under his racecar bed and fish out the baseball bat. Teddy's black eyes gaze at me. I shove him in my belt and move swiftly to the next room over. Annie growls and reaches for me.

"I'm so sorry," I say. I smash the bat across her cheek, snapping her jaw. I hit her two more times to cave in her skull. She drops to the floor, motionless. I couldn't leave her behind like that.

I take the stairs to the roof, emerging onto the deck, with its pots filled with wild grasses and stunted trees that have been forced to grow in spirals. 'Gangnam Style' plays. The place is surrounded by DNDs.

As the sun rises, I look to the rooftop deck one house over. It's about two feet away. I jump across. My sneakers thud dully as I land. I freeze, baseball bat ready. I also brought the screwdriver.

I traverse the entire block by hopping from roof to roof, taking me further and further from the DND horde behind me. I might just pull this off.

I reach the last house on the block. I jump. I land on the deck, right next to a DND, a chubby woman in a pinstripe dress. She's got curlers in her hair. She's lying there, one arm partially chewed off, legs splayed like she's waiting for her lover.

She growls and grabs my ankle. I stab her with the screwdriver. I yank the tool free and wipe black blood onto her dress. I hurry past the faded plastic patio furniture and the rusting barbecue to peer through the sliding door into the house. I tap on the glass. No DNDs respond.

Clear.

I step inside. The place looks like *Antiques Road Show* meets *Hoarders*. Doilies, vintage dolls in Victorian dresses, and Hummel figurines cover every square inch of the place.

180

Downstairs, I go out the back door. The yard is clear. I hop the fence, still hidden from the surge of DNDs just a block away. I take an indirect route to avoid them. On the plus side, the sound-and-light show has drawn them all to one spot.

I sprint for the cement walls of The Box.

I have no idea what to expect when I get there, but I imagine the worst—the gates open, smoke rising from the main building, and Gary and the others lurching towards me in the semblance of life, wanting to eat the flesh off my bones. Over it all, I hear Heidi's maniacal laugh. I run faster.

I encounter a lone DND in a mail deliverer's uniform. I smash her head in with the bat, barely breaking stride as she flops to the ground. A hearing aid clatters out of her ear, making a dull whine.

I round a corner, and The Box is in sight. The gates are closed. There's no smoke. Somehow, that freaks me out more. *Does Heidi have them chained up inside? Has she injected them—like she did to Andy and Annie? Like she did to Laleh?* I sprint faster. I hated running with a passion as a kid. My thighs were so badly internally rotated that my lower legs would swing out to the sides like a pair of propellers, making the other kids point, laugh, and call me a gimp.

Two hours a day of stretching for three years has opened up my groin and adductors; lunges, kettlebells, and step ups have taught my glutes how to fire, and I couldn't be more grateful as I race towards this finish line, praying I'm not too late.

I hear the blast of a rifle firing. *Fuck! Heidi's shooting them!* I'm ready to run faster—until a second shot rings out and a puff of dirt and asphalt fly into the air in front of me, stinging my knees and thighs.

I stumble to a halt. I pant, staring at the wall of the compound. It's still about 100 feet away, but I recognize Gary standing on the wall, hunting rifle in hand. He points the weapon at me, gazing through the site. Heidi stands next to him, holding Buddy to her breast. A bandage wraps around her forearm.

I take a step forward, and Gary fires again. I cover my face. Chunks of road smack my elbow. I stop.

"You have to listen to me!" I shout. A few blocks away, I see a couple of DNDs staggering towards me. The blasts have drawn their attention. I've got time, but not a lot. "She's infected!"

Gary uses the shotgun to point off to my right. I see a knapsack sitting there, with a piece of paper tied to it with an elastic. I go to it and pull the paper free. I instantly recognize Gary's neat calligraphy. My tears start to flow. After everything, this is just too much.

Broseph,
It breaks my heart to do this, even more than my heart has been breaking little by little as I've watched you deteriorate into someone I no longer recognize. You've grown paranoid and delusional. Now, you lure Heidi to a house you've set up for the two of you, and you try to hold her there against her will. You say you hate her. But, as I've long suspected, you're obsessed with her.

"Long suspected," I read out loud. *How long has he believed that? How could he believe that?*

You've grown increasingly violent, attacking her, playing off her better nature to trick her into letting you out of your room, stabbing her, and now trying to forcibly confine her. I'm sorry she broke your heart all those years ago, I am, but you're out of control.

I don't know if the strain has gotten to you or if you're infected. All I know is that you've become dangerous.

I have to look out for Buddy. He has to come first. I love you, bro. If you love me, if you love Buddy, and I know you do, you have to stay away. —Gary.

This isn't happening. I look at the bag on the ground. It's packed with canned goods, chocolate protein bars, and tetra paks of coconut water. A short sword pokes out. Next to it is the picture of me and Steph. This is it. This is my goodbye survival package. He means it. Gary lifts the barrel of the rifle again, pointing it at me—not at the ground in front of me, *at* me. I lift my hands in peace, tears streaming down my face.

I've lost everything. She wins.

No!

I take Teddy from my belt and place him on the ground in front of me. Buddy will demand that Gary come for the bear, and even though I'll be gone, part of me will remain, and the door will still be open, if only by a crack, for me to return.

I hear the shot, and Teddy explodes. I gape. Stuffing flies everywhere. I stare down at what's left of my over-loved childhood toy. His torso's ripped to shreds. His head, arms, and legs are barely held together by a scrap of tattered cloth.

In happier times, I'd paraphrase *Southpark,* screaming *Oh my God! You killed Teddy! You bastard!* Instead, I am speechless. My throat constricts.

Heidi is beaming. She kisses Buddy triumphantly on the cheek. He gives me a sad little wave. I wipe the tears from my eyes and wave back. I kneel down to zip up the bag and I see a manila envelope inside. From the weight and feel of it, I don't need to open it to know there's a gun inside. Heidi's curly cue script is on the envelope.

There's one bullet in the cartridge, it says. **Put it to good use.**

It's enough to make me charge the gate. There's no way Gary knows this is in here. If I show it to him...

Then what? I wonder.

Then nothing, Teddy replies. I stare into his glassy eyes. His head is intact, but his torso is a mess of stuffing and mangled fur. He looks like Toys 'R Us roadkill. *He's done with you*, Teddy says. *No stupid note from Heidi is going to change that.* With a sigh, he seals the deal. *You know when you're not wanted.*

His final words are a black maw of abandonment. The DNDs are getting closer. I grab what's left of Teddy, shove him into the knapsack, and swing it onto my back. Grasping the sword in one hand, the bat in the other, I run back the way I came.

Strike me down, and I will
become more powerful than
you could possibly imagine.
—Obi-Wan Kenobi

PART 5

CHAPTER 35

I'm splattered with blood by the time I get back to the house with the doilies and Hummel figurines. I hop the fence and let myself in the back door. I hear 'Gangnam Style' from the other side of the block. I hate that song.

I set the knapsack down. I crack open a coconut water and drink.

I pick up an electricity bill from the kitchen countertop and scan the name of the former occupant. Doris Mansbridge. Doris kept an immaculate, if dated, kitchen, with beige tiles for a backsplash, slat wooden cupboards that look like they belong in a western, and the kind of orange pots and pans my mom used when I was a kid. I find an unopened off-brand chocolate-hazelnut spread. I'd prefer Nutella, but beggars, choosers, etc… I crack the seal and shovel it into my mouth with my finger. I lose myself in its sweetness, if only briefly.

The real stuff is better, but I'm guessing Doris was on a pension. Maybe her son topped that up once a month, but it's not like he was making a killing.

I hate that I'm making up stories. That's Heidi's party game.

She's going to kill them. She's going to kill all of them. The not-quite-Nutella turns sour in my mouth.

I tried to warn them. They wouldn't listen. People like me can't beat people like her.

I find an unopened bottle of schnapps. I swig it, wincing at the sickly taste but enjoying the burn as it goes down my throat.

How could Gary take her side? I wonder. *How could he not see through her?*

"Because you've been acting crazy," I reply. "Frankly, so has he."

She's going to do worse than kill them, I realize. *She's going to make them like her.*

"And there's nothing I can do to stop her," I say out loud.

I see a women's fitness magazine on the table as well as coupons for a weight-loss supplement. It's a glorified diuretic. I wonder who Doris was, what her dreams were, how many times she tried to lose the weight and to change her life, only to end up back in her housecoat watching her *Golden Girls* DVDs on a Friday night.

I revise my earlier story. There was no son to write her a cheque once a month. There was no one for Doris. She lived the way she died. Alone.

"Just like me," I say.

I take another hit of the schnapps. I wander over to the washroom. There's room for a small vanity, the toilet, and an old-school TV with a built-in DVD player. It sits on a shelf above the sink, blocking the mirror. The red on light glares at me. She's still got power. There are no windows in the washroom. Should be safe to turn on the TV. DNDs won't see or hear. Maybe part of me hopes they do. I close the door, sit on the toilet, drop my knapsack, drink more schnapps and click on the set. The DVD player springs to life, spinning away, and up pops Dorothy, Blanche, Sophia, and Rose, the *Golden Girls* theme song thanking me for being a friend.

"I'll get the cheesecake," Gary used to say when we'd get home late from one of the gay bars he used to drag me to, and I knew he was going to force me to watch a *Golden Girls* disc from his box set.

This was after Heidi drained me of my savings, then left me with the lease for a two-bedroom apartment I didn't want in the first place and couldn't possibly afford. I needed a roommate to make ends meet. I put an ad up on Craigslist. Gary answered within the hour. As he put it, he needed a fast out from his "cohabitation situation." We bonded over bastard exes. One month's down payment, a hasty reference check, and a promise to be my personal trainer, and Gary was moving in.

I didn't know a guy could own so many tank tops.

He made me throw out my flashy nightclub shirts and forbade me from trolling the mall for girls.

He was only supposed to stay until my lease ran out, then we'd go our separate ways, maybe staying in touch via facebook, but probably not.

Three months turned into two years, and then a business, together. Strangers became bros.

Then came Chris, Buddy, and Steph.

I'm barely listening as Rose starts telling some story about St. Olaf.

I flip through pictures on my phone. There's one of Gary and me leading an exercise class, then me and Buddy playing *Battleship*, followed by Steph and me in Leia and Luke costumes for Halloween. She was Luke. Eventually, I get to pictures of Heidi and me. I keep going, stopping when I get to the photo shoot of me and my fake girlfriend from back in the day, the one I used to convince Heidi I was high value the first time we met. I laugh. What a time.

I take out the gun with its single bullet. I put my mouth around the nozzle, but it feels too much like I'm giving it a blow job. I press it to my temple instead. It's more masculine.

As I do, I get to a picture of me as a kid. I'm at a cottage my parents rented every year. I look like a bobble head with a bowl cut. I'm doing what I believed was a jaunty pose, leaning on an oar and sticking my hip out, a canoe at my side and the lake behind me. *My God, I looked gay.* Everyone said I was "so sensitive" back then. I smile as I scratch the side of my head with the tip of the gun.

I ponder the question, would the boy I was be proud of the man I've become? *I think he'd be blown away.* He always thought he was so useless, but he grew into me, and I can *do* things.

He found a way, Teddy notes.

"Yes," I muse out loud. "He did."

I think about that kid as if he were somebody else, just a random 10-year-old that I happened to meet. Would I think he was a loser? A sissy? Not worth the time of day? If I knew the shit that bludgeoned him day after day, internally and externally? The isolation? The rejection? The gnawing self-doubt? My God, the sheer weight of it, and the frequency, and the duration. Sensitive my ass. He was tough as fuck. He was a goddamn emotional CrossFit champion. How else could he have endured all that crap?

If he hadn't learned to endure all that crap, do you think you would've survived all this crap? Teddy asks.

Seen through that lens, for the first time, I admire my younger self. In fact, I wonder, *How did he do it?*

I wait for an answer, from Teddy, from Heidi, from any one of the voices in my crowded head. *It's busy in there*, my therapist used to say. But not today. I rub the gun with my thumb. Today, my mind is quiet. The could've, should've, would'ves melt away. Usually, the dark place descends with the heaviness of a low-pressure system. And yet...Nada. How weird is that?

I should be scared about the thought of putting a bullet through my brains. I should be recording a suicide video. I should be trapped on a rollercoaster of my spinning thoughts. I'm so floored by my stability that I can't help but say to myself, *Who are you, and what have you done with Marty Melon?*

Honestly, if ever there were a time I could justify killing myself, this is it. But I'm not going to kill myself. Because I finally see that's not who I am. That's not what I'm about. I'm going to do what I always do; I'm going to fight. For a second, I try to draw on Rambo, but who needs him? The kid in that picture is a fighter, and so am I. That is a core part of what makes me Marty.

The clarity is sunlight killing a vampire.

You're done, the voice of Heidi says to me. *Gary kicked you out. He wants nothing to do with you.*

I laugh.

"Oh sweetheart," I say, "you don't get it, do you? Rejected is what I do best."

CHAPTER 36

I sit at Doris' kitchen table. I eat Doris' expired granola bars and drink a can of Doris' Ensure. If this is what she considered diet food, it's no wonder she never lost weight. *The first ingredient is sugar, Doris! You have to look at the nutritional content.* Teddy stares at me with his black button eyes, head and limbs still intact, barely attached to the ragged strips of his shredded body. Next to him, on the kitchen table, are the gun and Heidi's note.

Infecting all I hold dear and making it her own isn't enough for Heidi. She couldn't bend me, so now she intends to break me. She gave me the gun and the bullet because she needs the satisfaction of knowing she's hollowed me out so completely that I end myself. And, if I don't?

She'll come for you, Teddy warns.

I could run. It's a big world out there. She can walk among the dead, but that's a lot of ground to cover. It would also leave the others at her mercy. How long before she does to them what she did to Andy and Annie? Maybe it's already too late.

That's not helpful, Teddy says.

I scratch him behind an ear.

Agreed.

So what are you going to do? he asks.

"Well," I reply, not even caring anymore that I'm talking out loud to a blown-up teddy bear, "Heidi wants me dead. Heidi wants to gloat over my corpse. I'm going to give Heidi what she wants."

Teddy's voice fades to the background. He knows I need to work. My brain is swirling. I open the music player on my phone and find a remix of the song *Defying Gravity* from the *Wicked* soundtrack. Gary downloaded it for me after I told him about Heidi's and my first date. "You need to reclaim that shit," he said. "Make it your own. 'Cause it's an awesome musical." This version takes the original score and adds a bass-heavy electro beat that's gotten me through some of my toughest workouts.

I put the headphones on and press PLAY.

Amidst the thunk-a-thunk-a meathead-at-a-rave beat, a pair of Broadway babes croons back and forth about their friendship falling apart because green-skinned Elphaba is rejecting societal prejudices (and the rewards that come with submitting to them) to stand up for what she believes in. I open the photo album on my phone. I flip through pictures of Steph, Gary, Buddy, The Box, my parents, my nephews and nieces, all the people I love most in the world, and who loved me.

Elphaba is singing loud and proud about how it's time for her to start defying gravity, and how no one can bring her down. I flip hurriedly through the pictures on my phone, faster and faster. I'm now in the period where Heidi and I dated. Most of the pictures are of her. She never really cared about pictures of the two of us together, as long as she got the perfect one of herself to post online. I didn't even know what to make of Steph when she'd insist on the two of us posing together because she wanted *shared* memories. She was the balm to my wounded soul.

And, there it is.

I stop on a picture of Heidi—one of the rare ones with me in it. My smile is forced, clearly uncomfortable, yet grateful to be included, settling for being a pauper in my own relationship because I figured it was more than I deserved. She's laughing, with her arms around her gay bestie Kevin. This is the picture that Heidi had framed in the house that was to be our love nest, complete with DND children. Kevin and I really do look alike. Now that I've muscled up, we're practically identical. It's like my before and after shot all in one.

You'll never pull it off, Heidi warns. *Elphaba's spells always go awry. And so do yours.*

"I'm not Elphaba," I say. "I'm the Wizard."

CHAPTER 37

The plan that I form is so fucked it's as likely to get me killed as a bullet to my brain. I use this as a source of courage. One way or the other, this will be over.

I open Doris' medicine cabinet. It's full of pill bottles.

"Doris, you nasty little prescription drug addict," I say. "I love you."

I rifle through them. Most of the prescriptions are foreign to me. They could be laxatives for all I know, but some stand out like neon at a funeral. Ativan (thank you Doris) and my nemesis, Ambien. The former is an anti-anxiety medication, which is wonderful for taking off the edge, especially with a glass of red wine. Not that I would know from experience—wink. The latter is the sleep aid with which Heidi drugged me. Doris has two full bottles of each, from prescriptions written by two separate doctors.

"Naughty girl," I tsk approvingly.

The pills go into my backpack. I find a bottle of red wine still in a gift bag, and I shove that in as well, next to the gun with the single bullet. My short sword I keep in hand.

I can't believe I'm doing this. I feel a manic thrill rush through me.

Just wait for the crash, Teddy warns.

Later, I reply.

Time for phase 2.

I leave through the back door and climb over the fence into the street. It's clear. I reach the perimeter of our "safety zone," comprised of cars blocking off intersections to encourage DNDs wandering out of downtown to keep on wandering.

Beyond, I find a parked hybrid car. A teen girl with a nasty bite on her forearm sits inside, pressing her palms to the window. I slide in behind her and stab the short sword through the back of her head.

193

The high I felt when I began this enterprise disappears during the drive deeper into hell. Flames lick dozens of homes and small businesses. House and car windows are smashed. Bodies are scattered about, their heads bludgeoned or blown off or ripped limb from limb. A few with craniums intact get up as they see me. I slam the car into one. I don't even wince at the crunch of bones.

My first stop is a pharmacy that's already been ransacked by other survivors. All the good stuff is gone—pain killers, antibiotics, Viagara. I find what I'm looking for—syringes and needles to match. I also snag a mortar and pestle. As I'm walking past the cash, I grab a packet of gum and an on-sale fanny pack. My gaze stops on a basket full of squirt guns. They look so authentic that for a second I think they're real.

I pick one up, so ludicrously light it might as well be made from aluminum foil. It's useless against a DND, and while it might fool Heidi and the others, why bother when I'm packing an actual firearm? I can't even hit anything with it.

Take it, Teddy says, wheels spinning in my mind. I slide the toy gun into my side pocket.

My next stop is a hardware store. I emerge with a crowbar and rope.

A few blocks away, I park in front of a row of businesses with apartments up top. I'm dreading what I'll find here. My plan is held together by spit and duct tape.

I stare at a tattoo studio with exotic designs in the window. It dredges the emotional swamp in my gut. This is where I met Steph.

I exit the car and approach the studio. With every step, the rotary slide reviewer in my mind flits faded strips of my past on my inner screen. I've been here many times, under many circumstances.

Heidi's best friend Kevin lives here, in the apartment above the tattoo shop—at least he did, back when Heidi and I dated. I'd drop her off so she could have "girl time" with him. After she dumped me, I would happen to find myself parking here, to get a frozen yogurt, never mind that it was completely out of my way. The fantasy was that she would see me, come to her senses, and throw herself into my arms, sobbing about what a mistake she'd made.

Funny not funny how things work out.

The internal slide shifts, filling me with the projection of what happened when I did run into her here. I was emerging from the restroom in the frozen yogurt shop. They were out of paper towels and the dryer was broken. I was left to wipe my wet hands on my pants. I was looking down at my feet when I heard her laugh. The sticky floors turned into Super Glue. Animal behavioralists talk about fight or flight. They need to add frozen to the list.

Move, you useless idiot! You can't let her see you like this! I raged.

I stepped back into the washroom.

I caught a glance of her with Kevin, taking spoonfuls of each others' yogurt, laughing like the couple Heidi and I could never be. The door to the unisex toilet clicked shut in my face. I sat on the can, trembling. *What am I doing here?* Someone tried the locked door.

"Busy!" I shouted. They went away.

I couldn't help but wonder if it was her on the other side.

The frozen yogurt shop is now dark and silent, except for the scurry of rats amidst the knocked-over tables and puddles of melted yogurt. There's a splatter of dried blood on the sidewalk out front. I go to the tattoo studio. There's a retro-style metal sign above the shop with an Asian-inspired dragon on it. The red paint of its scales is artfully weathered.

The front window's smashed from the inside out. The jagged pieces of glass look like a shark's jaws spread wide, its teeth covered in blood. I can guess how this went down.

Crowbar in one hand, short sword in the other, I step through the shattered window. My boots crunch on glass, and a growling DND covered in tattoos rushes me. She's got jet black hair, wears a tank top to show off her ink, and her face is smattered with piercings. I shove my sword up under her chin.

She slides off my blade. My heart hammers wildly. I think of Steph. How can I not? This is where I first met her. In a weird way, Heidi brought us together.

I sat in that toilet stall of the frozen yogurt shop for half an hour, staring at graffiti that promised hungry-college-jock oral sex, complete with an accompanying primitive illustration.

When I found the balls to walk robotically out, Heidi was gone. The acne-prone teen behind the counter stared at me as I crossed the floor. I think he clocked how long I'd spent in the crapper. It didn't matter. I knew this was the last time I would come here. Contrary to my fantasy, there was no joy to seeing Heidi. She'd been done with me long before we broke up. Did I want to go back to the psyche ward? Was this the loser I wanted to be? Cold clarity washed through me. On that day, in that fluorescent-lit frozen-yogurt purgatory, I was finished with her.

I walked out the door, ready to get into my car when my eyes saw the bevy of tattoo designs on the wall inside the studio next door. I stopped and stared. I went in. The buzz of a tattoo gun was like the drone of bees. Patterns filled the wall, of devils, Looney Tunes characters, hearts, broken and otherwise, roses with and without thorns, mermaids, sailors, and every other cliché imaginable.

I was about to give up when I saw the butterfly. It was barely more than an outline, like a single brushstroke.

The whine of the tattoo gun stopped, and the raven-haired artist asked, "See anything you like?"

"That one," I said, pointing at the winged creature.

"Me likey," another female voice said.

I turned around. I couldn't help it. A woman was talking to me. I'm a guy; dick on alert. I saw Steph for the first time.

"The design, I mean," she explained, blushing just enough to be adorable. "Simple. Timeless. Borderline feminine."

"Just like me," I said, having no idea where that was coming from. I was too raw to censor; I just said whatever shit came to my mouth. I was finally being myself because I was too tired to be anyone else.

"Allergies?" she asked, pointing at her eyes, then at me.

I realized how I must've looked.

"Meltdown," I winked.

"I hope he was worth it," Steph replied.

She thinks I'm gay, I realized. Not the first time that had happened, and as I'd come to learn, it wasn't the worst thing in the world. Hot chicks like gay guys.

"She wasn't," I said. The confusion on Steph's face was worth the world's gold. Did I mean an actual "she" or was this a gay-gender-fuck-around "she," which could actually be referring to a guy? Gary couldn't get enough teaching me about the gay use of female pronouns to refer to other dudes; I had to confess, it was growing on me. It clearly confused Steph. Fun.

"Girl," I said, "you look so cute trying to figure this out."

She laughed, and the tattooist had to pull the ink gun away from her arm. The artist gave me a dirty look.

"I'm sorry," I smiled, snorting involuntarily.

It was the first time I could joke about the breakup. I felt lighter than I had in months. Instead of darkness in my belly, I felt a ball of golden light—one that I'd never felt with Heidi because I was always waiting for her to be the Lucy to my Charlie Brown, pulling the football out from under me, both of us knowing I'd come back for more. My online pickup course promised to cure me of being an average frustrated chump. For that, I needed more than a few smooth lines and a cheat sheet on female psychology. In fact, I'd come across a growing movement within the pickup community that focused on "inner game," attracting quality women by becoming a better man from the inside out.

I noticed Steph's tattoos for the first time—swathes of color up and down her arms. I'd always hated tattoos on women, thinking them too rough and unseemly, fool that I was. On Steph, they looked exactly right.

"I'm going to be a while," the artist said. "If you'd rather come back later or make an appointment..."

I looked at the butterfly tattoo, then to Steph, whose name I did not yet know, and I replied, "I think I'll wait."

The tattoo chair in the front of the shop is now cut to ribbons and doused with blood. The artist is on her back, my blade stuck inside her skull. I pull the weapon free and kneel down next to her.

"Okay Marty, just do it," I say.

I unbuckle the tattoo artist's pants and wriggle them over her hips and down her thighs. After everything I've been through, the homes I've plundered, the DNDs I've put down, I still feel like a perv. For someone so Goth, her underwear is surprisingly girly—pink lace. The label says Victoria's Secret. Her thighs are just as covered in ink as her torso. I won't be able to practice on her.

"Shit."

I poke my head out the back door, and I see a lone dead not dead feasting on what's left of a cat. He's got a thick beard, and my guess is he was homeless and rough around the edges before the world went to shit. I'm pretty sure I've given him change before.

"Hey!" I hiss quietly.

He looks at me as if he's unsure if I'm talking to him or some other guy. Then a switch goes off, and he runs at me on all fours. He bears his teeth, bloodshot eyes craving the kill. I end him with my blade and drag him inside. I'm panting, and I wipe the sweat from my brow as I let him fall to the floor.

I now have a canvas.

CHAPTER 38

What follows are the three most frustrating hours of my life. My plan was coming together so well; I started to believe I was going to pull it off.

I scan the wall of designs and spot the pattern for the butterfly tattoo embedded on my shoulder. There's an index number at the bottom. I find it's match on a folder in a filing cabinet. There are half-a-dozen copies of it. Bingo. Or so I think.

I don a pair of latex gloves, transfer the design onto my dead dead hobo using a clear gel, and fire up a tattoo gun. I then proceed to butcher his shoulder. Maybe I'm using too much pressure; maybe twice dead skin doesn't take to needles being repeatedly jabbed in it; maybe I don't know what I'm doing. Whatever the case, the needle is slicing as I move it along the butterfly's wing rather than delicately depositing ink beneath the epidermis. The black tar that is the hobo's blood pools underneath, some of it blistering to the surface.

"Shit."

I turn off the tattoo gun and grasp Doris' bottle of wine. I unscrew it and take a swig.

"Thinking caps on," I say to myself. The clock on the wall ticks away. *You still have that gun with a single bullet*, Heidi assures me. *I'm saving that for you*, I reply. My eyes alight on a permanent marker sitting on the front desk. I smile. Could it be that easy? I grab the marker and use it to trace over the pattern.

"Huh," I grunt. "Not bad."

This may work after all.

With my tweaked plan in place, I remove the mortar, pestle, and meds from my bag. I dump the pills into the bowl and crush them with the pestle. I take another swig of wine then pour some into the bowl, mixing the dark liquid with the powder. I fill three syringes with the concoction.

I have no idea if my downer delight will have any effect, but after Heidi dosed Laleh with heroine, even as a DND, she seemed high. Parts of her brain and nervous system still worked enough that she was fucked up on drugs—I think.

Now the real question. *Can I find Kevin? Can I find my gay twin?*

Heidi's GBF could've survived the initial outbreak and be holed up in some militarized safe zone. Or, he could be torn to pieces. Maybe he wasn't even in the city when all this shit went down. So many maybes. I have plan B of course—which is to find someone of relatively the same height and build as myself, then hack his face just enough to make him unidentifiable. Then it's all on the tattoo, and too much is at stake to rely so heavily on my skills with an indelible marker.

I go out front. There's a wooden door with three buzzers right next to the tattoo shop's entrance. I pry the door open with the crowbar. A DND stumbles down the stairwell—a man in his 50s in head-to-toe camouflage. He missteps and tumbles. I crack his head open, then wait for a count of five ragged breaths. I hear fumbling movement upstairs. No one else comes forward. I drag camo guy out of the way; up I go.

A filthy, worn carpet covers the stairs. Blood's on the wall. A dead woman in a pair of tight jeans, and nothing else, is face down at the top of the stairs. I nudge her with the sword, just in case; she doesn't move. I step over her, through the beam of light sneaking in from a tiny window.

There are three doors. One is open. One is closed and still. The doorknob of the third apartment is rattling like crazy. Someone—some*thing*—is trying to get out.

Kevin's home.

He must hear me because the door shaking grows more frenetic. I'm about to wedge the crowbar between the door and the frame when a thought occurs to me. "You have to unlock the deadbolt!" I shout.

The rattling stops. I step back, lifting the crowbar over one shoulder. The deadbolt pops back with a click. There's a dramatic pause of disbelief, and then the door jerks open.

There he is, Kevin, Heidi's bestie, my gay "twin." He's an inch shorter than me, the teeth bigger and covered in blood; a gaping bite marks the side of his biceps. I'm basically staring at myself. It's uncanny. He's dressed in jeans and a t-shirt. His feet are bare. He lumbers at me. I squeeze the crowbar, almost forgetting that I need him almost dead, not *really* dead.

I turn and run.

CHAPTER 39

He lunges at me as I round the banister. I duck then trip over the corpse at the top of the stairs.

Idiot! I think as I grab the handrail and save myself from a nasty fall. *Move the fucking body from your escape route!*

I run down the stairs two at a time. My DND twin leaps over the dead body, his pounding feet closing in. As Heidi liked to say, "the bitch is agile." I beat him to the door, barely. I yank and hold it closed behind me. He grabs the knob, pulling on it, grunting wildly, as if to say, *Not again!*

He's pulling harder and harder. I wait for the pressure to build, and then I let go. The door flies open, and he goes stumbling back. I run into the tattoo studio. He's up and only a few steps behind. I grab a syringe off the counter and hoof it to the back of the shop. I glance over my shoulder. He's reaching for me. In one fluid motion, I drop, swivel, and kick his legs out from under him. He lands on his back, and I pounce on top of him.

My hand presses into either side of his jaw, clamping it tight. Priority one: control his bite. If he gets his teeth into me, it's game over. Today, loser or not, I play to win.

His fingers close about my throat. Even now, I marvel at a DND's brain capacity. Why the throat? Why not my arm? What hardwiring makes him go for the jugular over all else? Not that it matters. It's his undoing.

My free hand presses the needle of the syringe into the corner of his eye. Laleh was alive when Heidi drugged her. Laleh's circulation system was still working. A DND's blood is like tar. Whatever's keeping the nervous system firing and muscles contracting, I doubt oxygen distribution has anything to do with it. I'm guessing I've got to get my concoction of sedatives directly into the brain. I press the needle as deep as it will go, then push down on the plunger.

Black ooze bubbles up from where I've stuck the needle. It drips like a teardrop down Kevin's cheek. I keep pressing, praying the boozy depressants will leach into Kevin's gray matter, whatever's left of it, and that he's susceptible to their effects. I empty the syringe. Kevin's squeezing harder on my throat. I'm running out of oxygen. I see stars. I instinctively try to pull away. Instead, he yanks me closer. I lose my grip on his jaw.

I see a flash of his bloody teeth. My neck is exposed. I land on him, chest to chest. I try to push away, but my arm is like jelly, flopping uselessly. I brace for the pain of my neck being ripped out. Two seconds pass. I blink and roll off of him. I get to my knees and stare at my gay doppelganger. He's not even looking at me. His bloodshot eyes are glazed, transfixed by something only he can see. I wave my hand in front of him. He snorts. If I didn't know better, I'd say it was a giggle.

I pull the needle from his eye and toss it into the corner. I dab away the black tear from his cheek with a paper towel—and then I do what I must.

CHAPTER 40

Kevin's wonderfully stoned and docile. I transfer the butterfly pattern onto his delt and trace over it with the permanent marker. This is almost too easy.

Don't get cocky, Teddy warns.

He's right. This is far from the end game. I take a moment to admire my handiwork. Not bad. I fan it with a magazine to make sure it's dry, test it gently with my thumb to see if it will smudge (it does not), then I smear it lightly with blood.

"Perfect," I say.

Adequate, Teddy counters. The bear's being overly critical. I hope.

I change Kevin into my clothes—including my underwear. Even our junk is a decent match. My male ego is admittedly appeased. I bind his wrists and ankles with rope. I tie a bandana around his mouth. I'm not sure why I've bothered. He's so baked; it's eerie.

There's one last thing. A bit of insurance. I'm naked as I set the toy gun on the front counter. With a fresh needle, I draw my blood and use it to fill up the squirt gun. If I need it, hopefully it will work.

"Okay, Marty, game on."

I must be a sight as I drag Kevin to the car by his armpits, pop the trunk with the automated opener, and then dump him inside. I lift up his sleeve to check out the butterfly "tattoo" one last time. Screw Teddy. It's legit. Kevin coos at me through his gag, like a cat trying to lure a bird. I give him a second injection through the eye, then close the trunk.

Breathe Marty, breathe.

I go back to Kevin's apartment. I dress in a set of his clean clothes, all of which fit tighter than I'd normally dare—even the track pants. I adjust their padded crotch. The t-shirt I don says *Truvada Whore*.

I never clicked with Kevin, but I salute his sense of humor.

He didn't deserve to die like this, Teddy says.

Neither does Heidi, I admit. Nobody does.

Teddy doesn't argue.

Like any good gay, Kevin's got vodka in the freezer and Red Bull in the fridge. I put both into a reusable shopping bag from under the sink. Also in the freezer are two glass vials, with plastic lids, filled with a clear liquid. It's GHB, colloquially known as the date-rape drug, at least when poured into a victim's drink. But self-administering is a thing. When the alcohol is subtracted, it creates a sexual high not unlike ecstasy.

Kevin once assured me that a sex party was incomplete without it. He also laughingly told me that one of the main ingredients was paint thinner. Didn't stop me from doing it with Heidi. Our best sex, admittedly, was high—until I woke up in the hospital after doing too much. Her text told me to call when I came to. She was at brunch.

I steal both vials.

In the cupboard, I find a banned pre-workout energy supplement— an investigation linked it to heart attacks. I grab it. On my way out, I see the picture of Kevin, me, and Heidi on a bookshelf—except in this print, I've been cropped out.

I wait for that to sting. It does not. I'm adapting.

Night has fallen by the time I park in front of the cars we've used to discourage the downtown zombies from wandering into the safe zone around The Box. I drink one of the cans of Red Bull, praying it will, indeed, give me wings. The short sword is in my lap. I pull out the mortar and pestle. I pour a can of Red Bull into the mortar, then a generous helping of the neon pink crystallized pre-workout supplement. I used to joke that it was basically cocaine. Only then do I realize Kevin likely had actual cocaine in his place. Maybe even meth. Whatever, I'm not going back. I let the pink crystals dissolve, then fill three syringes with the concoction. I put the needles in the money bag around my waist. Over my shoulder goes the backpack with Teddy's head, paws, and shredded torso inside.

I pop open the trunk. Kevin blinks at me like a baby bird woken from a nap. He's so compliant; I almost forget what he is and what he isn't.

Sedation is not a cure, I remind myself.

I grab him under the arms and pull him out. He's heavy. *You're stronger than you think*. It's Gary's voice. *It's you who's holding you back*. I smile despite the circumstances. *True 'dat, brother*. I drag Kevin over to the cars blocking the road and grunt as I clamber onto a hood, pulling him up and across in my wake. I pant and sweat. My feet touch down on the other side. Kevin lies at my feet.

Heidi turned my friends against me. Let's see how she likes it when I do the same to her.

'Gangnam Style' no longer plays in the distance. DNDs moan and shuffle towards me, their outlines emerging from the darkness.

The crowbar pokes out of my knapsack. I squeeze the short sword and cut through the rope binding Kevin's ankles. I leave his wrists tied. I force him to his feet. I nudge him, and he stumbles towards the compound. I follow close behind.

A DND steps into a circle of sputtering light five feet away. She's got long brown hair, hunched shoulders, and a taste for Walmart's discount rack. She spots us and staggers in our direction. I angle Kevin between her and myself.

She cocks her head at Kevin, confused. I end her with my blade and yank it free—swift, efficient, and merciless.

I push Kevin forward.

Five DNDs come next. They're all soldiers. Two of them are Chris-clones, or what Gary would describe as "just his type." The third guy is as big and brutal-looking as a silverback. The last two are women, one of whom reminds me of Steph.

My sword goes under her jaw and into her brain. The remaining four step wide and come at me from different angles. Are they working as a team? I use Kevin as a shield against one Chris while taking out the other. My sword sticks in his eye socket. Silverback shoves Kevin out of the way and jumps me.

I fall to the ground, yank the crowbar from my knapsack and swing the hook right into his skull. His dead weight crushes against me. Kevin's getting ahead of me. His outline disappears beyond the cone of a flickering streetlight.

Shit!

I'm pinned under Silverback's massive body.

The last two soldiers close in.

I pull out my gun. It's light in my hand.

Wait for it, I tell myself.

When they are a foot away, I fire at the remaining Chris. The gun makes ph-zzttt ph-zztt sounds as I squirt the DND with blood from the water pistol. The way he bunches up his face, he looks like a cat punished with a spray bottle. The female soldier's nose twitches excitedly.

Come on, I beg.

She turns on him, biting into his face and neck where my blood is dripping. I wriggle and push at the mass on top of me, like I'm bench pressing for my life—which I am.

The female DND pulls away from her meal, a sour expression creasing her brow.

Sorry, not sorry.

The Chris lookalike shoves her away. I'm painfully aware of Kevin shuffling further away. "Kevin!" I hiss.

I growl. With a final explosive effort, I shove Silverback off of me. The remaining soldiers come at me. They both trip on Silverback's corpse. The woman falls to her knees and grabs at my pant leg as I cut down her companion.

She hisses triumphantly. I smash the heel of my other foot into her half-eaten face—once, twice, three times. She lies still in a pool of black blood.

It's dark. The streetlight beams are too far to reach me. I pant. A fresh set of shuffling steps closes in on me. I turn, blade lifted, ready to stab; I stop myself at the last second. It's Kevin.

"You came back for me," I smile.

He gnaws on the bandana tied around his mouth.

You said it, I think to myself, and I give him a push back towards the compound.

I take out two more DNDs (an old guy I nickname Bad Grandpa, and a 10-year-old who may or may not be his grandson). Sweat and blood soak my Truvada Whore t-shirt.

Kevin and I reach The Box. I lift a commanding finger.

"Stay."

He blinks at me and sways uncertainly.

I set down my knapsack, move Teddy's head to the side, and I pull out a metal bar that I've twisted into an S. Bending a metal bar, if you know what you're doing, isn't as hard as it looks. Gary taught me how. I've padded the top of my do-it-yourself hook with strips of towel, which I've duct taped in place, to reduce any noise when I toss it to the top of the gate. A knotted rope dangles from the end.

I grasp the metal and mutter a quick prayer. My first toss is too low, and I wince as the hook thuds to the ground. I wait for any response beyond the gate.

My second throw goes over the gate, but the hook fails to catch; down it comes. Still no response from inside. On the third attempt, I nail it. I yank the rope, and it holds.

"Okay, Marty Melon," I tell myself, "easy peasy."

I climb. The hardest part is getting myself up and over the top. When Gary does stuff like this, it's like he's enhanced with ape DNA. I, on the other hand, almost fall over the other side, making sloths look graceful.

I land on my feet—barely. There's a thud, and fire runs up my ankles into my knees, hips, and lower back. I wince. *Bend the knees and absorb the impact, asshole.* All the same, I did it. I take a few test steps. I'm limping slightly as I make my way to Steph's Prius, still parked in the training yard. It's unlocked. From underneath the driver-side foot mat, I take out a spare key for The Box. I use it to unlock the gym's boarded-up front door. I'm almost walking normally as I get back to the gate. I open it. Kevin stares at me. It's so creepy the way he doesn't blink. I yank the hook down and stuff it into the knapsack.

I wave to Kevin and he shuffles in.

I don latex gloves and scratch him up with some spare barbed wire that's lying around—a detail I hadn't thought of until now. Next, I carefully untie the bandana in Kevin's mouth, gently pulling the cloth free of his lips. The fabric is covered in spit, blood, and (I'm pretty sure) a bit of grizzled flesh. I drop the bandana into a ziplock bag and stuff it into the knapsack.

He sways and smiles his creepy smile.

I take the picture of Steph and slide it into Kevin's back pocket. Kevin's jaw hangs slack as I untie his wrists.

"One more thing," I say, regretfully undoing the arrowhead necklace from around my throat. I place it about his neck. *It's okay*, Steph assures me. Her voice is comfortingly real, stronger even than Teddy's. It's a weird moment. I stare at this zombie version of myself, knowing that this could've been my fate, and may yet be.

"Okay mister," I say, "it's up to you now. Do me proud."

Kevin stares at me, drool running down his chin.

The guy is *baked*. I'm starting to worry that he's *too* baked.

The plan is for Gary and the others to see a DND inside the compound, freak the fuck out, and then put him down, fast. On closer inspection, they will (hopefully) think it's me. If he's just standing there drooling, they might realize something's wrong. They might take a closer look. They might figure out that it's someone else.

I take a nervous breath and open up my fanny pack. I withdraw one of the needles with the gray-pink mixture of Red Bull and heart-stopping pre-workout crystals. I'm convinced this would kill an elephant.

"Do *not* bite me," I say. "Understand?"

I'm keenly aware that Kevin is now untethered, and I'm about to fill him with the gym bunny equivalent of crack-cocaine.

I slide the needle into the corner of Kevin's eye. He couldn't care less. I press on the plunger, forcing the combination of caffeine, Taurine and guarana into his brain. Hopefully, they'll soak through whatever's left of the cell walls to bind to receptor sites in his central nervous system.

I pull the needle out, and the moment it pops free his whole body gives a shake. And then, nothing. He stares and drools.

"Kevin?" I say. "Come on buddy. Wakey wakey."

I snap my fingers in his face. Nada. I reach into the fanny pack to take out another syringe of stimulants. As I do, I notice his eyes open wide, and his lips spread into a snarl.

"Oh, fuck," I whisper.

He growls and lunges at me. I stumble back and drop the needle. *Fuck, fuck, fuck!*

He's on top of me, jaws snapping an inch from my throat. I hold him back with my elbow against his chest. The only thought on his mind is of his teeth ripping into my jugular. He doesn't even use his hands to help. I bend my knee and wiggle my foot up to press into his chest. I shove him off, grab the needle from the ground, scramble to my feet, and I run. He's chasing, grunting. I spare a glance behind me. He's too close. I turn around. He reaches for me, clawing at the air in front of my face. I kung fu chop his thrashing arms aside again and again. He rushes me. I side step and shove him into the wall. It only buys me a few seconds—time enough for me to yank open the door of The Box, step into the gym, and jerk the barrier shut behind me.

I hear Kevin pounding on the other side, blotting out the sounds of DNDs in the distance.

Holy shit, I realize, *I think that actually worked!*

CHAPTER 41

I lock the door and run across the gym. I trip on a kettlebell that fuckwad Chris no doubt left in the middle of the floor. He's always leaving shit lying around! I fall, roll, and I'm back on my feet, dodging around a stretch cage and the cable machines. Kevin's pounding fists echo in my ears. I unlock the back door, slide into the alley between The Box and the loft, and jam the spare key into the lock.

Careful, Teddy warns.

I can hear a chain rattling behind me, just beyond the door to the loft.

Hurry, Teddy says.

Careful. Hurry. He's a slew of contradictory instructions. I lock The Box and pull the key free. I hide behind the dumpster just as the emergency exit on this side of the loft opens. Glowing beams of light search the darkness. My lungs are heaving. Sweat drenches me. My heart is pounding away. On a primal level, I know I'm not supposed to be here. I was cast out. The tribe made it clear; I am not wanted.

Please, don't let them hear me. Being thrown out once was humiliating. But, there are worse things they can—and will—do if they find out I'm not willing to stay away. The playground taught me that.

"Clear," Gary says, voice tense and low.

I hear him unlocking The Box. My heart beat is a lub-a-dub chorus in my quivering ribcage. *How can't they hear it?* The door to The Box closes behind them.

Move! Teddy orders.

I race from behind the dumpster. I grasp the handle on the loft's emergency exit and pull it open. I'm about to start up the stairs when I hear the shouting from the courtyard—and the first gunshot.

Kevin's growl pierces the night, followed by a second blast. There's a yelp, a third shot, and then silence. That is the end of Kevin.

"Are there any others?" It's Chris talking.

"Clear," Gary finally says.

"How the hell did he get in here?" Chris asks.

"He must've climbed through the barbed wire somehow," Gary replies. "We'll have to attach something to the top of the wall so no more of them can get in that way."

There's a tired calmness to his voice. One more thing to deal with, and one more sense of security chipped away.

"Gary," Chris says.

"What?" Gary asks.

"I think it's Marty," Chris replies.

There's a moment of quiet. I imagine Gary standing over my body, a bullet hole in my head, a look of incredulity on his face. I hear his sobs.

"I got you," Chris says.

"I shot him," Gary says. "I killed him."

"Babe, he was already dead. You did what you had to do," Chris says.

"He came back," Gary says between his tears. "Whatever was left of him, it brought him back here."

I fight the urge to call over, to let him know that I'm okay.

"Come on," Chris says. "There's nothing more you can do. We'll give him a proper burial in the morning."

You're not even going to look at the tattoo? I wonder. For a second, I'm pissed. I worked really hard on that. I remind myself that sometimes people don't notice what's there, but they would notice if it weren't.

You don't have time for this, Teddy says. The bear's right. I run up the stairs two at a time.

CHAPTER 42

I slide into the second-floor hallway.

If they continue following the protocol we established before I was banished, Buddy will be with Heidi and Bob the Builder, locked inside Chris and Gary's apartment.

I hurry to the unit I once occupied. The deadbolt is still switched around, with the latch on the hallway side of the door. If they catch me, they'll put me in there, but it won't be like before. That was voluntary. This time, I'd be a prisoner. I'd be at Heidi's mercy—and so would they; they just wouldn't know it. The thought makes my lungs constrict. I see myself tied to a chair, trying to warn the people I care most about in the world about the danger they refuse to see, begging Gary to listen, sobbing as I asked him, "Why won't anybody believe me?"

Stop imagining, Teddy hisses, *and start doing.*

I let myself into my old unit. I gag on the smell of rot and body odor. *What the hell did I leave in here?* The click of the door behind me is both reassuring and terrifying.

If they notice that the latch is unlocked...

Hurry! Teddy snaps.

I rush over to the Winnie the Pooh cookie jar in the kitchen, take the head off the container, reach in and pull out a key dangling from a pink ribbon. It's the spare key to Heidi's apartment. It's still here.

I could hide in her flat right now, but it's risky. Her apartment *might* be clear, but might isn't good enough. What if she's not following protocol? What if the protocol's changed? What if she's in her apartment with Buddy? I can't take the chance of putting him in more danger. Thanks to Kevin, I won't have to. For now, I'll hide upstairs. Gary and Chris will come back and tell her I'm dead. That will draw her out. She'll insist on seeing the body. That's the main reason they had to think it was me, and not some random DND.

I'm done fighting fair. I'm ready to play by your rules, Heidi. Tonight, you die in your sleep.

I hear a low, animalistic growl behind me. I wheel around, pointing my flashlight at Bob the Builder. He's tied to a chair. His hairy, hulking body is naked except for a pair of dirty underwear. Sweat drips down him. He's covered in bites. Gauze pads and bandage are wrapped all over his arms, legs, and torso, soaked through with pus and blood. When did *this* happen? He must have been caught by a mob of DNDs. His eyes are snaked with red as he stares at me. The smell of rot comes off of him in waves.

He whines, the sound muted by the red bandana pulled tight into his mouth. He struggles against the bonds, his shoulders heaving.

Poor fucking bastard. He's still alive—if barely. My guess is they have him quarantined here until he changes into a dead not dead. Seong had the stones to end herself. Bob's not like that.

Bob stops struggling. His expression transforms, going from rabid to imploring. I remember how Steph's moods changed after she was bit, swearing like a sailor one instant, her sweet, sassy self the next. He's transitioning.

"Bob, can you hear me?" I ask.

He nods.

The look in his eyes, it's going to haunt me for the rest of my life. All that's left is pain, misery, and despair. The man is utterly broken, mentally and physically. That's me if I'm caught. Being a prisoner of those I love, while Heidi's velvet-covered claws prepare to dig in, my sanity will crack like an egg destined for a morning omelet.

"You're probably wondering what I'm doing here," I say.

His eyes widen and he jerks his head to one side. There's a click as the deadbolt snaps into place. I'm locked in.

Fuck!

My temperature drops. *They know I'm here.* My insides desiccate and my throat tightens. I'm trapped.

I look to Bob for confirmation. The terror in his eyes mirrors my own.

Why is he *so scared?*

He's chewing the kerchief in his mouth and jerking his head to one side more forcefully. The door rattles as someone attempts to open it. Bob's head is still yanking to the right, towards the bathroom.

Hide! Teddy yells.

I suddenly get it. They're trying to let themselves in. I slide behind the washroom door just as the front lock turns open.

In steps Heidi.

CHAPTER 43

Her perfume reeks worse than a teenage boy who's just discovered body spray.

She's covering up her slowly growing stench.

She holds a burning candle in a teacup. I catch a whiff of vanilla. She taps the door handle as if it's been naughty.

"I have got to start remembering to lock you when I leave. Blond problems, am I right?" she says to Bob with a sigh.

He squirms against his bindings, his squeals muffled by the gag.

She walks toward him. He jerks so hard on his restraints, he tips over.

"Ooopsy," Heidi says.

She reaches his side and easily lifts the chair with him in it. She sets it right. She sits on his lap and dangles her arm around his neck. He's sobbing. His teary eyes find me through the gap in the washroom door. I take the gun from the knapsack. The *real* gun.

I can do this, I think to myself.

It's too risky, Teddy counters. *You only have one bullet. What if you miss?*

I won't miss, I reply.

You don't know that, Teddy says. *You're not Gary. She needs to be asleep. That's the plan.*

I can finish this, I counter. *Right here, right now. I can do this.*

Heidi wipes away Bob's tears. She nibbles on his ear, like the sweetest of lovers. "Hush now," she says, "I know it hurts, but not for much longer. This will all be over soon." She bites down on the lobe and gives a sharp jerk of her head, tearing a piece of his ear off. The gag muffles his screams, his whole body bouncing up and down. Her mandibles gnash on the fatty adipose tissue as if it were a piece of Bazooka Joe bubble gum. He chokes on his sobs. That's when I realize, he wasn't attacked by a mob of DNDs. Those bites all over his body—while I've been giving Kevin a makeover, Heidi's been feeding on Bob.

Please, his eyes beg me. She chews on his flesh, grimaces, and spits it out. There's a bloody plop as the piece of Bob hits the floor.

"You're turning rancid." She takes a tissue out of her pocket and dabs the blood from her lips. His ear is bleeding. She tosses her hair over one shoulder.

He stares at me pleadingly.

"What are you looking at?" she asks, grabbing his chin. He jerks his gaze away from me and forces it onto hers. She looks at him, then back at me.

"Is someone there?" she asks. It's dark. I've got one shot. Is now the time to take it? Do I have a choice?

She laughs. "Got ya!" she says, tapping Bob on the nose with her finger. "Who would ever come to rescue dead weight like you? The others are glad that you're gone."

The way she's talking to him, it's like they're dating. She kisses him on the forehead, places her hands on either side of his temples, and she gives his head a sharp jerk. I hear his spine snap. She gets up, yanks a curtain from its moorings and tosses the fabric over him.

"Now what am I supposed to have for dinner?"

She shakes her head at him and heads for the door. She grasps the handle and stops. Something's caught her eye. Her head swivels toward the kitchen.

She looks back at Bob. "I know that I am literally losing my mind, but did you leave Winnie the Pooh's head off the cookie jar?"

Fuck me, I think.

She stares at the bathroom door, open just enough for me to make out her silhouette. I step back. Did she see me? I point the gun at the mostly-closed door. My hands are shaking.

Come on, I think. *Come on.*

She's backlit by the candle. In the mirror, I see her outline walking towards me. *Closer, closer.* At this range, even I can get a clean shot. I think. I mean, how hard could it be? She starts opening the door. My finger tightens on the trigger.

Not yet! Not yet! Teddy screams in a panic.

You're going to fuck this up, the voice of Heidi whispers.

Behind her, I hear someone coming into the apartment. She stops and turns. Is it Gary?

"Auntie Heidi, what are you doing?"

Fuck-tard!

It's Buddy. He's pointing his Sponge Bob flashlight into the apartment.

I lower the gun. I can't take the risk.

"What are you doing here?" she demands angrily. "I told you to stay put."

"I heard a noise. Daddy Chris and Daddy Gary aren't back yet. I got scared."

"Oh, for fuck's sake, stop being such a sissy," she yells.

I feel a shift inside of me. Teddy's voice comes through loud and clear. *Shoot the bitch.*

I step closer, trying to figure out how I can make the shot without putting the kid at risk.

"What's that?" Buddy asks.

He's pointing his flashlight at what's left of Bob under the curtain. It twitches.

"That's our little secret my delicious pumpkin," she says. Her tone shifts. Bark and bite transform into a saccharine drip. "If I read you a story, do you promise not to say a word to either of your daddies?"

He thinks about it. "I want two stories."

"Well, sure," Heidi says.

"Two *long* stories," Buddy insists.

"Yes, yes, two *long* stories," Heidi agrees, mirroring his inflection as she scoops him into her arms. He's just become her human shield. I lower the gun. Did I miss my moment? Was it my moment? He wriggles uncomfortably in her arms, his nose scrunching up.

"You smell funny," he says.

218

"You're not exactly a bed of fucking daisies yourself," she replies. There's a note of humor to the delivery. Even now, she knows how to laugh things off. But there's an edge to her tone as well.

"You're not supposed to use that word," Buddy says.

"Here's an idea," she replies. "How about you go fuck yourself? How about that?"

My rage eclipses everything else. I open the bathroom door, ready to charge forward. I need to be quick and decisive. Put the gun to her skull. Pull the trigger. Boom. Done. And that's when Buddy points his Sponge Bob flashlight directly at me.

"Uncle Marty?" he asks.

Fuck!

"What's that about Uncle Marty?" Heidi asks. My plan disintegrates. She doesn't look at me, though. Buddy says nothing, staring at me. I put my finger to my lips, the universal *shhh* sigh. He stays quiet. I step deeper into the shadows, maneuvering so I'm once more blocked by the door.

Be ready, I tell myself. *Be ready*. My palms are an assembly line of sweat.

"I miss him," Buddy replies, pointing the flashlight back towards Bob. The kid's good, I'll give him that, but will Heidi buy it? I feel like there's a Sigourney Weaver-style alien tail tightening around my throat, and the pounding in my chest is the embryo it implanted in my torso, ready to burst out of my ribcage.

"Well, sure," Heidi says, all sweet again. "We all do."

Breathe, I order myself.

"But, you said he did all those mean things to you," Buddy says.

I almost turn into a suicidal cowboy at that, charging out, guns blazing. Poisoning my relationship with Gary is one thing; poisoning Buddy against me will not be tolerated.

"Do you want me to read you that story or not?" she replies.

"Two stories," Buddy corrects her.

She sticks her nose into his hair and takes a big whiff.

"Dear God, you smell good," she says.

He wriggles in her arms, pushing himself away from her.

"I want down," he says.

"Hey!" she snaps, squeezing harder. "Be *very* careful little man. I can lock you in here if I choose, and then you can find out what's under that curtain. Is that what you want?"

He stops squirming, saying nothing. The movement under the curtain transfixes Buddy.

"Answer me!" she shouts.

"No," he says. His voice is low and afraid.

She laughs all of a sudden. The sound is too loud, too sharp, tinged with madness. She's a rabid wolf howling at a street lamp, thinking it the moon.

"Of course, I'll read you two stories," she says, opening the door. "Do you know the one about *Hansel and Gretel*? It's about two children, and a witch who wants to eat them."

"No," he says quietly, "I don't know that one."

"Oh good. Then you won't mind if I change the ending."

She eclipses the candlelight as the door whispers shut behind her.

CHAPTER 44

I hurry out of the bathroom. Through the closed apartment door, I hear voices coming from the hall.

"Gary, Chris, what's the matter?" Heidi asks. I peer through the peephole. In the glow of their flashlights, I see Chris and Gary. Gary is sobbing. Chris holds him. Heidi's face sours, and her nails dig into Buddy. He squirms again and pushes hard on her chest to get away.

She looks ready to yell at him but catches herself. Instead, she chews the insides of her cheeks so hard they must be bleeding. *Is she feeding on herself?* She sets the kid down, and he hides behind Gary, wrapping his arms around his dad's powerful leg.

"What happened out there?" Heidi asks. "Is it Bob? Did he come back?"

At the sound of his name, the thing under the sheets behind me jerks from side to side.

"It's Marty," Gary says between sobs. "He's...he's..."

"He's dead," Chris says. His tone is matter-of-fact—like it's a weather update.

"I shot him," Gary says, wiping the tears from his eyes. "I killed my best friend."

Heidi weeps.

"I have to see him," she says.

Of course, you do. Right on schedule.

"Don't do this to yourself," Chris argues.

"I *have* to see him," she repeats. Chris relents. "Okay."

My plan is working. The fly is turning the black widow's web against her. As soon as she goes, I can slip over to her apartment, let myself in, hide, and wait until she comes back. Once she falls asleep, I'll make sure she never wakes. If all goes well, I won't even need the gun. I can slip out before anyone realizes I was here. Now who's a ninja?

You are, Teddy assures me. *You are.*

"I'm just going to walk Gary and Buddy home; then I'll take you down," Chris says.

"You're such a dear," Heidi says. Her lips are pouty. If I didn't know better, I'd say she was going into seduction mode on Chris' gay ass.

Wrong tree, I think. *Wrong forest.*

"Come on, Buddy," Chris says, opening his arms to his son.

Buddy shakes his head. "I want Daddy Gary to carry me."

"Don't argue with me," Chris snaps.

"It's okay," Gary says. "I've got him."

Gary lifts the kid into his arms. Chris looks ready to chew the kid out, but Heidi gives a nearly imperceptible shake of her head.

"Let's go," Chris huffs.

This is going to work! I almost can't believe it. I'm the man. I am the sneakiest sneak there is. I am...

I hear the click of the deadbolt snapping into place. The sound is like an eraser swiping over the blackboard of my mind, turning the most brilliant mathematical formula of all time into dusty streaks. I'm locked in. Again. My heart is too afraid to beat. I peer through the peephole, and in the light from her flashlight, I see Heidi's leer. She links her arm into Chris', and they disappear into the stairwell.

I am well and truly fucked.

CHAPTER 45

I pace the apartment. Bob spasms under his curtain. The locked door mocks me.

Why the fuck did I leave my crowbar behind? I could shoot the lock, use my one bullet, announcing to everyone that I'm here. As crazy as it sounds, I'm considering it. I rifle amidst a junk drawer. It's full of elastic bands, twist ties, a deck of cards, two pairs of dated glasses, expired coupons for Bouncy Burger, and an old sour cream container full of random keys.

I contemplate the keys.

Could one of these be a spare? Could it be that easy?

I don't move.

What if none of them work?

My God, you're like an old woman. Do it already! Teddy snaps.

I take the container of keys over to the door. The first few don't fit. I put them aside. I get three in a row that do go in, but they won't turn. They hurt my soul the most, because there's an instant of hope, dashed a moment later. I put them in another pile. I go through the entire container, and none of them are a match. I stare angrily at the piles and start again.

I look over at Bob. He's rocking the chair from side to side. I end him with a sharpened pencil through the eye.

I am not going to wind up like him. I try another key, and I swear the lock starts to turn. In my excitement, I turn harder; it snaps.

"Fuck me," I whisper softly.

I wipe the sweat from my forehead, but before I can fully panic, the lock starts to turn from the other side. My eyes widen. Heidi's back. I point the gun at the door. My chest heaves. I'm so close to all of this being done.

The door opens, my finger tenses on the trigger, and there's Buddy blinding me with the beam from his Sponge Bob flashlight. I lower the gun and shield my eyes. I search for Gary, my brain scrambling to explain my presence.

I got nothing.

I'm about to aim the gun at Gary, but Buddy's alone.

"What's a True-vay-dah whore?" he asks, reading Kevin's t-shirt.

I don't dare laugh. "Can I get a hug?" I ask.

He opens his arms wide, and I take him into mine, squeezing him tightly. I fight my building tears. I can't break, not now. Buddy's wiry frame defies physics, clinging to me with the magnetic strength of a neutron star. His embrace crushes and fills me with love.

Reluctantly, painfully, I set him down.

"I came to let you out," he says.

"Thank you," I say. "Where's Daddy Gary?"

"He's lying down," Buddy replies. "He thinks you're dead."

"You didn't say anything to him? About me?" I ask.

He shakes his head and puts his finger to his lips.

"Good boy."

"Are you playing a joke on him?" Buddy asks.

"Something like that," I say.

"Buddy? Buddy where are you?" Gary calls from his apartment.

"You should go," I say. "Before you get in trouble. And, remember," I put my finger to my lips. He does the same, gives me one more hug, and then runs back to his place. I watch him disappear inside, and then I move. I lock up behind me, get to Heidi's, and let myself into her flat using the spare key she gave me what seems like a lifetime ago.

I immediately bang into something. Clattering glass chastises me. I shine my light on a recycling bin overflowing with empty wine bottles. On the counter, a half-full carafe sits alongside two large stem glasses; they're both filled. I feel like I'm interrupting a romantic evening. *But, between whom?* I pick up one of the glasses. It has lipstick on it. She found time to do her makeup. Come to think of it, shouldn't her bleached hair be showing roots by now?

I set the glass down and make my way to Laleh's old room. I step inside, flashing my light around to find a hiding place.

"What the fuck," I murmur.

Along an entire wall are unopened boxes of baby diapers piled from the floor all the way to the top of the 15-foot ceiling. The packaging forms a montage of toddlers. They gaze at me with their baby smiles. The contextual creepiness overshadows the promises of super absorbency.

"Jesus H.," I say, turning my light in a circle around the room.

Diagonal to the diapers, a warehouse's worth of baby wipes and formula lean precariously. Stuffed, chewable animals and hundreds of toddler jumpers in various colors are piled into a corner. There are four playpens in various states of assembly, and so many strollers piled one on top of the other against the drapes, it looks like a modern-art piece about the consumerism and pageantry of reproduction in western society. I feel like I've entered an episode of *Prenatal Hoarders*.

When did she have the time to do collect all this? And to sneak it in?

The bed is buried in a library of books that overflow onto the floor. I see titles like *Baby Makes Three*, *What to Expect When You're Expecting*, *The Terrible Twos*, and *Raising the Gifted Child*. The one that draws my eye is a copy of *Mommie Dearest*, with a hatchet stabbed into it. Gary made me watch the movie, "a camp classic," so when I flash my light onto the one wall that's not covered by baby paraphernalia, I recognize the quote scrawled there in giant letters in what looks like dried blood.

It's from the scene where Joan Crawford mercilessly bests her young adopted daughter in a swim race. My lips move as I read it:

I'm bigger, and I'm faster. I will *always* beat you.

It's as if Heidi wrote that just for me.

The bassinet is what makes my mouth run dry. It's rustic, possibly salvaged from a junk store. The curved wood's been restored with OCD determination. It's draped in soft fabrics of blue and yellow that remind me of Steph's tattoos, dangling like a ball gown to the floor. It swings gently from side to side.

"Oh Heidi," I whisper, "what have you done?"

I think of Andy and Annie. Did they have a baby brother or sister? Did she kill some other survivors and steal their infant? I approach the crib cautiously and peer inside. I see the small shape within, a blanket tucked around it. I poke it gently with the flat of my sword. It doesn't move. I use the blade to draw the blanket back. Glaring up at me is a doll in pink pajamas. It's stained with a child's bloody handprints. Red Bull pounds in my head, chest, and heaving gut.

I almost don't hear Heidi's voice in the hall.

"Thank you," she says, "for being so supportive. I'm such a wreck!"

I hastily turn off my flashlight and close the door to the bedroom. I hear her come into the apartment, the tread of her feet in sneakers a stark contrast to the clickity clack of the heels she favored before civilization ended.

"It's just so tragic," she says. "Poor Marty."

"Yeah," Chris agrees half-heartedly, "poor Marty."

Oh, come on man, I think. *Really?*

I open the closet door, thinking to hide in there. I'm blocked by a wall of breast pumps.

Fucking fuck.

I open the other closet door and stare at box upon box of Viagra. What does Heidi need erectile medication for? They're mixed in, Jenga-style, with boxes containing AndroGel—a form of testosterone absorbed through the skin. Gary says he used it during his clubbing days when certain party favors made boners impossible. There's another drug, too— dozens of bottles of Clomid. I've heard of it. Some of our former clients, who were on the juice, would use it in their off-cycle. It helped their

226

bodies start producing their own testosterone again after the 'roids shut their balls down. Is this for Chris?

"Can I top you up?" Heidi asks. I hear her gulp down her own glass and give the wine bottle a shake.

"I probably shouldn't," Chris replies.

I sneak over to crouch behind the far side of the bed. Something reeks of stale urine. The garbage can is full of little plastic cups and what looks like digital thermometers. I use my phone to light them up, and they are clearly *not* thermometers. They're pregnancy testers—dozens of them. All used. I flash back to the drug Clomid. Its legal application is for women to promote fertility. I look at the testers in the trash. My breath catches.

Is Heidi pregnant?

"It's been an upsetting evening," Heidi says, pouring refills for them both. "I think we could use the release."

"I should get back to Gary," Chris says. "He's pretty messed up."

"Naturally," Heidi says. I know that tone. She doesn't like someone else's needs coming ahead of her own.

I hear the clink of glasses.

"To Marty," Heidi says.

Chris says nothing.

"Is it weird that I miss him?" Heidi asks.

"He doesn't deserve you," Chris replies.

I'm reconsidering who I should shoot with my one bullet.

"He was different before," Heidi muses. "Kind, sweet. Well, he could be, when he wanted something."

Chris grunts, "I hear that."

I ignore them as I go through the testers. I think of Steph, of the unused pregnancy test she left behind. I wipe away a tear.

Heidi cries softly.

"There, there, Little Pea," Chris says.

"Gawd, I'm such a girl, no wonder you date men," she says.

"If only you had a cock," he says.

"I know, right? I'd be the top by the way," she laughs. I hear her give him a playful smack, probably on his pec.

227

"Just like you were with Marty," he laughs.

I pause in my work.

Seriously? She told him about that? I was being open minded! And, with Steph, it actually felt amazing.

"You're terrible!" Heidi giggles like a stuck pig.

"Too soon?" he asks.

"A little," says her words, though not her tone.

I forage quietly through the pregnancy testers. One line, one line, one line; negative, negative, negative. I'm about to shut off my phone when I see one more tester, alone, on the bedside table.

I look to the closed door. I look back at the tester. I pick it up. In the glow from my phone, I see the impossible. Two lines. Heidi's pregnant. I'm so stunned it takes a few moments to process what Chris is saying.

"Heidi, we can't. We promised each other that the last time was the last time."

I shake my head.

The last time for what?

They're not...

"So things are better between you and Gary?" she asks. There's a hint of taunting, a tiny vice on his balls, twisting his manhood, threatening to crush it—but not just yet. Heidi likes to play with her food.

Chris doesn't answer, which *is* an answer.

"It's the worst thing, isn't it?" Heidi asks. "Being with the one you used to love. You're lying next to him night after night, close enough to touch, and yet all you feel is the distance between you. It's more lonely than being alone." It's as if she's gotten her claws on a transcript of my therapy sessions.

"How can I miss someone so much when he's right there?" Chris' voice catches.

"Because you haven't fucked in six months," Heidi replies. "When's the last time you two even kissed?"

"I...I can't remember," Chris replies.

"I know, baby, I know," Heidi answers.

They stop talking. Instead, sounds I should not be hearing haunt me from the other room. Soft moans. The smack of lips. "That's it," coming from Heidi.

Your husband and son are just down the hall! I rage at Chris. Since she's infected, he most likely is too. Is Gary? Or Buddy?

I have no time to process. The door separating me from them creaks and whines. Without being touched, it opens a few inches, all on its own.

Fuck my life!

I turn off my phone. I see candlelight from the kitchen.

"What was that?" Chris asks.

Heidi laughs softly. "It's just Laleh's door. There's a draft. It always does that. Have some more wine." Chris does.

You too, Heidi, I think. *You too. Drink the fuck up.*

Chris moans again.

"There we go," Heidi coos. I see their silhouettes through the partially open door. Heidi's hand moves up and down Chris' crotch.

"Drink," Heidi encourages him. Her tone reminds me of when she got me to consume the drugged chamomile tea. The Viagra in the closet is for Chris. She's spiked the wine with vasodilators. She's probably using the testosterone gel for lube.

I hear a zipper being undone. Heidi's silhouette rides him standing up. Chris' head arches back. He leans against the counter and grasps it with his palms.

"Yes, fuck yes," he says.

It doesn't take long for his hips to jerk and a strangled gurgle to seep from his throat.

"Huh, huh..." he moans, biting his lower lip, followed by silence.

From Chris' outline, I can tell that he won't look at her. They zip up.

"I should go," he says.

Heidi nods. "Gary needs you."

She squeezes Chris' biceps. His shoulders are pathetically hunched as she closes the door behind him. She returns to the kitchen and pours herself another glass of wine. Swirling the glass, she looks down at her tummy and rubs it with circular motions.

"I'm going to be such a good mommy," she says. "We just have to get rid of the last two people in our way."

Now that she has her perfect family, there's no room for Buddy and Gary.

Sure there is, Teddy says. *They'll be dinner.*

I should shoot her right now.

Looks like you're about to get your chance, Teddy says.

He's right. Heidi's walking right towards me.

CHAPTER 46

I should duck behind the bed.

Fuck it. I'm done hiding.

She opens the door. I point the gun at her.

The look on her face, unable to believe what she's seeing, it's a victory unto itself. She recovers quickly, nonchalantly swirling the fresh glass of wine in her hand.

"You're looking well," she says. "Much better than that corpse down in the training yard. Clever, I guess. Cute t-shirt."

She's acting casual, buying herself time.

"Thanks," I force myself to say.

"Where did you find a DND that looks so much like you?"

"Where do you think?" I say.

It's the smugness in my voice that gives it away. She stares at my Truvada Whore shirt.

"Kevin," she whispers.

Her transformation is so fast, even though I'm counting on it, I'm unprepared.

"You fucker!"

She throws the wine in my face. My instinct is to shoot blindly, but I restrain myself. One bullet, and one bullet only. She's on top of me, knocking the gun from my grip. I swing the sword. She catches my wrist, squeezing so hard I hear a crack; I drop the weapon. Her fingers are a noose around my throat. She lifts me and slams me into the pile of books on the bed. I grab the kitchen hatchet stabbed into *Mommie Dearest*. She knocks it from my grip.

"I'm going to kill you," she says.

Other than herself, there was one person in this world she genuinely loved—Kevin. She squeezes on my jaw, forcing my mouth open.

"That's it," she says. "Nice and wide, cocksucker."

She leans over me, letting a dribble of spit dangle from her mouth. It's thicker and stickier than normal saliva, dripping like honey. She's not going to kill me; she's going to infect me. It drops towards my open mouth. I jerk my head to the side at the last moment, and it strikes my cheek.

She pushes my temple into the floor, exposing my neck. She licks from my collar bone all the way up to my ear. I remember what she did to Bob. She whispers to me, "I'm going to eat you slowly. I'm going to bite off your cock, and chew it, and swallow it right in front of you. But you won't die. Not for a very long time. I'll patch you up. I'll inject you with meds to slow down the virus. You'll still feel the infection, changing your brain, rewiring you. The hunger, oh Marty, you have no idea, but you will. You won't be able to control it. You'll need to eat, and eat you will. Gary will be your first taste of human flesh. I'll break his arms and legs, and I'll set you loose on him. You'll devour him, lost in the ecstasy. I know you don't believe me. You think, 'I would never do that to my best friend, to the man that I worship, to the man I wish to be.' But you will. And, while you do, I'll be holding Buddy, forcing him to watch, telling him that he's next—because he will be."

At the mention of harming Buddy, it's my turn to lose it.

I spring my hips from the ground, throwing her partially off of me. My ankle wraps around her neck, slamming her face into the side of the bed. I skitter away from her and hop to my feet. I search for the gun.

"Freeze," Heidi says.

She gets to her feet, pointing the weapon at me.

"I've always wanted to say that," she confesses. "Goodbye, Marty."

Her finger twitches, unable to pull the trigger. Her brow crinkles in confusion. She checks the safety and takes a lurching step, swaying from side to side. The gun falls from her listless fingers, clunking to the floor. She stumbles and collapses against me. I prop her up against the side of the bed.

"Marty, I...I don't feel so good. Everything's blurry." She grasps her belly. "I think it's the baby. I feel it kicking." She grabs my hand and places it on her still firm stomach. "Oh, honey, I think it's time. You're going to be a daddy!"

I pull away and pick up the gun.

"Honey?" she says. "What's wrong?"

"I think you've had too much to drink."

My words—and tone—cut through the haze of her dementia. She shakes her head. "What have you done to me?" she demands angrily. I look at her wine glass on the carpeted floor. Her lipstick print is clear on it.

"I did what you would've done," I reply.

Her eyelashes bat in confusion.

"I drugged you," I explain. I crush the glass with my foot as her eyes flutter shut.

CHAPTER 47

I drag Heidi into the living room and tie her to a chair. With all the crap I put in her glass of wine—the crushed sleeping pills, the Ativan, Kevin's GHB—I can't believe she drank the whole thing without realizing something was off. It must have tasted disgusting. I can only guess that her taste buds are shot—except when it comes to human flesh.

"So this is your plan?" she asks.

She's drowsy but coming to. Her system's metabolizing the cocktail I gave her faster than Kevin's did. He was a DND. She's in transition. Fuck me if I know what that means.

"You're going to bring the others in here, show them my baby room, make them think I'm crazy," she says.

"You are crazy," I reply.

She snorts. "Don't confuse people for their disease. Isn't that what you told me when I made that crack about your mom?"

"And you replied 'no wonder I don't let you fuck me anymore.'"

She pulls at her bindings. She could call for help, but she doesn't want the others seeing what's in Laleh's room.

Her eyes tear up. "I'm sick Marty. I'm doing what I can to slow it down, but I can feel it eating away at my brain. I want to live. I want to have a family. That's all I've ever wanted. Help me. Please, Marty. I...I love you."

I point the gun at her. Her face freezes. It occurs to her that my plan is *not* to bring the others—that I have something more permanent in mind.

"Marty," she says, "you're scaring me. This isn't you."

"You're right," I say. "This isn't me. Not the me that I thought I was, the one who believes that compassion is a strength. Maybe I could keep you tied up. Keep you medicated for as long as possible in the hopes that they," I point to the outside world, to an imaginary team of scientists working around the clock in a lab full of test tubes and computers, "can find a cure."

"Yes," she says. "Let's do that. You can lock me in your old flat. Put me in a straightjacket. I can get better, Marty. You'll see. You can help me. You can save me. You can be my hero."

"No, I can't. You're too dangerous," I say. "If it were Steph, I would risk it. I would risk everything, even them," I jerk my head in the direction of Gary's loft, "but not for you."

"Please!" she begs. "I'm pregnant. Don't hurt my baby!"

I lower my gun. Hope springs in her eyes; mine fill with pity.

"You must be hungry," I say.

She nods vigorously. Tears cavort in her eyes—real ones, maybe.

"I've got something for you," I say, opening my fanny pack. I take out an unused needle and syringe. They're still in the package.

"Marty, what..."

"It's okay," I say. In the candlelight, I slide the needle into my forearm and fill the syringe with my blood. She stares at it like a junkie waiting for her fix. I withdraw the needle and walk towards her. She bites her lower lip and moans. Her eyes are fixed on the needle. I hold it above her. Without prompting, she cranes her head back, mouth open, a baby bird waiting to be fed.

I squeeze the blood out, drop by drop, into her mouth.

Her neck undulates as she swallows. Her eyes flutter, and her skin twitches. My blood, it's a drug to her, like she once was for me. When the syringe is empty, I throw it aside.

"More," she says.

"Okay," I say.

I remove another syringe from my fanny pack. This one is already full of a dark liquid. I slide its needle into her arm. She gasps a bit.

"I want to drink it," she says.

"This way, it should hit you faster."

I press on the plunger, and the liquid starts going inside of her. She's not a DND, not yet, so her circulation system is presumably still working; I don't have to go through her eye as I did with Kevin.

"Marty," she struggles. The ropes hold. "What do you mean? What are you putting into me?"

I finish injecting her, pull the needle free, and I toss it aside. It clatters in the darkness.

"Answer me, Marty. What was that?" She still sounds like a queen.

"Stimulants," I say.

Her brow crinkles in confusion.

"Why?"

"Because, Heidi, after you die, there's something I need you to do for me," I say. "I need you to kill me."

"I...I don't understand," she replies.

There's fear in her eyes. She struggles against her bonds. The straps groan. The cocktail of caffeine, guarana, and Red Bull is kicking in fast.

"Focus on how much you hate me," I tell her, aiming the gun. "Think about what I did to Kevin. How I took him from you. Think about your deepest, darkest secrets, your vulnerabilities, the ones you've hidden from the world, and which I'm about to lay bare. You're going to lose everything you cherish—Chris, your baby, your life, and it's all my fault. I'm taking everything from you."

"So that's what this is?" she shouts. "You're revenge, you pathetic piece of shit?"

Her arm snaps one of the bindings, and she uses her free hand to claw her other limb free.

"I *am* going to kill you!" she screams. She charges.

"Most of all," I say, "remember the smell and taste of my blood."

I pull the trigger. The blast booms. The bullet hits her in the chest and throws her off her feet. She wheezes. Whatever I hit, it's not an immediate kill.

She barks a laugh. "You're a shit shot," she says. "Just like everything you do."

"Game's not over yet," I say.

She tries to get to her feet but falls to her knees. Gobs of red sputter from her mouth. Maybe I grazed her heart. Possible collapsed lung. Could be she's choking on her own blood.

Shouts fill the hallway. Chris is calling her name. She looks at me with her beautiful Bambi eyes.

I get it, Teddy says.

Get what? I ask.

Why you fell for her, he responds.

Her gaze is imploring.

"Goodbye," I say, and I turn away.

I step into the hallway. Flashlights bob like glowing insects, swarming towards me. I shield my eyes with one hand.

It's Chris and Gary. The dynamic duo. Gary's wearing my arrowhead necklace, dangling between his muscled pecs. It looks better on him. Motherfucker.

"Hey," I say, "'sup?"

They freeze, their lights on my face. Gary points a gun at me. Chris is holding his sledgehammer. Buddy is behind them.

"Get back to the room," Gary says to Buddy.

"Hi, Uncle Marty," Buddy says.

"I said, get back to your room!" Gary shouts.

"Do as your father says," I tell him gently.

"Okay," he complies, running back the way he came.

"You're alive," Gary says. "But, I shot you, I..."

"It wasn't me," I say.

"Well, shoot him now!" Chris shouts. "He's obviously infected."

Gary, thankfully, doesn't seem to be buying it. Has he been second guessing turning me out? I point my gun at Chris.

"Settle down," I say.

He snorts. "We only gave you one bullet, and you just used it."

"What do you mean, you gave him one bullet?" Gary demands.

Chris is so busted, and I'm relieved to know, for sure, that Gary knew nothing about the suicide note.

"I...Heidi...we felt bad sending him out there alone," Chris stammers. "We were doing him a favor."

"Is that why you were fucking her?" I ask.

Chris' face sags with shock and guilt; Gary sees.

"You shut your shit mouth!" Chris shouts. He charges, mallet raised.

I fire my gun. He freezes, only now realizing I may have found more bullets out in the world or broke into their armory. The gun doesn't boom. It barely makes a sound, just a faint squelching noise; out shoots a liquid, all over Chris' face, neck, and chest. I'm firing the squirt gun from the hardware store. He's so surprised, he stops. I keep squeezing until the toy is empty. He wipes the liquid from his face and rubs it onto his shirt and pants; more dribbles down his neck, soaking into his collar.

"I am going to kill you," he growls.

Gary yanks the sledgehammer from his husband's hands.

"What are you..."

"Go check on Heidi," Gary says coldly.

"I..." Chris hesitates. "He'll say anything to save himself."

Gary glares at him.

"You're a terrible liar," Gary seethes, "and nowhere near as sneaky as you think."

Chris can't look him in the eyes. To me, he gives the stare of death. He shoves me against the wall as he passes. He opens Heidi's door and goes in. Before Gary can say or do anything, I stick the key in the lock, turn it shut, and I twist the key so hard it snaps.

"Marty," Gary begins.

"You knew about them," I say.

"I...I suspected," he says.

"No!" we hear Chris shout. "No, no, no!"

He's sobbing so loud it carries through the door. He's found Heidi. Dying. Possibly already dead.

"I am going to fucking kill you, Marty!" Chris yells.

"He's infected," I say.

"You don't know that," Gary replies.

I don't have the patience to argue over the obvious.

"Has he kissed you lately?" I ask. "Have you shared plates or glasses or bottles of water? Think! Buddy's life is at stake."

The Buddy card works.

"No," Gary says. "I've been careful. I...was worried."

Not worried enough, I want to snap back. *And when you were, it was about the wrong person.*

"It's okay," I lie. "I've taken care of it."

"Taken care of what?" Gary asks. "Marty, what have you done?"

"When I used the squirt gun on Chris, it wasn't filled with water. It was filled with my blood. Heidi won't be able to resist. I doubt she'll even realize it's him. She'll smell and taste me."

Chris screams, not from emotional heartache, but pure physical pain. Gary is as fast as ever. He shoots the lock off and kicks the door open. Heidi is ripping into Chris' throat with her teeth.

"No!" Gary shouts.

She leers—as if mocking him. He fires a single shot, right above the bridge of her nose. Her head snaps back, and she collapses to the ground —dead dead. Gary runs to Chris' side.

"Baby, no!" he cries.

"It's too late," I say.

"Shut the fuck up!" Gary yells.

"I'm so sorry," I say.

"Fuck you," he replies. "You killed him!"

I consider telling him that we don't have time for this, that Chris killed himself when he made out with her, that what Heidi just did to Chris, ripping his throat out in a DND frenzy, Chris will soon do to Gary.

If positions were reversed, I wonder, *if that were me on the floor, with Steph in my arms, about to get killed by the love of my life, what would Gary do?*

The answer comes as action. I grip my real pistol and smash the butt into the back of Gary's head. It dazes him. He looks at me, confused, vision hazy, and I roundhouse kick him in the face. Gary is Goliath; I am no David. I could never beat him in a fair fight. So, I don't play fair. I sucker punch him, and it works. I catch him as he falls, and I drag his unconscious form away from his dying husband.

Chris looks up at me as I come back and tower over him. He's struggling to breathe, choking on his own blood. Our gazes meet. His eyes fill with loathing. If hate were life, he'd be immortal. I press the tip of Gary's gun to Chris' temple.

"She was going to kill Buddy," I explain. "It was your duty to protect him, but you were too blind to do it. You failed as a husband, and you failed as a father. Goodbye, Chris."

He mumbles something; I'm not sure what. They're his dying words. I don't ask him to repeat them. What's done is done, and this is done.

I pull the trigger.

True friendship can afford
true knowledge. It does
not depend on darkness
and ignorance.
—*Henry David Thoreau*

PART 6

CHAPTER 48

When Gary wakes, he grimaces and sits up in bed. We're in the apartment he, Chris, and Buddy took over. Gary groans and slides back down.

"Is your head ringing?" I ask.

"Yes," he says.

"Possible concussion." I'm stating the obvious.

I slouch in a reclining chair. Buddy is curled in my lap, asleep. He's got what's left of Teddy clutched in his arms. The mini-dose of Ativan I gave the kid is doing its job. Me, I'm wide awake. I'm too wired for anything else. According to my watch, the sun must be coming up. A single candle lights our bunker.

"How much do you remember?" I ask.

"Everything," Gary replies.

"Good," I say. "I was afraid I was going to have to tell you."

"That you killed my husband?"

"Yes," I say. "That I killed your husband."

He's quiet. I think he's fallen back asleep.

"Thank you," he says.

"For what?" I ask.

"I suspected," he answers. "That Chris was infected. I even packed a bag of supplies. Thought of taking Buddy and just disappearing."

"Why didn't you?"

"Would you? If it were Steph? Would you have just left her?"

I don't need to answer.

"Thank you," Gary repeats, "for doing what I couldn't."

I can tell from the way his breathing changes that this time he has drifted off. I put Buddy into bed next to him, along with Teddy.

I walk down the hall to Heidi's apartment. I shine a light inside. I'm expecting her to be gone. To have survived. To have some super-zombie virus that even a bullet to the brain won't put down.

But she is there. Her body is as I left it. She's mortal, her remains surprisingly fragile in death for all her ruthlessness in life. Chris is still a hulk.

I go back to Gary's apartment. I watch him and Buddy sleeping for a while, sad for their broken family. I saved them, but at what cost? In the candlelight, Teddy stares at me, and I hear him say, *If you have to ask the price, you can't afford it.* I killed Gary's husband and Buddy's other Daddy. If I lose them because of that, if that's the price I pay, then so be it.

Outside, I hear the groans of the DNDs drawn by the gunfire. Now that I know Gary's okay, the weight of my exhaustion is like a building imploding. I crawl into bed next to Buddy, Gary on the far side of him.

Their breathing soothes me. I sleep.

CHAPTER 49

The next day, when Gary tells Buddy about Daddy Chris and Auntie Heidi, the kid cries, but less than I expected. I think he suspected something was wrong with them. Aside from believing in Santa Claus (which, let's face it, is dumb as fuck), kids are smarter than they look.

"I have a place where you can go," I say. "Safer than this and without the bad memories." For them, anyway.

"That would be good for Buddy," Gary agrees. "And, for me. And, for you."

That last part is guy speak for *we're cool*. I know bridging the rift between us is not that easy, not that quick, and may not even be possible. But, he's willing to try, so I choose to believe.

I leave them in The Box for the day to pack up supplies. While they do that, I hop rooftops and return to the DJ's home. The entry to the top deck is unlocked like I left it.

Even without the light and sound show, a few DNDs shuffle listlessly around the house.

Armed with rubber gloves, I shove what's left of Andy and Annie, along with their parents, into industrial garbage bags. I stash them in the garage. I'll bury them later. I stare at the blood stains in both Andy's and Annie's rooms. We're going to need bleach and cover up paint for that. I doubt we'll ever use these rooms, but still. I take all of Andy's Lego and set the plastic bricks up on the kitchen table for Buddy. I'm guessing Gary will want to burn sage and his other traditional medicines to, I'm not sure, purify the place? I'm not opposed. I may set up some positive-energy crystals in a healing grid. The DJ had books on that. Can't hurt.

Gary and Buddy arrive as the sun starts to set. When Buddy sees the Lego, his eyes light up.

Good, I think. *There's still a kid in there.*

Over the next few days, we fall into domestic routines.

In the middle of the afternoon, Buddy passes out on the couch. While he snoozes, I work on sewing Teddy back together with some fun fur I scrounged from the basement craft room.

"There's something I need to ask you," I say to Gary, wincing as I poke myself with the needle. "About Chris."

Gary's hunched over the kitchen sink, skinning a squirrel that he caught in a trap up on the roof.

"Do you think we could've saved him? Medicated him the way Heidi was medicating herself?"

"No, I don't think that," Gary replies. "The Chris I loved died as soon as he was infected."

His tone is harsh. Angry. Not with me, I think. With Chris. For the betrayal. For the way in which he became infected. I should let it go, but I can't help but wonder if...

"You're overthinking, aren't you?" Gary asks. He knows me well.

I shrug, neither confirming nor denying; I certainly don't tell him how determined I am to prove that I'm different from Heidi, that unlike her, I wouldn't do anything to survive. I *will* take responsibility for my actions because honey badger does, in fact, give a shit.

Gary reads me.

"I loved Chris, with all my heart, but he was selfish, always has been. And he was weak. That weakness got him killed," he says. "My denial almost got you killed." I open my mouth to say more. With a rip, Gary yanks off the animal's pelt. "That's the end of that conversation," he says.

He knows it had to be done, Teddy councils. *This is how you survive a plague where the dead feed on the living.*

He's conveniently leaving out the fact that both Heidi and Chris were alive when I shot them. A court might accept that it was triage. I know it was also personal.

I think of a Darwin quote that I almost used in a blog post, back in the days of blogs, tweets, and hashtags. *A moral being is one who is capable of reflecting on his past actions and their motives—of approving of some and disapproving of others.*

246

I know what Heidi would say. *Success is the sole earthly judge of right and wrong.* She did like quoting Hitler.

Over the next few weeks, we scavenge the neighboring houses for paint (and paint thinner) to clean up Andy's and Annie's rooms (the carpet we just rip up and don't replace). There's a basement pantry stocked with so much freeze-dried food we could probably last the next two years. There's a cistern that's almost full and solar panels for hot water and electricity. Heidi really fucked these poor fools over.

We pass the time by playing board games, reading stories, and working out. The latter includes devising a new martial arts system specifically for fighting DNDs, taking into account their strength, lack of pain, and affinity for biting. It's weird to say, but I'm oddly happy. I know this reprieve won't last, so I tell myself to soak it up and store it, like a rechargeable battery.

It's not all rainbows and unicorn ponies. Gary and I make a pact. I'm going to keep an eye on him and his behavior in case he's infected. He's going to do the same for me. Neither of us talks about what we'll do if Buddy's infected. I think we both know that without him, we're done.

For now, we enjoy the time out. In the dining room, Buddy rolls the dice on the *Settlers of Catan* board game before us and moves the gray Robber piece right onto one of my octagonal territories. "Please be wheat, please be wheat," he says as he steals one of my resource cards at random. Teddy sits next to him, patched together with mismatched fun fur and filled with goose feather stuffing from a pillow. He's like the rest of us—odd pieces stitched together to form a Frankenstein whole.

"Yes!" Buddy says as he gets the resource he wanted. He trades in a couple of cards to the bank and sets down a simple red wooden piece, about an inch long and a quarter inch square. "Longest-road card, please," he says.

"He's getting good at this game," I say, fiddling with the arrowhead necklace that is back around my neck.

Gary takes a break from adjusting the dial on the radio. Over the static, he ticks off the skills of the game on his finger. "Acquire resources, trade, build alliances..."

"You mean gang up on me," I say.

"Abso-effing-lutely," Gary smiles.

"He'll turn on you if you start to win," I warn.

"Counting on it," Gary says. "The kid's a survivor."

"Your turn," Buddy says, handing me the dice.

I use my knight card to move the robber onto one of Buddy's resource octagons, and I steal one of his cards. It's ore.

"Oh, come on!" he says. It's become one of his catch phrases, along with "Yum yum yum!" when we manage to cook up something special like Rice Krispy squares. I roll, collect a couple of resource cards, then hand the dice to Gary.

"Your turn," I say.

His fingertips graze my palm as he takes the dice. He shakes them in his hands and is about to release them when something breaks through the static on the radio. Gary drops the dice, and they clatter on the floor. He tweaks the dial until the voice comes through more clearly.

"...safe zone," a woman says. There's a pause, and then she starts again. "For anyone who can receive this message. We have established numerous safe zones, quarantine areas, and helicopter drop sites. We will begin aerial searches for survivors over the next few weeks. All survivors will be subject to a mandatory Z1M1 viral antibody screening. Please note, current anti-viral medications are not effective against Z1M1."

Gary and I look at each other.

"Safe zones," he says with an almost holy reverence.

Viral screening, I mouth.

No more freaking out over every hypochondriac symptom (inflamed gums, bad breath, pink eye) that we might be infected, not to mention the mental red alerts (panic attacks, suicidal thoughts, a gaping maw of loneliness). There's a saliva culture they can do or blood work; I don't care if it's a urethral swab as long as it's definitive. One way or the other, we'll know.

248

Gary is crying.

"What's the matter?" Buddy asks him. "Do you miss Daddy Chris?"

He nods. "Very much. Every day."

"Me too," Buddy says.

It's going to be okay, I reassure myself. The words are not spawned from a sense of relief at the prospect of rescue. It's coming to an end, our little artificial family, just like when Gary met Chris.

Enjoy it, Teddy tells me. *This moment will never happen again, not exactly like this.* If Gary had any idea how sentimental I was being, he'd send me to a gynecologist.

"We should make a sign to let them know we're here," Gary says.

"Can't we finish the game first?" Buddy asks.

"This is more important, right Uncle Marty?" Gary asks.

Buddy looks to me with big eyes.

"You know what, I'm with Buddy," I say. "We're almost done. Let's finish what we started."

Gary appears ready to argue, and he'd be right of course. It's just a silly board game. It doesn't mean anything, but if I test positive, or Gary, or (please God, no) Buddy, then this is our last moment untainted. One or more of us will be diseased. We'll be one of *them*.

Gary's mouth closes. There's been a shift since he kicked me out of The Box. Since I came back. Since I...did the things I did. He sees me differently. *I* see me differently. He's always respected me, but I was several rungs below him. Now, I think he's a little afraid of me. I know I am. At the least, he gets that this is important to me and that's enough.

"Okay," he says.

When it's my turn, Buddy hands me the dice.

"Your move," Gary says.

I roll, collect some sweet resources (two bricks and an ore), and trade some of them to acquire another "road." I hold it between my fingers. It's just a little bit of colored wood. What a stupid purchase.

"Put it on the board," Gary says. I do. "Looks like you have something that belongs to Uncle Marty," Gary says to his son.

"Oh, come on!" Buddy says in that cute kid way of his. I smile regretfully as he hands me the card for longest road. Add that to the cities I've built, and I now have a total of 10 Victory Points.

"I guess that makes me the winner," I say. "Game over."

Regret tinges my voice. I got caught up in winning when I should've been dragging the moment out to enjoy it for as long as possible. I used to hate board games because I usually lost. It took me a while, but I finally realized it was the time spent with others that mattered, the laughs, the teasing, the warmth, all chasing the shadows in my mind back to their corners, lighting up the dark place.

"Till we play again," Gary says, squeezing my shoulder reassuringly.

Buddy comes and sits in my lap, and we carefully put the game pieces into their respective ziplock bags. His hair smells of baby shampoo. I've always thought of baby powder as the scent of innocence, but this will do. I take in a deep lungful.

"You're mixing the resource cards with the development cards," Buddy whines.

His OCD makes me laugh. Gary looks at me weird, and I wonder, am I laughing too hard? Too loud? Too long? Am I just normal elated or infected crazy? *Pull it together*, Teddy says.

I pick up a Xanax blister pack and break free two pills. I swallow one and give the other to Gary.

I know the dark place is still there, waiting—always waiting—but for right now, I can't feel it. My shadow hole of doubt is sleeping. I get to belong—for a little while.

If you enjoyed this book, please take a moment to write a positive review on **AMAZON.COM** and **GOODREADS.COM**. This makes a big difference in selling copies, which allows the author to spend less time at his day job and more time on writing a new novel for your reading pleasure.

Shares on social media are also greatly appreciated.

Check out the author's other books:

I Want Superpowers
The Girl with Green Scales (forthcoming)
The Adventures of Philippe and the Outside World
The Adventures of Philippe and the Swirling Vortex
The Adventures of Philippe and the Hailstorm
The Adventures of Philippe and the Big City
The Adventures of Philippe and the Magic Spell
Gay and Single…Forever?—10 Things Every Gay Guy Looking for Love (and Not Finding It) Needs to Know
Queeroes
Queeroes 2

Author's Bio:

Steven Bereznai is the bestselling author of *I Want Superpowers*, about a teen girl who dreams of being more than DNA regular in a dystopian future where only Supergenics can be heroes. Critics have described it as "The love child of *1984* and *The Chrysalids*." The author was aiming for *Divergent* meets *Kick-Ass*.

When he's not writing novels, Steven loves traveling the world (he's an avid travel writer), competing in water polo with the Toronto Triggerfish (he's a three-time medalist at international LGBTQ2S aquatics championships), and watching way too much TV (preferably sci fi).

He's currently working on the sequel to *I Want Superpowers* and hopes to one day release his YA fantasy novel, if he can decide on a title.

Join his mailing list at stevenbereznai.com and follow him on Instagram, Goodreads.com and Amazon.com.